PRAISE FOR THE CAIT MORGAN MYSTERIES

"In the finest tradition of Agatha Christie . . . Ace brings us the closed-room drama, with a dollop of romantic suspense and historical intrigue." —*Library Journal*

"Touches of Christie or Marsh but with a bouquet of Kinsey Millhone." —*Globe and Mail*

"A sparkling, well-plotted, and quite devious mystery in the cozy tradition." —*Hamilton Spectator*

"Perfect comfort reading. You could call it Agatha Christie set in the modern world, with great dollops of lovingly described food and drink." —CrimeFictionLover.com

THE Corpse WITH THE Sapphire Eyes

CATHY ACE

TouchWood
Editions

TouchWood Editions
touchwoodeditions.com

LIBRARY AND ARCHIVES CANADA CATALOGUING IN PUBLICATION
Ace, Cathy, 1960–, author
The corpse with the sapphire eyes / Cathy Ace.

(A Cait Morgan mystery)
Issued in print and electronic formats.
ISBN 978-1-77151-120-9

I. Title. II. Series: Ace, Cathy, 1960– Cait Morgan mystery.

PS8601.C41C667 2015   C813'.6   C2014-908217-7

Editor: Frances Thorsen
Copy editor: Cailey Cavallin
Proofreader: Lenore Hietkamp
Design: Pete Kohut
Cover image: *Mock norman. Penrhyn castle*, Christopher Rowlands, 123rf.com
Author photo: Nick Beaulieu Photography

We gratefully acknowledge the financial support for our publishing activities
from the Government of Canada through the Canada Book Fund and the Canada
Council for the Arts, and from the Province of British Columbia through the
British Columbia Arts Council and the Book Publishing Tax Credit.

The interior pages of this book have been printed on 100% post-consumer
recycled paper, processed chlorine free, and printed with vegetable-based inks.

1 2 3 4 5 19 18 17 16 15

PRINTED IN CANADA

This book is dedicated to my sister, Sue.

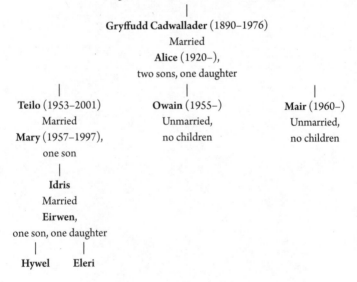

Hywel ap Idris Cadwaladr (1815–1885)
Married
Eleri,
one son
He built the family fortune on copper, and was inspired by the
Norman Keep at Cardiff Castle to build a Norman-style castle on
a clifftop in the Gower Peninsula, near Swansea, South Wales.

Ieuan ap Hywel Cadwaladr (1855–1935),
anglicized name to **Powell Cadwallader**
Married
Iris,
one son
He continued the family business, building it from just copper to also include steel,
nickel plating, slate, and coal. He was very successful and mixed in the highest society.
He built the Gothic-revival wing of the castle, where the "guest rooms" are situated,
between 1880 and 1889, then built the final wing from 1889 to 1899 for his new wife,
Iris, who loved the Jacobethan style because she was obsessed by Hatfield House. As
well as building onto the castle, he added Tudor-style stables.

Gryffudd Cadwallader (1890–1976)
Married
Alice (1920–),
two sons, one daughter

Teilo (1953–2001)
Married
Mary (1957–1997),
one son

Owain (1955–)
Unmarried,
no children

Mair (1960–)
Unmarried,
no children

Idris
Married
Eirwen,
one son, one daughter

Hywel   **Eleri**

**See the end of the book for some hints and tips for
pronouncing Welsh names and words.**

Un

GENERALLY SPEAKING, I BELIEVE THAT when life gives you lemons, you should make yourself a large gin and tonic. Or a lemon mousse. Okay, preferably both. There's always a bright side. But here I was, due to marry Bud Anderson in two days' time at a clifftop castle in Wales, and the apocalyptic weather system swirling above us didn't seem to have a silver lining. It had turned my wedding venue into a creepy place to be. All my romantic notions about Gothic-revival architecture had been blown away.

As I shivered in the drafty bridal boudoir of Castell Llwyd, my sister, Siân, tried to comfort me, but my mood was as gloomy as the skies.

"Buck up, sis. The storm will blow itself out by Monday. It didn't stop you and Bud getting here from Canada, or me from Australia. We're all here, safe. Though why you chose this place to get married, I'll never know. It's like something out of a Vincent Price movie."

"Why here? Because I allowed myself to believe I could celebrate the start of my new life in a fairytale castle. For once, just once, I wanted to be a giddy, giggly romantic and wallow in luxury. I suppose it serves me right for trying to do something just a bit impractical, for a change."

"Come on," said Siân gently, rubbing my back as though I were a sick child. "It'll be alright. It can't get any worse. Now, show me your wedding dress, I can't wait to see it."

As if on cue, there was a knock at the door. I raced across the glacial room and perked up immediately when I heard Bud's voice in the hall outside.

"Cait, can I come in?" His tone was urgent. As I pulled open the heavy oak door, smiling expectantly, Bud set my nerves on edge by using his calming voice. "Now, don't panic, Cait. And don't get cross. You don't need to do anything. Mrs. Jones has everything under control. Besides, he's dead anyway, so there's no real rush. Don't panic. Right? This death will *not* spoil our wedding on Monday. I promise."

"Death? What death? *Who's* dead?"

Siân gasped. "Someone's dead? Oh, Cait, not this weekend."

Bud hugged me tight, then drew back, held onto my hands, and sighed as he spoke. "The choirmaster fell down the stairs to the kitchen and broke his neck, Cait. He's dead. I'm very sorry for the guy, of course, but we won't let this terrible accident affect our wedding."

His tone was measured and sounded almost matter-of-fact. Decades in law enforcement will allow you that ability, and I knew that Bud had delivered difficult news to too many people over the years, especially during the latter part of his career when he'd held a command post in homicide in British Columbia. However, a year or so of retirement seemed to have softened him around the edges a little, and his facial expression as he spoke showed concern and real sadness. I dared to hope this was for *us*.

Bud said quietly, "I'll tell you about it, once we get off this drafty landing. Let's all go into your room, Cait."

I replied, "It's not much better inside, but you're right, let's go in." My voice had as much spark in it as the dead choirmaster now had. I shut the door behind Bud, who sat in an oversized wingback chair upholstered in the same deep pink brocade that hung in front of the sadly inadequate shutters. Siân perched on a stool next to the dark wood dressing table. I pushed back one of the drapes surrounding the massive four-poster bed and jumped up onto the high mattress, dangling my legs, shoulders hunched.

Bud said, "I booked a male choir to sing at the ceremony on Monday. You enjoyed the concert at Brangwyn Hall in Swansea in October so much, I thought it would be a good idea. You know, a special treat from the groom for the bride." He adopted his "cute puppy" expression, but he could obviously see he wasn't winning me over because he added quickly, "Not a whole bunch of guys like we saw on stage, just a chorale, he said. They do it all the time, he said. But he fell, and, well . . . there you are."

As Bud talked, I could feel my chin pucker. The past twelve weeks had comprised a heavy teaching schedule, clearing out the house that had been my home for a decade, selling it, finding a new one to live in with Bud, buying it, moving in, *and* planning our wedding in Wales. As a psychologist I knew that I had not coped well with the strain. I'd even lost my stress-reliever of decades past—my cigarettes. I'd given them up when Bud and I had set a date for the wedding.

Suddenly, I felt the wall of exhaustion I'd been pushing back for months smack me in the face, and I burst into tears. These should have been the most romantic days of my life. I'd fully expected that returning to Wales, where I was born and raised, to start my new life as the wife of the man I loved would be an excellent idea.

But my dreams of a fairytale wedding were falling to pieces. So far our trip had been a litany of trials and frustration. A flight delayed by four hours in Vancouver; the panic-inducing temporary disappearance of the suitcase containing my wedding outfit; a motorway awash because of the record-breaking rainfall; no time for a nap when we'd arrived; a wedding venue that had seemed more than acceptable at our October viewing, but which was clearly lacking in adequate heating and insulation against the inclement winter conditions—and now the corpse of a choirmaster. As I let it all flow over me, I miserably accepted a tissue from Siân, who then gave me the whole box. For several moments I blubbered like a child.

Dau

LEARNING OF THE UNEXPECTED DEATH of a stranger is not unusual for me, so I was surprised at how poorly I was taking this. Bud and I had met when he decided his Integrated Homicide Investigation Team could use my expertise as a victim profiler, which is my chosen field of research as a professor of criminology at the University of Vancouver. I suppose it could be said that death was how we met, and it's a thread running through our lives. Certainly it was what brought us together as a couple—if Bud's wife, Jan, hadn't been tragically killed, we'd have remained simply colleagues.

Eventually, my sobbing subsided. I sighed determinedly. "You know what, Bud Anderson? Nature in all its wrathful glory has done its best to stop us from getting to Wales. But here we all are. Storms or no storms, dead body or no dead body, you and I *will* be married on Monday. I'm very sorry for the choirmaster, and for those who will be more personally impacted by his death than us. But—let's be practical. Are you sure we don't need to do anything? I know we're just paying guests here, but should we really just stay in our rooms and let the folks who live here get on with it?" My tummy rumbled. I looked at my watch. "Oh heck, we were due to have dinner in an hour or so, and I'm starving. I wonder how a fatal accident will affect that plan." I stopped myself before I said more. "That's a terrible thing to say. I know I shouldn't be thinking about food at a time like this. You're one hundred percent sure that it *was* an accident?"

"Of course it was an accident." Bud sounded very sure of himself. *Maybe a bit too sure?* "I'm glad to see you've pulled yourself together enough to be thinking about your stomach." He smiled, but I noticed Siân shaking her head in disbelief. "Cait, you need to drop this idea of yours that there are hordes of murderers all around the world just waiting for you to show up so they can go ahead and kill someone."

His grin widened, and I finally returned his smile; my habit of encountering foul play was our little "joke," though not a very amusing one to an outsider, or the victims in question, of course.

Bud looked serious as he continued, "We managed to be here in Wales for a whole eight days in October without so much as a hint of a body showing up, so let's just accept that this is a very unfortunate accident and move on as best we can."

I nodded, though there was something about his tone that made me feel uncertain.

"Besides," he continued, fiddling with one of the buttons on the arm of his chair, "I cannot imagine that anyone would have a good reason to push a choirmaster down a flight of stairs—unless he was a terrible conductor, of course." He tried raising an eyebrow in my direction, but merely ended up looking surprised. *He's not a pro at eyebrow manipulation, like me.*

"Bless you for trying to cheer me up, Bud Anderson," I said. "It's working."

He cocked his head lovingly and said, "Good, I'm glad. You deserve to be happy, especially this weekend—the only time in your life you'll be a bride. Besides, I happen to know he lived here, so you'd think anyone who wanted him out of the way would have chosen a time to kill him when there wasn't a retired homicide detective and a famous criminal psychologist staying here, right?"

I shrugged my agreement. *You've thought this through, Bud. Why?*

"Don't forget me. I'm here too," added Siân. "I might not be a super-sleuth like you two seem to be, but I could do my bit in an emergency. Remember, before I had the kids I was a very accomplished theatre nurse. I could do the medical assessment of a body."

Bud tilted his head toward Siân and winked. "If we happen to find a corpse that needs a physical exam, we'll call you, Siân. But Mrs. Jones told me she found the body and it was clear he'd fallen. So let's leave it at that. This is nothing for us to get involved with, Cait. It's terribly sad, but there's nothing we can do and no need for us to get involved *at all*. I dare say the authorities might want to speak to us when they get here, because we were on the premises when the poor guy fell. I cannot imagine it will affect anything important that we've arranged but—you know what—?"

"What, oh my dearest fiancé?" I quipped feebly.

"If, for some reason, it looks like all this is going to get in the way of us having our ceremony here on Monday, the way we want, then we three will just find ourselves some hotel rooms in Swansea, and we'll do it there. At the register office itself, if necessary. It might not be your dream wedding, but we will, at least, be married on time."

My practical nature kicked in. "Look, Bud, the location of the marriage is specific to the license. They are very particular about that sort of thing. The rules say we must each have been resident in Swansea for seven consecutive days to be able to apply for the license in the first place. That's why I had to negotiate cover for my lectures so we could come here to visit for a week back in October. The rules also say that we have to be married at the location listed, so in other words here, at Castell Llwyd, within one year of that week of residency, or else get another license."

Bud looked grim for a moment, then brightened. "That's that then. It has to be here, and while we've technically got until next October to be married, Monday is the last day of the year, and I *will* marry you this year, Cait Morgan. We will begin the New Year as a married couple. Got it?"

We each left our respective seats and met in the middle of the room. As we hugged, I heard a melodramatic sigh from Siân, then she added, "If we weren't all in your bridal boudoir, Cait, I'd say 'get a room,' but that's enough of the mush for now, okay?"

I gave her a sisterly pout. "Hey, there's no such thing as too much mush when a girl is getting married," I said. "And I do know that, at forty-eight, I am stretching the meaning of the word 'girl' to its limit—" Siân nodded vigorously, "but I suppose we can restrain ourselves, if we must."

We perched on the edge of the bed beside each other. "So, Bud, tell us how you happened to find out about the accident."

"Well, after we'd all met up and chatted over coffee, I went back to my groom's room knowing I could manage with just a quick shower and a shave, so I'd look my best for my bride." Bud's eyes twinkled wickedly. "Then I rushed downstairs for a secret meeting I was due to have with the choirmaster, whose name was David Davies by the way—"

I interrupted. "It's pronounced Day-*vis*, not Day-*vees* as you said it. The name 'Davies' is pronounced Day-*vis* here in Wales."

Bud rolled his eyes in mock annoyance. "Okay, David *Day-vis* didn't show for our meeting, so I went to look for him. This place is vast, and parts of it are like a rabbit warren. I don't think they planned how to join the wings to the main body very carefully. So I got a bit lost. It's weird, my sense of direction is usually excellent, but I got completely turned around."

I nodded. "You're not wrong about the construction. I read up on the history of the place before we got here. Castell Llwyd was built by two generations of the Cadwallader family, in three different architectural styles, between 1845 and 1900. It's why it looks like three entirely different places from both outside and inside."

"You can give us our lesson on architecture, history, and culture later—*much* later—" piped up Siân, her now-Australian twang very pronounced, "because I know you well enough to know there'll be one. But, for now, I want to hear what happened next."

Bud nodded. "When he didn't show, I wandered about a bit and I ended up pushing open a swinging door tucked underneath the main staircase, where I quite literally bumped into Mrs. Jones, who was just about to come out through the same door. I told her I was trying to find David Davies, and she told me I wouldn't find him because he'd just fallen down the kitchen stairs and broken his neck."

"Did she seem upset by his death?" I asked. *Sometimes I can't help myself.*

To be fair to him, Bud gave my question a moment's thought before he replied, "Cait Morgan, do *not* go there. Her demeanor is irrelevant. In any case, people react to a sudden death in many different ways. But that's not the point—this is not our problem. Got it?"

Bud gave me a warning glance as he continued. "Of course I asked if there was anything I could do, but Mrs. Jones said no, she was quite sure he was dead. Then she shooed me away and said she was off to let the Cadwalladers know, and they'd call the doctor. I suggested she call the ambulance and the cops, saying I really didn't think that a family doctor would be the right person to contact in the case of an accidental death, but she implied that, as a foreigner, I wouldn't know the right thing to do. Well, okay, she didn't imply it, she just straight out said it. And she made it clear that it was a family matter, so I left it at that."

"Not possessed of the most winning manner, is she?" I observed wryly.

Bud sighed. "You're right. Acerbic, to say the least. But that's that, Cait. It's a blow, my darling, but, like I said, it's over to the family and the authorities to sort it all out."

Siân's tone was sympathetic. "I'm so sorry, you two. It's a great shame. Who's Mrs. Jones, by the way?"

I turned my attention to her. "Of course, you only met Idris Cadwallader, when he greeted you. You don't know anyone else who lives here. Bud and I met Mrs. Jones when we visited in October. She's the cook. A face like a hatchet and a tongue just as sharp. Wears one of those old-fashioned crossover pinafores. Hair in a net. Like Gramma Morgan used to wear. In fact—you'll get this, though Bud won't—she looks just like Ryan Davies, from *Ryan and Ronnie*, you know, when he used to dress up as that 'Mam' character?"

Siân's mouth made a big O. "You're kidding?"

I shook my head, and we shared a chuckle.

"I'm guessing this is a Welsh thing?" asked Bud.

Still grinning, I replied, "A TV show we used to watch back in the 1970s. Very funny."

Bud shook his head. "I knew I was going to feel like an outsider on this trip, where you know the culture, and all that, but I guess I'll get used to it." He sounded resigned.

"So," said Siân, "other than this Mrs. Jones, who'll probably now make me want to laugh out loud when I meet her, who else is there here? I promise to listen carefully and try to keep up, but I haven't got a photographic memory like yours, Cait, so I might forget one or two details."

"Then I'll keep them to a minimum," I replied, arching my right eyebrow in its most disdainful manner.

"Does that eyebrow thing of hers work on you, Bud?" asked Siân.

Bud shook his head, smiling. "Not anymore."

"Me neither, sis, so you can cut it out," said Siân with a grin.

I conceded defeat. "There's the family, then there are those who live and work here. First, the family. Alice Cadwallader is the matriarch. She's very old now, in her nineties, I believe, but I gather she was a real beauty in her day. The parties she and her husband, Gryffudd Cadwallader, hosted here were legendary. Alice's son, Owain, and daughter, Mair, live here as well. He's got a reputation as a historian and a scholar; I know nothing about the daughter. Neither are married, and no children. Also living here are Alice's grandson, Idris, and his wife, Eirwen. Bud and I have met both of them, but not the rest of the family. We were all supposed to get together at dinner tonight. Idris is Alice Cadwallader's grandson by her late son, Teilo. Idris and Eirwen have two children, though I was told by Idris when we arrived today that they have gone to stay with his wife's family for the New Year, having just enjoyed Christmas here at Castell Llwyd. So there won't be any children running around the place, which is just fine by me."

"This must be a great place for kids to spend Christmas," Siân said, quite wistfully. She had traveled alone, leaving her husband in charge of their two offspring. "I know it's gloomy and brooding, but they'd love its quirkiness, and that massive tree in the main hallway is quite something. I took a look at the decorations earlier on—they must go back some years. Very intricate, some of them." Siân smiled a little as she added, "We have a little Christmas tree made of silver foil, back home in Perth. But, of course, it's all a bit different there. Christmas Day this year it was over thirty degrees in the morning—we couldn't wait for the Fremantle Doctor to blow in. Too hot to roast a bird, so we had fish on the barbecue."

"Not shrimp?" I grinned.

"Ha ha, sis, very funny," replied Siân. "No, there wasn't any room next to the kangaroo steaks," she quipped.

"The doctor? Was someone sick?" asked Bud, sounding concerned.

"You're sweet, Bud," replied Siân, "but no, no one was sick. The Doctor is a wind that blows into Perth every afternoon; it makes us all feel better when it's hot. It's very special. You two should come and feel it one day, and meet the children. They'll be off to university before you've so much as met them face to face, Auntie Cait," she chided lovingly.

"I'd like that," replied Bud seriously, "and I'm sure Cait would too. I bet she could arrange a good, long break from her teaching, or maybe a couple of semesters of sabbatical?" He was slyly tackling a topic we'd touched upon several times before—and it never ended well. For him.

"Not now, Bud. Let's get this trip over with first, eh? I mean, let's enjoy our wedding as best we can, right?"

I returned my attention to Siân. "So, to continue—that's the Cadwallader family. Then there's Rhian Davies, the woman who's the event planner here—she's the one I've been emailing about all the arrangements. And, of course, Mrs. Jones, who'll be preparing our wedding luncheon. Other than that, I have no idea who else lives in, or helps out. Though I dare say we'll find out over time. Or maybe at dinner, if we dine. But that's enough about them and my ever-sharpening appetite. Bud, how did you get hold of the late David Davies in the first place?"

"Remember you went to the washroom in the interval of that concert in the Brangwyn Hall?" I nodded. "Well, he came and had a pint of beer in the bar where I was getting you a drink. I'd seen your face as you listened to the men singing on the stage and you looked transported—when you weren't admiring the art on the walls, of course. I got the idea right away, so I approached him and got his card. We later exchanged a few emails, and he told me he had a pared-down chorale that often performs at weddings here, so it was an easy thing for me to organize. He mentioned that he lived here, though he never told me why, and I guess I just didn't think to ask. There's been so much going on back home I was just glad it seemed such a simple thing to arrange."

Every time I looked at Bud, I knew how lucky I was to be marrying him. "You're a thoughtful, loving man, Bud Anderson, and it was, indeed, a delightful idea. I adore the sound of male voice choirs, and that night was as wonderful as I had imagined it would be. I know that my eidetic memory allows me to recall things at will, but it's always a joy to be able to experience them again. I often sang in that very hall when I was in the West Glamorgan Youth Choir, back when I lived in Swansea, as did Siân, years later. I attended a good number of other concerts there over the years, too. As for admiring the paintings, I have never, ever taken Frank Brangwyn's incredible work for granted, whether the performance was André Previn conducting Vladimir Ashkenazy, David Essex, or even Queen." I reached over and took Bud's hand. "But it's not the end of the world, my darling. And thank you for trying."

"I tell you what," said Bud, leaping up from the bed. "I'm going to go hang about downstairs so I can see whoever needs to take my statement as soon as possible, and I'll check with them whether they even need to talk to you two at all. You can get yourselves all gussied up for dinner and ready to join me downstairs. By the way, are you going to be okay in this room, Cait? It's not as warm as mine. Of course, it's three times the size. Mine seems a good deal cozier—wood paneling is more welcoming than the painted plaster you have in here. Though those scenes on the walls are quite something. Amazing. I expect you're enjoying them."

"You're right," I replied, looking up at the scenes from Welsh mythology that had been painstakingly composed and expertly painted onto the walls above the chair rail, and across the ceiling of my circular bedroom. "I'll be fine, thanks. I've never spent a night in my very own turret before, so this is an opportunity not to be missed. I could do without the windows rattling behind the shutters; however, so long as none of the figures from the Mabinogion step down from their painted scenes, I'll probably survive."

"I don't know how you could bear to sleep in here," Siân said as she looked around the room. "All those eyes staring down at me would freak me out. Weird characters to have painted in here in any case. Ancient stories full of death, retribution, and lots and lots of begetting."

"The Mabinogion?" Bud mangled the pronunciation a little. "I guess that's something I'll get the chance to learn about when you school me later?" he asked, looking wary.

I could feel the corners of my eyes crinkle as I replied, "I'll catch you up on millennia of Welsh history, including medieval mythologies, before you know it. Then you can do the same for me one day about Swedish culture—how about that?"

Bud shook his head vigorously. "I'd have to learn about Swedish stuff first, Cait. I might have been born there, but my parents never saw fit to immerse me in my birth culture, just my adopted one of Canada. Now, Canadian history? Well, there I *am* pretty good. You get a real sense of place and history being in the Royal Canadian Mounted Police—you have to, or you won't understand all the communities you're dealing with, all the cultural variations, you know? I could tell you tales from ancient, and more modern, Canadian history that would make your hair curl. You could test me if you like."

I grinned. "This is only for tonight and tomorrow. Then you can leave your cozy groom's room and join me here, where we can snuggle for warmth in the conjugal bed." I threw Bud an impish grin.

"Two nights is a long, long time," he sighed.

"Well, two nights it is," I replied, wagging my finger at him. Then, in a slightly more serious tone, I said, "Okay, Bud, while I try to make myself acceptable for public consumption, maybe you could find out what's happening about everything downstairs. I hope this doesn't mean that we won't be able to eat here at all tonight. It's the best part of an hour by car back into Swansea for food. We're really out in the wilds here—on the edge of civilization to be sure."

"I'll go and sort everything right now, and you can come find me when you're ready. You'd better get on with it, you've got a lot of work ahead of you." Bud chuckled as he moved to leave.

"Hey, before you leave us, Bud," Siân said, "I promised Mattie and Beccie that I'd give you this right away. Go on, open it." Her face was alight with anticipation, so I took the package she'd thrust toward us, and pulled at the packaging. "Careful," she warned, watching my every move.

As the paper fell open I found myself looking at a framed photograph of an apple-cheeked little girl with innocent, cornflower eyes, holding an infant in her tiny arms as though it were a doll. Sitting, once again, on the edge of the bed, I felt my face—and my heart—smile. We made a pretty picture, my sister Siân and I, all those decades ago. Unfortunately, the frame surrounding the image was less appealing. Its ugliness belied the undoubted enthusiasm with which Siân's children, Mattie and Beccie, had constructed it in Perth, and the care with which Siân had transported it halfway around the world. Youthful fingers had studded gaudily painted papier-mâché with an array of tiny shells and stones that should have spelled out, in celebratory capitals, the word *family*. Sadly, the items forming the two down-strokes of the letter M had fallen off, so the frame seemed to make an accusation. FAIIILY.

I was aware that Siân was monitoring my expression as I looked at the photograph. When I looked up, I knew my eyes were full of tears.

"I didn't mean to upset you, sis," she said quickly. "I thought you'd like it. I know you don't have many photos of us from when we were little. You got Mum and Dad's ashes; I got the photo albums. As we agreed after their funeral, you don't really need photos, with that memory you've got. But I thought this would be a nice gesture. And the kids loved making the frame for Auntie Cait. Do you remember when the photo was taken?"

I wiped my eyes. "It was Whitsun Sunday, before you turned one year old. Dad had that new instant camera. It seemed like magic to me at the time. He clicked a box, ripped some paper, counted, and there it was—a color photograph. Magic." I looked at our faces again, well, my face really, because Siân wasn't much more than a forehead, a cap, and a blanket. "It's faded a lot, hasn't it?"

"Yes, it has," replied Siân sadly. "But our sisterly love hasn't, right?"

"Absolutely not. Here you go, Bud, what do you think of me when I was a child?"

Bud took the photograph from me and smiled. "I haven't seen one of you this young," he remarked. "Cute as a button. Yes, cute. Funnily enough, that was what Mrs. Jones said about David Davies . . ." He paused, looking embarrassed. "Sorry, I didn't mean to break the moment by mentioning him again."

I sighed, then shrugged. "Well, you have now. Mrs. Jones said he was 'cute'? That's an odd thing to say about a body."

"I thought that too," replied Bud.

Tri

FIVE MINUTES LATER, I'D MANAGED to slap on some makeup, jump into my new stretchy-bouncy charcoal pantsuit, tie my hair into a neat ponytail finished with a charcoal silk scarf, and spritz myself with some of my favorite perfume—Coco by Chanel, Bud's Christmas gift to me. The mirror in my delightfully art deco, but woefully chilly, bathroom informed me that I needed sleep. I shoved my reading specs into my evening purse and headed off to see how Siân was doing.

My hesitant knock at her door was greeted with a loud, "Come on in!"

The vast oak door to my sister's room creaked as I pushed it open. Siân was clearly ready.

"You look great," I said. She did. My baby sister was slim and trim, tanned and toned, and looking effortlessly elegant in a long-sleeved amethyst jersey shift, belted with a gold chain. I sighed.

"You look lovely too," said Siân lightly.

"Thanks, sis, but I know I don't." I couldn't help but sound down.

"Oh come on, Cait, I'd give anything to have your curves," she said almost kindly as we left the room. "No matter how I exercise, I can't make myself look as good as you could. I mean, yes, you could lose a few pounds, but who couldn't?"

"You," I said, a little enviously.

"So do something about it then," she replied sharply.

Our entrance into the drawing room meant I didn't have time to utter a single sisterly expletive, which also meant I wasn't in the best of moods when Idris Cadwallader greeted us. I forced a smile as I shook hands with Idris, and then his wife, Eirwen.

I'd expected the tone of the room to reflect the seriousness of a recent death on the premises. Once it was clear that, surprisingly, this wasn't the first topic of conversation, I tuned out of the general chitchat between Siân and our hosts. It meant I had a chance to take in the rest of my surroundings.

Upon entering the room, the fire that roared and crackled in the massive carved-stone fireplace had been the first thing to catch my attention. It glittered in its surrounding of gold-backed tiles, filling the space with light and warmth. It was certainly a grand room. The oak paneling reflected the glow of the flames, the eclectic furnishings looked as though they'd lived together for decades, lamps added subtle pools of light throughout the space, and the ornate plaster ceiling danced with shadows. Watched over by the dead-eyed portraits with which the room was hung, Bud was warming himself beside the hearth and seemed to be enjoying a joke with a woman who, from the back, looked to be about seventy, with stooped shoulders and short, grayish hair. She was wearing a wooly black cardigan spotted with black sequins, atop a black jersey skirt, which skimmed her unfortunately thick ankles. I wondered who she was.

Idris Cadwallader, who stood no more than a couple of feet from me, was a pleasant-looking man of average size, about thirty-five years of age. He was an animated speaker, making liberal use of his hands as he spoke. His coal black curls and even white teeth weren't so unusual for a Welshman, but the darkness of his chocolate eyes was remarkable. Bud and I had met Idris during our visit in October, and he'd also been the one who'd welcomed us when we'd arrived earlier that day. Castell Llwyd wasn't a hotel by any means, and we'd known to not expect many staff. He'd graciously welcomed us into his home, and he'd given Bud a hand with the bags. He'd led us to our rooms, reminded us that there wasn't any room service, and shown us how to operate the beautifully chromed, if temperamental, bathroom fittings.

We'd learned in October that Idris was the person who ran Castell Llwyd as a business, much against the wishes of his grandmother, Alice

Cadwallader, who hated having paying guests in her home. While we walked through the gardens on a crisp autumn morning, he'd told us it was a choice between selling up or accepting paying guests and holding events at the place, so Alice had withdrawn to the west wing of the house, where she was able to maintain her privacy, and the rest of the place had been "commercialized." He seemed to be an amiable young man, with a winning smile and a head for profit, which wasn't entirely surprising, given the family's background of making its fortune from mining and minerals, in the days when Swansea had been known as "Copperopolis."

Standing beside him was his wife. When I'd told Bud her name, and he'd tried to pronounce it, he'd ended up growling like a pirate. He's not that good at rolling his Rs, so to push "Eye-rrr-wen" out had been a struggle for him. I suspected he would be doing all he could to avoid having to say the poor woman's name aloud throughout our entire visit.

Compared with her husband, Eirwen Cadwallader seemed almost insubstantial. Her straw-colored hair blended with her pallid skin, making her look very drab. Though short, she also seemed bowed, which, for a woman who I guessed was also in her mid-thirties, was interesting. Sometimes tall people will develop a stoop, particularly when they've sprouted as teens, because they are trying to fulfill a psychological need to, quite literally, "not stand out from the crowd." In short people, like Eirwen Cadwallader, I've grown to suspect that stooping is a posture they've adopted in order to meet a psychological desire to "disappear." I wondered who in her life had made her feel that she had to.

"Isn't that exciting, Cait?" asked Siân.

I tried to not give away the fact that I hadn't been listening to a word the three of them had been saying by replying, "Absolutely."

Siân's eyes rounded with annoyance as she said, "Cait was probably off in her own little world, Idris, or she'd have sounded much more excited to know there's a hidden treasure here at the castle, wouldn't you, Cait?"

"I had no idea," I said truthfully. "There's no mention of it on your website, is there?"

"Oh no," said Eirwen quickly. "Imagine what would happen. There'd be people poking around the place, damaging the ancient ruins in the front, or the gardens at the back. It would be a disaster. Alice would probably have a stroke. She'll be here any minute, I expect. Are we ready, Idris?" The woman looked twitchy and seemed to hunch even more. I suspected I had discovered whom it was who made her so keen to be invisible.

"I can understand your concerns, Eirwen," I said, resigning myself to the conversation about the castle. "I read that the stone circle surrounding the Roman ruins, just outside your front door, was put in place at about the same time as the bluestones and sarsens at Stonehenge. So about forty-five hundred years ago, *and* with stones from the same bluestone quarry in the Preseli Hills in Pembroke, no less. You wouldn't want those being damaged or disturbed, nor the remains of the Roman temple to Neptune. I understand the layout of the temple is either unique, or puzzling, depending upon whose opinion one believes." I noticed Eirwen's eyes begin to glaze over.

"That's Uncle Owain's field," Eirwen said. "He's just over there." She waved toward a gloomy corner of the room. "He'll know everything you could ever want to know about the ancient history here, and even more about the modern stuff. He's a real fount of knowledge, is Owain." Her tone told me she didn't think that was a good thing.

I meant it when I said, "I hope I get the chance to have a good talk with him. History fascinates me, always has. And here? Well, you have layer upon layer of it—quite literally."

"That's a very transatlantic accent you've developed there, Cait," said Idris, anxious to change the subject, I thought. "I know I shouldn't say 'American,' because you're Canadian, but it's hard for us Brits to tell the difference."

I smiled pleasantly as I replied, "It's funny you say that, because back in Canada, most people think I've still got a noticeable Welsh accent, though I often have to tell them it's Welsh—they just know it's British. But you don't have a very strong Swansea accent yourself."

Idris nodded. "My father sent me off to an English public school when I was a small boy, which is a shame, because I think this castle would have been a great place to grow up. It's why Eirwen and I have decided that our children, Eleri and Hywel, will attend local schools. They're both at a Welsh medium school—you know, everything's taught in Welsh. It's not far from Gowerton, so it's a bit of a drive for poor Eirwen every day, but it means they have a real home life. Of course, they still speak English here at home, because Eirwen and I are just learning Welsh, and other than Mrs. Jones, our cook, and Rhian, no one else here speaks the language."

"Tell me more about the treasure," said Siân, seeming to want to regain control of the talking points. "Cait, there's even a big dish, from the Swansea Pottery, with a set of clues painted on it. A set of clues about a hidden treasure. Isn't that wonderful? We could have a treasure hunt. A very careful, non-invasive one, of course," she added, looking at a panicked Eirwen.

"Really?" I was surprised. "Is this true?" *I love puzzles.*

Both Idris and his wife nodded. "If you believe what Uncle Owain says, that is," added Idris. "He's spent most of his life following his passion for researching this place, the ruins in the grounds, and the stories about the 'Cadwallader Cache,' as he calls it. Personally, I think it's a load of rubbish, but he's happy, and he's harmless, so we just let him get on with it. I'm sure he'll tell you more than you could ever wish to know about the plate and what he thinks the clues on it mean." Idris glanced in his uncle's direction with an indulgent expression softening his face.

"It's because of him choosing to never earn a living, and Mair never having been allowed to, that Idris has to work so hard to make this place pay," said Eirwen as quietly as though she were uttering a blasphemy.

"Oh, come on now." Idris hugged his wife to his side and smiled broadly. "We're doing just fine. In fact, we might even have a film crew coming here for a couple of months in the spring. I can't say too much about it, but we could end up with our home being seen around the world on TV before you know it. They don't want it for a whole series, or anything like that, just a few episodes where they can make use of the fact that the castle looks like three different places. I expect it would save them a great deal of money—so I think that means I can charge them more for the time they want to be here. The negotiations are at a delicate stage."

"It would be wonderful," said Eirwen. She looked around nervously as she added, "But don't say anything for now, please—we haven't told the rest of the family yet. We want to be certain before we do. It would make a big difference to us."

Idris also checked to see if anyone was in earshot before he spoke. "Yes, it could change things, for all of us, but Alice isn't good with change, so we'll have to manage it all very carefully. In fact, I think that the biggest problem might be that the episodes they want to film here are about hidden treasure. Not ours, of course, but a fictional one in their story, so we'll have to see if it's going to work at all. We really don't want the world and all their shovels to arrive one fine morning, as Eirwen said."

Seemingly out of the blue Eirwen announced, "Come on, you two ladies, let Idris get you a drink. His grandmother will be here soon, so we'd better get you sorted before that."

I said, "Thanks, a gin and tonic, please," just as Siân said, "Fizzy water," which resulted in a group grin, but before we had reached the drinks' table, the door to the drawing room was flung open. An ancient woman draped in velvet and sitting, very upright, in one of those motorized wheelchairs, rolled into the room. Although I'd never met her, I was sure this was the matriarch of the family. The impressive chair almost enveloped the tiny, wizened figure. It was bedecked with brocade bags, each stuffed with myriad items.

Having positioned herself in the center of the room, Alice Cadwallader said, "I see we have guests. Let's meet them, then."

I moved closer to her, and she offered me the tips of her ancient fingers, which I squeezed gently. Her wrist didn't look as though it would survive my shaking her hand. She was a woman with a storied past, and I'd been looking forward to meeting her. Rheumy yet still-green eyes glittered in the firelight and examined me keenly. Crepe-like skin hung in folds beneath her chin and around her emaciated wrists, and her snow white hair was coiled in a fleecy bun. Lipstick the color of dried blood emphasized how narrow her lips had become. Despite all these signs of great age, she had an energy about her. I suspected she was used to getting her own way. And there was something else—what was it? Hunger. Yes, she was hungry for something—or maybe everything—and she wanted it now.

"Professor Cait Morgan, allow me to introduce my esteemed grandmother, Alice Cadwallader." Idris spoke the name as though it were an incantation.

"Come closer, girl, I want to see you." Her voice could have etched glass.

"Alice is a little deaf, and a little blind," whispered Idris close to my ear.

"No, I'm not," exploded the woman. She cackled a laugh. "I might be ninety-two, but I can see and hear as well as I ever could," she shouted. "Not unless I want to be deaf and blind, and then I can put it on as I please. Ha!"

Her cold, dry, arthritically curled claw-hands pulled me toward her. She smelled of rose perfume and old age. It was an unpleasant, heady mix. As she peered at me, I peered back. Seemingly satisfied, she pushed my hand away.

"A professor? Of what?"

I replied, "I'm a criminal psychologist who specializes in building profiles of victims. I teach and carry out my research at the University of Vancouver, in British Columbia." I made sure I spoke clearly, though I didn't raise my voice.

"I expect you're very clever. Are you? I hope you are," she said.

I knew from my reading that Alice Cadwallader had been born and raised in Philadelphia, where she'd met and married Gryffudd Cadwallader when she was very young. She spoke with a very refined Welsh accent, the sort you might hear in the dress circle at a performance by the Welsh National Opera—from those who spoke English as a first language.

I was so taken aback I didn't say anything for a second or two, which is a long time for me. "It has been said that I am," I replied. "Why do you hope I'm clever?" It seemed like a reasonable question, but it drew a sharp intake of breath from Idris. I was immediately on my guard. I probably should have been before I opened my mouth.

"You aren't pretty. If a girl isn't pretty, she should be clever," she replied simply.

It took me a millisecond to reply, "Pretty isn't everyone's cup of tea, and beauty is subjective. If it's only external, it can fade. Quickly. Cleverness, insight, and an ability to be interesting, because you're interested, can linger, and even develop over the years." This time I sensed the entire room take a breath.

"Not backwards in coming forwards, are you?" replied the woman. No one breathed out.

"Good for you!" she added as she slapped the armrest of her wheelchair with surprising vigor.

I could have sworn I heard a collective sigh.

Pedwar

A SORT OF TRUCE HAVING been established between Alice Cadwallader and myself, she once again took center stage.

"If you need proof that what you just said is true," she announced, "take a look at the portrait of me above the fireplace. Stunning, wasn't I? Now, I'm this pile of skin and bones. But I was lucky, girl. Pretty *and* clever."

I looked in the direction that Alice Cadwallader's talon indicated, and there it was, the only portrait in the room of a person with life in their eyes and blood in their veins. The artist had captured what I could see was still the spirit of the woman, as well as her undoubted good looks. Red locks lay tousled upon bare, milky shoulders, and green eyes were highlighted by a green velvet gown that draped around voluptuous curves. Her full lips were parted in delight, and her hands were elegant, almost animated—one laying, gloved, in her lap, the other pointing toward some distant object that had caught her attention. Her haughty, knowing expression challenged me from the canvas. It made me think of Rita Hayworth in her *Gilda* days.

The setting for the portrait was obviously a woman's bedroom. A large dressing table with an oval mirror was partially obscured by a screen, delicately painted with very realistic representations of a host of exotic animals. Over one of her milky shoulders was a window that allowed a vista of a bizarre landscape—flat and white, with little brown "islands" poking up out of it, it looked like something from a Salvador Dali painting, strangely surreal, and seemed out of place in a realistic portrait.

I turned to face the shriveled figure she had become. "I disagree, I don't think you were pretty, Mrs. Cadwallader." Again I heard Idris inhale sharply. "You were a very beautiful woman, and your strength of character shines through in your portrait. Whoever painted it was a very talented artist."

"Handsome devil, he was." Alice smiled. "Irish. Younger than me. Not much more than a boy. But gifted. Gryffudd, my late husband, had it painted for my thirty-second birthday. By that time I'd been his wife for half my life. It was 1952, and we'd only been back in this place for a couple of years. The War Office took it over for The Duration, stayed longer, and left it in a terrible mess when they finally decamped. Gryffudd had to do a lot of work to the place to bring it back up to snuff. Something very hush-hush they did here during the war. The sort of thing no one would talk about. Gryffudd had moved me out to a cottage up in the Brecon Beacons in 1940, not far from Brecon itself. It was a lonely time for me, the war. I was very young, of course, and Wales and the Welsh still seemed alien to me. I did what I could, by way of mixing in, joining committees and so forth, but I wasn't able to really help, I felt. Gryffudd wouldn't let me."

Alice Cadwallader was feeling the loneliness all over again, I could tell. Her gaze was looking back across the years, not across the room to her portrait.

She seemed to suddenly become aware of us and continued. "He wanted me to be safe, you see. We'd traveled so much after we married that I'd barely set foot in this place before I was packed off to the back of beyond, so it didn't become my home until afterwards. Of course, Gryffudd stayed on in Swansea through it all, managing his mines and his factories from his offices near the docks. He was nearly killed in the Swansea Blitz in '41. A lot of his friends, and many of his workers, were. It made moving back here a very sweet homecoming for him, and for me, because I felt I could finally make a home. He always liked that portrait. It was painted before the children came along, so I think I looked about my best."

"Well, I might not have as much to lose as you did in the looks department, Mrs. Cadwallader, but I hope I end up as sharp as you, if I live as long as you have, and with a quarter the stories to tell." I didn't mean to flatter her; I spoke the truth.

Alice Cadwallader said, "Firstly, it's Alice, and secondly, if that grandson of mine can't make you a drink, I'll get out of this chair all on my own and do it myself. Idris? What are you doing there, boy?"

"I was just about to check which gin Cait would like," he replied sheepishly.

"My money's on Bombay Sapphire, right, Cait?"

"As it happens, you'd win your bet, Alice," I said, glancing toward Idris. "Bombay and tonic, please, not too much ice, and with lemon, if you have it. Thanks. And while you're very kindly doing that for me, Idris, I'd like to introduce my sister, Siân, to you, Alice."

Siân stepped into the aged woman's line of vision and reached forward to take her hand.

"G'day. A pleasure to meet you," said Siân very politely, on the verge of curtseying.

Alice Cadwallader peered at Siân in the same way she'd peered at me. "So you got the looks in the family," she said flatly. "How were the brains distributed? What do you do, my girl? One of those full-time helicopter mothers as they call them nowadays, like her?" Alice jerked her head toward Eirwen as she spoke. Eirwen stooped a little more.

Siân looked uneasy. "I chose to take a break from my career, as a nurse trained to work with surgeons, to raise my children," she said defensively. "It was a rewarding career, but I believe that raising your children can be equally fulfilling. And while I can't claim to be a genius like my sister, I'm no slouch when it comes to learning and applying that knowledge."

Alice nodded her head slowly and allowed Siân to remove her hand from her grasp. "You're lying about enjoying raising your children," the woman observed, "and I bet you'll be back to work before long. I raised three children. One ran through money as though it were milk and he owned the cow, and then he died. The other two are in this room. Maybe meeting them will give you an idea of just how *un*fulfilling it can be to raise children."

Siân had no response, and I noticed that Idris was avoiding making eye contact with his grandmother by busying himself at the drinks table.

"Owain, come here, boy," called Alice. "Come and meet Siân and her sister, Cait. It's a shame Cait's here to marry someone else because she'd be just right for you. Brainy. Mind you, past her childbearing years, so not much use to you really. Siân, Cait, this is my son, Owain. Not much of a specimen, but he doesn't do anyone any harm, so I suppose I should be grateful for that. Owain, show yourself!"

At first, all I glimpsed was a long, white hand emerging from the shadows, but the rest of Owain Cadwallader soon followed. A wild and wiry full white beard covered the bottom half of the man's face. Thick-lensed spectacles, which reduced the size of his eyes to almost nothing, perched on his bulbous nose; his heavily tufted, still-dark arching eyebrows looked almost like wings. He was completely bald. His suit shone like anthracite in places, and I guessed it had seen many years of service. His beard hardly moved when he spoke.

"A pleasure to meet you . . . um . . ." He put out his hand toward me.

"Cait!" snapped his mother. "That one's name is Cait Morgan, Owain. It's no wonder women never take a second look at you if you can't even be bothered to remember their names."

"Of course. *Cait.* I suspect that's an abbreviation of Caitlin. Means 'pure.' Irish originally. Are you Irish?" Owain spoke quickly, his high register and rapid delivery making everything he said sound like it was of the utmost urgency.

"No, I'm Welsh. Through and through. As is Siân."

"Ah, now very few people are that, Cait. Surprisingly few, in fact. What do you mean by that statement, exactly?" Like Idris, Owain's tone was clipped, informing me that the Cadwallader clan favored English public schools for its menfolk.

I decided to play along; after all, his nephew had finally handed me my drink, so I had to do something while I sipped it. "Well, Owain, what I mean is that our family tree was once traced back to the 1500s, and both of our parents' families were entirely Welsh, for all that time. They produced just us two sisters. I have no children, and Siân has married an Australian, so I'm afraid that the blood will be diluted for the next generation." I felt I'd done all I needed to prove my point.

Owain looked excited. "I've put together a full genealogy for our family, you know. It's been fascinating work. I'd enjoy discussing it with you some time. Maybe tonight, over dinner?"

The woman who'd been standing with her back to me while talking to Bud beside the fire moved to shake hands with Siân and myself. "I'm sure Cait doesn't want to be bothered with all that, Owain. I'm sorry, my brother isn't terribly good at social interaction. He'll bore you to death with our family history, if you let him. I'm Mair, by the way. I'm Owain's little sister, Alice's youngest child. Her 'spinster daughter,' as she likes to refer to me."

"The one who nearly killed me," said Alice, accepting a glass of something that looked like sherry from her grandson.

"Yes, Mother, the one who nearly killed you," replied Mair with a terse patience I suspected was born of practice. "Mother was forty when I came along, and she's never really recovered. Though she's managed to linger on these past fifty-two years quite well."

"Never got my strength back, and began to lose my looks almost immediately. All my hair fell out a month after I had her," announced the old woman.

"I'm terribly sorry about that, Mother," Mair sounded annoyed, yet bored. I suspected the apology was well rehearsed.

Mair had taken up a position behind her mother, and her hand rested lightly on the back of the wheelchair. She was in her early fifties, rather than her seventies as I'd judged from her back view. Mair was no beauty. Her mother's portrait, and the old woman herself, had

27

a fire in the eyes that Mair just didn't possess. Though, in her favor, she did have a hint of her mother's original hair color, and her blue eyes matched those of her brother. I sensed a tension about her that I couldn't name. It worried me.

Mair turned her attention from her mother to me. "Cait, the young lady hovering back here is my mother's nurse, Janet Roberts. She joined our household about six months ago, was it, Janet?"

"She's an angel," said Alice, beaming at the pink-faced, fair-haired girl, who was in her late twenties. "Lifts me very nicely, and tends to me much better than Mair ever did. Better than Danuta too. Danuta was my last nurse. Danuta Mazur, a Polish girl. She kept secrets from me, which is why I got rid of her."

"Are you local, Janet?" I asked by way of conversation filler.

"Reynoldston, originally," the nurse replied, referring to a village less than fifteen miles away. "So, pretty close. Funny really, I used to see this old place when I was little, and now I live here. Right turn up for the books, isn't it?"

I smiled. "It certainly is a small world. I used to see this castle from up on top of the common that abuts the Cadwallader Estate when I was young, and the first time I saw it I thought it would be a wonderful place to be married."

"Sounds like my cue," said Bud, joining us.

"Dinner is served," shouted Mrs. Jones from the doorway. "On the table in exactly five minutes."

"What is it tonight, Dilys?" called back Alice.

"You'll find out at the table," replied the cook, who was wearing a navy blue dress that looked like a tent. She looked more presentable than I remembered her, though still sour-faced.

"And the police phoned," she added. "They won't be here tonight after all. Can't. Nasty accident on the M4. Them coaches, big old buses, taking Arsenal fans back to London from the Swansea City game—four of them have run into each other on the motorway, they have. Terrible bad, they say. Hundreds were hurt. They did a news flash about it on the telly. They've had to cut some of the bodies out of the wreckage." The cook sounded almost gleeful. "Pound to a penny, no seat belts. Too busy drinking themselves silly. The Swans won, see. Tidy. Probably blood all over the place. Hours, they'll be. Maybe days. Amb'lances everywhere. My friend Audrey Williams phoned me about it too. She'll have to have her grandchildren overnight. Daughter's a nurse, see, and the hospital won't let her go home. Telling people to stay away from the emergency wards, they are, unless they're at death's door. Morriston's overflowing, she said, and Singleton's not much better. Overwhelmed. Sending some of them to Cardiff, she told me. Must be bad for them to do that. Terrible. So, now the police have said they can't come till tomorrow, could Idris please come downstairs and help me move him to the back kitchen? Not sanitary having him lying there like that, it's not. Dangerous."

Before Alice had a chance to reply, the cook disappeared. Idris prepared to follow her.

Alice remarked to Siân, Bud, and myself, "So cheeky. Never changes. The Joneses and the Cadwalladers go back for generations. Dilys, that's Mrs. Jones, was born and raised in this very house. Her mother and father both lived in. To be fair, she's a very good cook, and I hear they are not easy to find, these days. Idris informs me it's the age of the chef, and that 'cook' is a very unfashionable word."

"That's not what I said, Alice," replied Idris as he left the room.

"Never mind what you said, I know what I heard," said Alice abruptly. Then she added, even more sharply, "This sherry is not good, Idris. Get me another, and make sure it's my proper one."

"That *is* the proper one, Alice," replied Eirwen on behalf of her absent husband. "Your Amontillado as always. Only you drink it, and it's the only bottle we have."

"Well it's too warm then," she replied testily. "Cool it down, but don't you dare dilute it with ice, and bring me a glass to the table. I'll drink it in the dining room. Let's go."

"Right-o," shouted the young blond nurse.

Alice took off at speed across the drawing room toward the door. "You'd all better get a move on because I don't like anyone being late to the table," she added, then she was gone.

It was as though a particularly effective collie had yapped at a herd of sheep, because within about thirty seconds, everyone had left. Siân, Bud, and I had a moment alone. I gulped my drink, which was very refreshing. My mouth was dry, and I knew I was probably still dehydrated from the flight. Too late, I wondered if a gin and tonic had been the best choice of thirst-quencher. As soon as I put my empty glass onto the little table beside me, Bud and I squeezed hands.

I noted quietly, "No one seems very upset about the passing of David Davies. In fact, everyone seems to be in quite good spirits."

"You're not kidding," he said. "When I came down for drinks, it was as though no one had died. It was surreal. I kept wondering if I'd imagined it all. It's a really strange atmosphere here. I'm not one to believe in ghosts, but if they did exist, I guess they'd hang out in a place like this. And, of course, the weather's not helping. The storm doesn't seem to be letting up at all. Can you hear that wind whistling at the windows? Spooky enough for you?" Bud grinned.

"Mattie and Beccie would love it here," said Siân wistfully. "There'd be no stopping them from hunting for secret doors all over the place."

I patted my sister on the back as I said, "At least the windows in here don't rattle like mine."

"Let's just hope that Mrs. Dilys Jones is as good a cook as she is a you-know-what," quipped Bud, "because she's very, very good at being one of those!"

We crossed the great hall holding hands, with Siân beside us. Right on cue, my tummy rumbled.

I could have sworn I heard it echo off the stained glass roof that arced high above our heads.

Pump

THE DINING ROOM AT CASTELL Llwyd was positioned directly beneath my very own bridal boudoir, so when the three of us walked into the round room, its scale and layout were already familiar to us. As in my bedroom, the dining room had windows almost all the way around—here curtained with dark burgundy velvet—interspersed with wooden panels below painted plaster walls. Rather than the Mabinogion myths that graced my walls, the dining room showcased scenes from nature, with a heavy emphasis on fruits and vegetables. Cute furry creatures poked their attractive little faces through various stems and tufts of edible vegetation, while spectacular birds and iridescent insects hovered in the sky—which was the ceiling. There was a vast rectangular table at the room's center, surrounded by eighteen dark wooden chairs with tall, Gothic-arched backs. As in my room, the segment of the circle adjoining the rest of the wing was windowless, but here it featured a monumental fireplace. It was tiled, buttressed, painted with a good deal of red paint, and highlighted with glinting gold leaf. Beside it was a massive door. My room had a little door in the same spot that led to a bathroom. I wondered what was behind the door in this room.

"Sit to my right, Cait," called Alice Cadwallader from across the room. Her rasping tones bounced around, and it was immediately clear that any sound of chatter would do the same beneath the high ceiling, which was beamed like a spider web, with a massive iron chandelier hanging from its mid-point. "And you, the fiancé, sit to my left. I want to find out more about you. You look rather interesting. Mair, Owain, move along."

I felt awkward as I took the seat vacated by the daughter of the house, and my embarrassment was heightened when Alice's imperious demands resulted in everyone shuffling from seat to seat. We eventually all settled with Alice at the head of the table, Bud to her left, next to Mair, then Idris, who'd just rushed in to join us, having presumably finished his grisly task in the kitchen. I sat to Alice's right, next to Owain, then Siân, then Janet. The rest of the table stretched away, unused, making us look like a very feeble gathering.

Dilys Jones entered from the great hall carrying a huge tray, which she placed on a discreet sideboard. She placed platters of pâté, toast, and butter in the center of the table. She rather ungraciously plopped the plates down, reaching between us as though we were in the way.

"It's not what you were supposed to be having," the cook announced grumpily, "but with all that fuss about David I wasn't able to do a roast. I managed to get some toast done, and this was ready for tomorrow, but you're having it now. It's rabbit pâté. The main will be cawl, which should have been your starter, but you can have bigger bowls. Then there'll be trifle. Not really appropriate, but it'll have to do. I can make *teisen lap* for tomorrow instead, but I didn't have time to do the rice pudding I'd planned." It seemed that David Davies's death had been an imposition.

"Mair, come and serve me," said Alice loudly, "and tell me again what happened to David. Was it a nasty fall?"

I heard Mair sigh heavily, clearly holding back anger, as she left her seat. "I told you, Mother, he's dead. He died. He broke his neck. Of course it was a nasty fall."

"You never said he was *dead*." Alice's shock changed to horror. "You mean he *died*? Why didn't anyone tell me? It is my house, you know. I just let the rest of you live in it. I have every right to know. I should have been informed. Was it instant?"

As Mair piled pâté and butter onto a plate, then balanced a few slices of toast beside the glistening mounds, she almost hissed, "He fell down the servants' stairs, Mother, and his neck was broken in the fall. He was dead before he hit the bottom."

"You don't know that," said Owain. "He might have been alive for some time, then died just before he was found. Or even after he was found."

As Dilys circled the table she replied to Owain, "He must have been dead by the time he hit the bottom. The way his neck was broken, he couldn't have lasted the fall. Seen enough birds with broken necks in my time to know he was dead."

"I hope it was a quick, clean death," said Mair quietly and thoughtfully.

"Death is death," snapped Alice. "There's nothing clean about it. It's a filthy business. Even when it's just an accident."

"Mother." Mair sounded shocked.

"Grow up, girl. I think I made a mistake with you—you don't seem to have matured at all, you've just grown older. I should have sent you out into the world. But I needed you near me." I caught Mair's expression of silent rage at her mother's words. "He was lucky he didn't suffer, like some of us do."

Mair snapped, "You don't suffer, Mother. You live in luxury, with people tending to your every need. Since Father met you when you were sixteen, you have never wanted for anything. You are in excellent health for a woman of your age."

"Mair, sit down and eat your dinner, so you don't embarrass our guests." Alice spoke as though her daughter was five years old, and Mair acted accordingly, quietly sitting and doing as she was told.

Bud and I dared to exchange a knowing glance across the table, but our attention was then immediately captured by Owain, who pressed the cook with, "So how did he look? I've never seen a dead body. Not a fresh one. Lots of very ancient ones, of course."

"Not appropriate, Owain," commented Mair.

"Why not?" he asked plaintively.

"We're eating," replied his mother.

Everyone applied themselves to their loaded plates in silence for a few moments. I was assessing the family dynamic—*it's what I do, I can't help myself*—as I slathered my whole-wheat toast with what I was pretty sure was salted butter, then topped that with a thick dollop of moist, rough, rich pâté. The sensation as I bit into it was exquisite, the flavors a delight. It was definitely salted butter, and the pâté—oh the pâté! The rabbit was almost sweet, and there were hints of pepper and raspberry, a distinct note of salty acidity from capers, and finally, triumphantly, the richness of brandy in there somewhere. It seemed that Mrs. Dilys Jones was, indeed, a good cook. I was pleased and relieved, and I gave myself up to the pleasure of enjoying the first course in happy anticipation of an excellent meal.

Siân had decided that half a slice of toast with a smear of pâté was enough for her, so while the rest of us were still nibbling and munching, she had nothing to do but chatter. "Of course we were all very sorry to hear about the accident. I gather Mr. Davies lived here, is that right?" *I wish she'd picked a different topic.*

Eirwen answered, which I suspected was a brave move on her part. "He arrived after he married Rhian, that's Dilys's daughter, about six years ago. You'll have met Rhian, Cait; she's the person who's been planning your wedding. They have . . . um, had . . . well, Rhian still *has*, an apartment in the private wing. As do we all. Alice has the floor above the drawing room, and Janet has a room there too. Owain and Mair have the next floor up, then Idris and me, and the children of course, have the next, with Dilys, and Rhian and David on the top floor. We all manage very nicely."

As I continued trying to swallow the mouthful I'd taken, my heart became a big lump in my chest. Rhian Davies. *Of course.* It was *her* husband who'd died. I'd grown to like Rhian—we'd been in touch for months, planning the wedding.

Bud was smiling at Eirwen just a little too brightly as he said, "Let me see if I've got this right. You call the entry level the 'ground floor,' then the first upstairs floor is the 'first floor'? Right?"

Eirwen nodded eagerly.

Bud blustered on, "It sounds as though you have a different number of floors in each wing."

Eirwen smiled, pleased to have a change in topic. "Yes, we have a very unusual layout here. It's all a bit confusing because each part of the castle has a different number of floors. This wing has three floors, our wing has five, and the middle of the castle, the oldest part, only has two floors, properly speaking, plus the basement, which houses the kitchens. So, in this wing is this floor, which houses the morning room, this dining room, and the library, through there"—she waved an arm in the direction of the "mystery" door—"then there are the four guest rooms on the floor you're using: the bridal boudoir above our heads, the groom's room, and two more guest rooms. But there is another floor above that, where we could open up more guest rooms. To do that we'd need to remodel to allow for ensuite facilities, and all the new health and safety regulations. That would take a lot of money, so the floor is shut up for now. But—" She stopped speaking and literally bit her lip. I felt sorry for her. I suspected that the income from a possible contract with a television company would provide the cash necessary for the updating of the potential additional guest facilities.

"You mentioned my private library, Eirwen," said Owain. "Please don't give the impression that the room is open to the public." He nodded in our general direction. "I'm sure you appreciate that a man's library is his own domain."

"It's *my* library, Owain," said Alice Cadwallader, wiping the corners of her mouth with an embroidered napkin. She picked up her glass of sherry and drained the last few drops. "I'll take some wine now, Mair," she called.

"Yes, Mother," replied her daughter patiently, pushing aside her plate and rising from her seat. Mair moved to a second sideboard set so perfectly against the rounded wall that it must have been made for the room, just like the one upon which Dilys had carefully placed her serving tray. I thought it odd that Mair didn't serve her mother from the bottles of wine that sat upon the table, and from which we'd been invited to pour for ourselves. I began to wonder why she would do that, when my attention was taken by a sudden gust of wind that blew open the shutters on the window next to the sideboard, sending the curtain billowing into Mair. The bottle fell from her hand and shattered on the worn rug covering the flagstones.

A general hubbub ensued, which only ended when Dilys Jones, initially summoned by means of a bell-rope beside the fireplace, came rushing back in again with a dustpan and brush, and a copious amount of salt. "That's all I can do for the stain right now," she announced glumly, shooting an accusing glance toward Mair, who was ensuring that the window was closed. Mair took her seat when she was finished.

Alice, whose wheelchair had remained in place at the head of the table, called to her grandson, "Check she's done that right, Idris. You know what she's like."

"It's shut, Mother," said Mair.

"I'm sure it's just fine, Alice," added Idris, obviously not wanting to be used to belittle his aunt.

"Check it, Idris, we don't want another mess. Look at all that over there," snapped Alice imperiously.

Idris succumbed.

"It wasn't my fault, Mother," bleated Mair. "The wind blew it open. It is a terrible night out there, or haven't you noticed?"

"You are the housekeeper, Mair, and, as such, you were responsible for preparing this room for dinner. The fire is hardly alight; the shutters are blowing open every two minutes. Are you trying to make me catch my death of cold? Trying to kill me off? Is that it? Are you trying to get your hands on your inheritance that way?"

Just as Dilys Jones re-entered the dining room carrying another wide tray bearing an impressive tureen, Mair Cadwallader leapt from her seat, and completely lost it.

Chwech

"MOTHER—I AM NOTHING MORE, NOTHING less, than your unpaid skivvy. I am living the nineteenth-century life of a slave-daughter in the twenty-first century. It's ridiculous. A man is dead. *David* is dead. It's a terrible loss. And all you can worry about is yourself."

Mair clenched her fists as she spoke, her chest heaving with emotion. "Doesn't it occur to you that he will be missed? We're all grieving him in our own way. Rhian is so upset she can't even leave her room. Poor Rhian. Yes, Mother, poor *Rhian*, not poor *you*. You insisted that dinner go ahead when I'm sure that Dilys would rather be comforting her daughter. I know that Gwen's stayed on to be with her, but it's not the same as having your mother with you at a time like this. But that wouldn't occur to you, would it? Because you have no idea how that feels—to want to comfort someone. God forbid you'd think of your daughter that way, as someone who needs something from her mother, rather than as a thing, a servant, who can tend to her mother's every whim."

I wondered who "Gwen" might be, but it didn't seem to be the right time to ask.

Mair's anger seemed to subside into regret as she continued, "You never, ever showed me any affection, Mother. You didn't *need* me with you all these years, you just wanted a lapdog you didn't have to pet. Someone you could order around who couldn't resign. That's why all the nurses leave, Mother. They cannot put up with you. *You*. You're a pain in the . . . everything. But most of all you're a pain in the heart. *My* heart. I've only ever wanted you to love me. But I don't think you know the meaning of the word." Mair wiped away what I judged to be tears of anger and sadness, in equal measure, with her napkin.

"And you do, do you?" Alice's voice had a cruel edge.

"What?" Mair sounded impatient, to say the least.

"You think you know what love is, do you, girl? And how would that be, then? What secret life have you been living that would allow you to know that?" Alice managed to throw this barb in her daughter's direction while moving to one side so that Dilys could reach to place a bowl in front of her.

Mair plopped down into her seat, seemingly defeated. "Oh, Mother, not that again. Please?"

We'd all been embarrassed spectators, and it took Dilys's serving of the cawl to break the tension. For once the cook seemed quite jolly, at least proud of her offering.

As we all ate, with maybe a little too much gusto, there were lots of compliments about the hearty soup.

"This is delicious," said Bud with great enthusiasm. "What's in it?" I allowed my surprise to show. Bud never knows, or cares, what's in his food.

"It's cawl," replied Siân. "It could be anything." I could tell by her tone of voice that she was very tired. I suspected that her jetlag was kicking in.

"Dilys makes beef cawl," added Eirwen. "She's very good at it. Hearty, but not heavy."

"What's the green?" asked Bud.

"Leek tops," I replied. "And the yellow is swede."

"Swede?" asked Bud.

"We call it rutabaga in Canada; it's Swedish turnip—which is quite appropriate for a Swedish cop." I flashed a smile as wide as I could, and Bud reciprocated.

"You're a policeman?" asked Alice, sounding surprised.

"Used to be," replied Bud, "but I retired. It was time."

"Lost your nerve?" asked Alice dismissively.

Bud didn't miss a beat. "No, I lost my wife, then I decided it was time to quit." My heart went out to him.

"By 'lost,' I assume you mean she died?" asked Alice. I wanted to hit the woman, no matter her age.

"Sadly, yes," replied Bud. Realizing it was best to be direct, he added, "Cait and I were colleagues when my wife was alive. In case anyone gets the wrong idea, Cait and I were never anything more than respectful, friendly workmates during my wife's lifetime. It wasn't until Jan, my wife, was gone that Cait and I began to get to know each other as more than friends. We've been together as a couple for over a year now, and we are very much looking forward to our wedding here on Monday. Does that answer all your questions?"

Bud's good at being quiet when it's the right thing to do, but he's just as good at taking the bull by the horns when that's appropriate.

"Good for you," said Alice. "People don't often get a second chance. You should take them when they come along. I never had one. I was too old and ugly when Gryffudd died to turn any heads."

No one dared say anything, except Janet, who seemed to have been grinning for the whole evening. "Oh come on with you, Alice, you'd have any man you wanted wrapped around your little finger in an instant, I bet."

It was exactly what Alice had been fishing for, and she smiled at her nurse like a naughty child. "Oh, I don't know about that."

"Oh, yes you do." Janet's grin grew. She seemed to be the only person in the room with the energy and will to buoy up Alice. I suspected that the Cadwallader family was completely worn out by fulfilling the matriarch's desperate need for attention, and that maybe each nurse she hired gradually reached the same conclusion and left, the aged woman having fed upon their energy like a vampire, finally sucking them dry. I wondered how long the nurses lasted before they reached the "husk" stage and resigned.

As I sipped my tasty broth and nibbled on the delicious meat and vegetables it held, I contemplated the dysfunction of the Cadwallader clan.

Breaking the no-longer-heavy silence, Siân piped up with, "Do you have a very Swedish name, Bud? I've just realized that Cait's never told me your surname. Will I be able to pronounce it? Or will I need lessons?"

"Oh, I should think so," replied Bud smiling. "It's Anderson. Not so very exotic."

"You're kidding," exclaimed Siân. "An-der-son?"

Bud nodded. "Yes. Why? Is that an unusual name in Australia?"

"Not very," replied Siân. "In the town and shire of Dowerin, where my husband is from, there are a lot of Andersons. And it's especially popular at our house. It's my husband's name. It's my name, and my children's name. We're 'Anderson' too. I'm Siân Anderson. And my big sister will become Cait Anderson. Strewth. We'll have the same name again."

"No, we won't," I replied. "I'm keeping 'Morgan.'"

"You didn't tell me Siân's married name was 'Anderson,'" said Bud, at roughly the same time that Siân said, "You didn't tell me Bud's name was 'Anderson.'"

It hadn't occurred to me to tell either of them about the other's name. To be honest, I've never thought of Siân as an "Anderson" at all. She's always just been Siân to me.

"I'm glad we're not the only family that keeps secrets," said Mair.

I must have been feeling defensive, because I snapped, "A name's just a name, it's no big deal." *Stupid of me.*

"I have to disagree with that," replied Owain, who'd been largely silent since we'd entered the dining room. "A name is a signifier of belonging, of rights, of ownership, and of heritage. It can mark your place in society, in geography, and in history. It is a part of you. It's a vital part of everyone. You shouldn't belittle the importance of a name. Just look at us, the Cadwalladers. My grandfather changed his name from Ieuan ap Hywel Cadwaladr to Powell Cadwallader just so he'd be better accepted in the world of business, especially by the English. Even mother here changed her name from Alicia, her given name, to Alice, in order to be better accepted. Less Roman Catholic, I believe, isn't that right, Mother?"

Alice stared at her son. It was difficult to read the emotion in her glittering eyes, but I settled upon interpreting it as contempt.

"None of your cheek, Owain. Your father preferred Alice. That was that."

Her response made me wonder if her dismissiveness was directed toward her son or her late husband.

"Why will you be keeping 'Morgan,' Cait?" asked Siân.

Bud and I had covered this ground pretty comprehensively, so I smiled warmly at him and felt able to say, quite lightly, "It's the name I'm known by in my professional life, and it would be confusing to change it, given that it's the name that appears on all the research I've done to date. Cait Anderson didn't get a PhD, or put forward theories that challenged the criminology community, so she doesn't exist in my working world. Cait Morgan does. I'll be better off sticking with the name that's known."

"But you could be Mrs. Anderson too, like me," said Siân. As she spoke she allowed her spoon to plop into her still half-full soup bowl. It seemed she wasn't going to make the most of her main course, either.

"Jan was Mrs. Anderson," I snapped, immediately wishing I could recall the anger with which I'd spoken Jan's name. I made sure my tone was gentler as I said, "And Bud's mother is Mrs. Anderson. I'll be Cait Morgan. It's who I know how to be."

"Ah-ha! You prove my point for me. Exactly," said Owain triumphantly, "names define us."

"Like 'Davies the Eyes' defined poor David Davies?" asked Eirwen.

And we were back to the topic of the dead man. *Inevitable, I suppose.*

"Only in that he used those eyes to get whatever he wanted, from everybody," said Dilys Jones as she re-entered the dining room to gather our used dishes.

"What do you mean?" asked Eirwen and Mair in chorus.

"You know very well what I mean," said Dilys spitefully. "After that treasure he was, and made no bones about it."

"Our treasure?" exploded Owain. "He's been hunting for our treasure?"

"*My* treasure," said Alice. "And what do you mean exactly, Dilys?"

"I know what I knows," said the cook, tapping her nose. Thrusting herself between diners, she picked up the priceless nineteenth-century Swansea china soup plates and allowed the silver spoons we'd been lucky enough to use to clatter about in them as though they weren't worth a fortune.

"And what would that be?" asked Mair.

Dilys looked across the room toward the impressive, dark oak dresser that stood between two of the sets of curtains. "Never could take his eyes off that, could he? Always staring at it, mumbling, he was."

I followed her gaze and noticed the large, rectangular platter that had pride of place on the middle shelf of the dresser.

"Is that the puzzle plate you were all talking about before dinner?" I asked.

"It is indeed," replied Owain. "Please, feel free to take a good look at it, Cait. It is there for anyone to see, though of course we remove it, along with all the other china, before members of the public are allowed to troop through this room. Some people are very light fingered, you know."

I took my chance, left my place at the table, and was peering at the plate in less than a moment. It measured about two feet long by eighteen inches high, with slightly rounded corners. All the decoration was in a mid-blue on a white background, typical of Swansea willow-pattern china, and its border was painted with a pseudo-Chinese design, which I found curious. The center was hand painted with a verse:

> Where the fire meets the earth, where the water meets
>   the air,
> Where the face of beauty smiles, the treasures will
>   be there.
> Black gold in a seam, now popping with a spray,
> For every humble man, there is a time to pray.
> The breath of Llŷr and Neptune's tears—the same, there
>   is no doubt,
> When they are gone, what gold is left, we cannot live
>   without.
> The worthy man sees treasure through the silver and
>   through glass,
> The vain man only ever sees the beauty that will pass.
> Cadwalladers will never leave the castle of the gray,
> As long as ancients rest in peace and old walls not
>   give way.
> By the rushing of my lifeblood, I swear this on my grave,
> The wise man will discover them, and my kin be ever
>   saved.

"It's beautifully painted," I noted.

"It is a good deal more than that," said Owain proudly. "It is proof that the original Cadwalladers hid a treasure hereabouts, and I intend to find it. The clues are tantalizing, and I believe I am making headway."

"You say it's from the Swansea Pottery?" I asked.

Owain nodded. "Founded in 1790, closed in 1870. Very sad. Produced the best wares between 1814 and 1817. I'm pretty confident that was when this plate was made."

He looked very pleased with himself, which rankled me. I felt like telling him what I really thought, but I satisfied myself with a polite, "Surely it can't be that old."

"Know a lot about the Swansea Pottery, do you?" challenged Owain.

Bud glared at me, but it was too late. I bit. "I'm familiar with the writings and collections of W. J. Grant-Davidson, as well as the Glynn Vivian and Swansea Museum collections. I would say this plate is much later than the true period, dating to maybe the late nineteenth century, or maybe even the twentieth. The glaze is all wrong, and the body seems far too thick." *Maybe I bit a little too hard.*

Owain was red in the face. "Preposterous!"

Bud looked horrified, Siân worried and strangely tense, and I noticed a wicked smile play at the corners of Mair's mouth.

"That's shut you up for a while," said Owain's mother to him, as though he were a naughty boy. "Told you she was brainy, that one. Been here two minutes and she's already seen something you couldn't, even though it was staring you right in the face."

"True," said Mair quietly, though I got the impression she wasn't referring to the puzzle plate.

"What do you make of the puzzle then, Cait?" continued Alice. "Does that gibberish mean anything to you?"

"She barely looked at it, Mother, what can you expect?" was Owain's angry retort.

Having retaken my seat at the table I decided that I didn't want to play nice anymore; I'd give the overbearing Owain a run for his money. "I can come up with several theories," I replied.

I think Bud wanted to kick me under the table, but he couldn't reach.

I began quietly enough. "I believe that the first couplet is a very general introduction, telling us that there is treasure in three different places, those being where some sort of fire meets some sort of earth, where air and water meet, and where 'beauty smiles,' which might be a literal place, such as on a face, or could be more metaphorical, meaning a natural beauty of some sort, rather than a human being. I believe that each of the next three couplets then refers to each one of the three different places in turn—following the order of the introduction. So, 'Black gold in a seam, now popping with a spray / For every humble man, there is a time to pray' refers to the location introduced as 'Where the fire meets the earth,' and so on. I see the final four lines as an acknowledgment that the discovery of the treasure would allow the Cadwalladers, somehow, to retain ownership of the 'castle of the gray,' or Castell Llwyd."

"Rubbish," said Owain. "All the treasure is in one place—why would anyone spread it around? It's quite clear that all three clues have to be taken as a whole. Believe me, Mother, I have spent years researching this. With respect to our guest, she's given it no more than a few moments' thought."

"And yet she's said more about it in those minutes than you have in all those years," said Alice. She turned from her son in disgust and said to me, "Tell us more, Cait. What do you think the treasure might be?"

Bud was glaring at me, and I took the hint. We weren't on a treasure hunt.

"Oh, now there's a turn up for the books," interrupted Dilys, who'd been listening with lively eyes alight with scandal, "her just being here a little while. I think David thought a bit different about them clues than you did too, Owain."

"Don't say anything to this lot, Dilys," said Alice quickly. "If anyone should know what David Davies was up to under my roof, it should be me. You can tell me after dinner. Now serve the trifle and let's be done with this evening. I'm very tired and I want to go to bed."

It seemed that Alice was determined to shut down the conversation.

From the far end of our group Janet called, "You won't be able to go to bed for an hour after you've eaten, and you know that. So why not give the trifle a miss for now, Alice, and I'll wheel you to your little chair lift. Then I can get you some nice hot milk with a drop of something in it, and you can sip that while your dinner settles, alright?" She smiled indulgently at her charge as she spoke, and, as always seemed to be the case when Janet said anything, there was a chuckle in her voice.

"Can I have a drop of my special whiskey in it?" Alice brightened.

"If you're a good girl, yes." Janet smiled.

"Right then," said Alice with determination, "goodnight all, I'll see you in the morning. Help me reverse, Janet, then I'll meet you at my lift." As soon as she was out from under the table, Alice pushed a little stick on her armrest and zoomed off across the dining room. I was pretty sure I could hear the squeal of brakes echo in the great hall as she took corners.

"She'll be the death of me, that one," said Janet as she rushed after Alice.

I realized that Dilys Jones had vanished too, and we were all left to contemplate what she'd meant about David Davies hunting for the treasure. I couldn't help but wonder if it might have something to do with his death. Then I told myself off and turned my attention to the dessert that Dilys had plopped in front of each of us before she'd dashed away.

Saith

I ENJOYED EVERY MOUTHFUL OF the small portion of sherry trifle. I hadn't tasted a real trifle in years, so the thick, golden custard topped with smoothly whipped cream, the sponge fingers generously soaked in sherry, and the scarlet fruit—strawberries, raspberries, and cherries—suspended in the blackcurrant-flavored jelly were a joy in which I reveled for a few, brief moments.

Too brief, it seemed, because I was called back from taste bud heaven by my sister saying, "I can't keep my eyes open any more, folks. I'm sorry, I'm going to have to hit the hay." It looked as though she'd eaten half a spoonful of jelly, and that was it. *No wonder she's so thin, she hardly eats at all.*

As Siân stood to leave the table, she swayed alarmingly. Both Bud and I jumped to our feet and rushed to her side.

Owain's reaction was surprising. "It's a heck of a trip from Oz. She'll need a good sleep, and no mistake."

Siân rallied and replied, "Been there, have you?" She spoke as though the idea seemed unlikely, and swatted Bud and me away at the same time.

"Once or twice," replied Owain. "Geology is a passion of mine, along with history. The two are so inextricably linked. And, of course, both my father and grandfather were well known for their geological knowledge, and their ability to exploit it. I'm afraid I'm rather lacking in that particular ability." He sounded as disappointed about this circumstance as I suspected his mother might be.

"Todd's in mining. My husband," responded Siân groggily. "You two would probably get on like a house on fire. He's never happier than when he's talking about sediment, formations, strata, and deposits.

Serves him right I've left him alone with the kids for once." I'd never heard Siân say anything along these lines before, and I couldn't help but feel that she was in a particularly vulnerable state. "Flies all over the place he does, for weeks on end. He has no idea what it's like to spend real time with them. Up country to the iron area, off to Newman and Tom Price, and inland to Kalgoorlie for the gold and God only knows what else—I dare say the topless bars there keep him entertained."

I had to act, so I steadied Siân, nodded to Bud for him to do the same, and we steered her toward the door. "I'm taking Siân to bed now. I think she needs some sleep. As Owain noted, she's very tired. I'm sorry we're all leaving so abruptly. Dinner was delightful . . ." By the time the last words were out of my mouth the three of us were in the great hall and beginning to negotiate the first few steps of the staircase.

I realized then that Siân had more or less been a non-participant in the table conversation for some time, but it was almost as though she'd gone from stone cold sober, if disengaged, to falling down drunk in the space of about five minutes. Such is jetlag. It never warns you when it's about to bash you over the head with a brick—it just does it, and down you go.

"Is she going to be okay?" mouthed Bud as we dragged Siân, who now seemed to be almost unconscious, up each step. She looked slim enough, but she was a dead weight. It wasn't an easy trip to her room, but eventually we managed to get her inside and lying down on her bed, underneath the old-fashioned eiderdown.

"Let's just leave her in her clothes," I said, motioning for Bud to leave with me. "She should be warm enough under that quilt. It's not as drafty in here as it is in my room. Fewer windows, for a start, and I might be imagining it, but I think that the wind's died down a bit, too."

I shut her door as quietly as possible, and Bud and I both let out a huge sigh of relief.

"Leaving the light on inside her bathroom was a good idea, Cait," he said quietly. "If she's disoriented when she wakes, at least she'll be able to navigate her way there."

I nodded. "Who knows if she'll sleep until morning. It's still only nine-thirty, so if she can sleep in until at least eight, she should be refreshed. How about you? How do you feel?"

Bud rubbed his temple. "To be honest, I've got a bit of a headache, and I think I could at least do with lying down. I just need to stretch out, you know?"

"I know exactly what you mean," I replied. I did. My back was aching, as were my neck, shoulders, and legs. "I know it's early, but I don't think I can keep going any longer, Bud. However intriguing the death of David Davies, that wonderful plate, and the Cadwalladers' dysfunction might be, I need my bed. So let's just call it a day?"

Our parting embrace quickly resulted in each of us supporting the other, which led to giggling.

"Off to your bed, young lady," said Bud, chuckling.

"My bridal boudoir, you mean." I smiled as I waved to Bud from my door. "Goodnight, husband-to-be. Love you lots."

"Love you more," replied Bud from his own doorway.

"Love you most," I whispered back and shut my door so that I became the clear winner.

The massive bed looked inviting, but so did my bathroom, so I changed in there, where the radiator allowed for the smaller square footage to be a little less chilly, then scampered across the expanse of the room and dove under the covers. I was almost asleep by the time I switched off the bedside lamp four seconds later. Then . . . nothing.

I awoke with a start and grabbed the bedclothes to my chest. I probably looked like a right twit as I stared into the darkness, trying to work out what had woken me. The wind howled around my turret. The windows rattled. But, other than that, I couldn't hear anything else.

I looked at my wristwatch. It was 2:37 AM, and, lo and behold, I was wide awake. I snuggled back down, but I was restless. My mind raced. The characters painted on the walls and ceiling seemed to be moving in the shadows. It was disquieting. I knew it was all a trick of the dim light that seeped through the crack at the bottom of the door, but it didn't help. My mouth was dry, and my fingers and ankles were still painful and swollen from the flight. I lay there trying to make spit, twirling my ankles, and clenching and unclenching my fists. The knock at my door startled me so much that I bit my tongue.

I leapt out of the bed, switched on the lamp, and scampered across the room. "Who is it?" I hissed.

"It's me, Bud."

I opened the door, relieved to see Bud's tousled silver hair and wide-eyed expression. "Cait, what's happened?" He pushed me into my room. "Let me look at you. What is that? Is it blood? Oh my word—what have you done?"

"I bit my tongue when you knocked on the door. You frightened the life out of me. I'll get some tissue. It'll stop."

"I'm sorry. I didn't mean to . . . Oh, you know I didn't mean to startle you. Were you asleep? Stick it out, it'll help," suggested Bud unhelpfully.

"You're just taking the mickey now, right?" I hurled my most aggressively arched eyebrow at him, and he flinched. I felt triumphant. But I did as he suggested and kept my tongue out, as much as I could.

Bud steered me to the edge of the bed and, once I was settled, dashed to my bathroom. He returned quickly, trailing a length of loo paper. As I dabbed at the bloody mess I'd made, he explained, "I woke up, I don't know why. I think I heard something. This place is full of such strange noises, and the storm isn't helping. Anyway, I just couldn't get back to sleep. I'll admit that this place has spooked me a little. Back home, it would be the evening for us, not the early hours of the morning, so maybe our bodies think we should be up and about. So I came to see if you were awake too."

I replied, "Ny pubby hinksh ish pimmer pime." *How do dentists ever understand a word you say in their chair? Do they get lessons at dental school?*

"Are you speaking Welsh?" asked Bud.

I shook my head. "Ny pubby hinksh ish pimmer pime," I repeated.

Bud interpreted, "Your body thinks it's dinner time?"

I nodded.

"Oddly enough, so does mine," admitted Bud. "You haven't got any snacks hidden in your luggage, have you? I know you like to have snacks at hand."

I shook my head. "Kishen?" I managed.

Bud looked alarmed. "What, risk going into Mrs. Dilys Jones's domain without her express approval? Are you nuts? She'd probably have us garroted with some kitchen twine before we got the fridge open. *Phooey!*"

"Wha?" I croaked. My throat was getting dry.

"Now I've mentioned the fridge, I can imagine it full of leftovers. That trifle was really good. Not too sweet. You know I don't like really sweet desserts. I could do with another serving of that. Or that pâté. Or anything really."

A few moments later I was dressed and armed with a flickering flashlight that looked as though it had been in the bathroom since the plumbing was installed in the 1930s. In the darkness, the great hall felt like a huge, black pit, and we held hands as we made our way down the stairs, which seemed to go on forever. At the bottom of the stairs I almost butted heads with one of the suits of armor that stood guard there. Bud pulled me to safety, and we headed to a swinging door beneath the stairs, close to the dining room. Beside the door was a stuffed bear that seemed to rear up out of the darkness and threaten me. I gave it a wide berth as Bud pushed open the door as quietly as he could. Unlike almost every other door I'd encountered in the castle, this one didn't squeak at all. With two flashlights at our disposal, Bud shone his at the floor, while I kept mine pointing ahead of us as we made our way along a little corridor. Eventually we reached the steps down which I assumed David Davies had taken his fatal plunge.

"Be careful, Cait," whispered Bud, very close to my ear. "These look as though they are very steep, and you're not the best on your feet, especially when it comes to precipitous steps, or heights."

I set off, gripping the piece of thick rope looped through metal rings along one wall that acted as a pretty inadequate handrail. I could hear Bud breathing behind me, so I knew he was close.

"I wish you'd let me go first," he whispered.

"I'm nearly at the bottom, I think," I replied calmly. My tongue was finally allowing me to speak properly. When I reached the stone flags of the flooring, I stood still and shone my light onto the last couple of steps for Bud.

"It looks like it's this way to the food," said Bud eagerly as he joined me, and he pulled me into Mrs. Jones's inner sanctum. We moved carefully into a gaping black chasm. Bud flicked a switch, and fluorescent tubes sputtered to life above our heads. The kitchen was a cavernous room—stone walls; high, small barred windows; and a selection of outdated, well-used cupboards and work surfaces. It felt as unwelcoming as the woman who used it. Even so, five minutes later we were both sitting on the edge of the big wooden table in the middle of the room, swinging our legs like children, greedily scoffing trifle off fine Swansea blue-and-white willow-pattern china I'd taken from the pile of dishes that had been left to air-dry on a long draining board beside the deep, ceramic Belfast sink. I felt like a character from an Enid Blyton book. It was great fun. Bud and I were having an adventure. *With food.*

When we'd finished, which didn't take long, I rinsed off the dishes and placed them back on the draining board. We'd both acknowledged that we'd have to admit to our sins in the morning, when food was found to be missing, but that we'd charm Mrs. Jones into forgiving us.

We each had a glass of milk, agreeing it was too dangerous to try to carry full glasses back to our rooms, but then we were at a loss as to what to do next. We were both not only wide awake but now buoyed up by the sugar we'd just consumed.

Just as I was about to suggest that we should leave and go back to our rooms, because I knew it was the right thing to do, I saw the unmistakable sweep of a flashlight in the corridor beyond the kitchen by which Bud and I had entered. I grabbed Bud's arm.

A figure, dressed all in white, appeared noiselessly at the doorway. I froze.

Wyth

"WHAT THE——?" GASPED BUD AS he leapt down from the table.

"It's only me," said Siân.

"What do you think you're playing at?" I snapped. I could have hit her.

"I'm sorry I frightened you," she said sheepishly, as I too jumped down from the table. "I didn't think there'd be anyone here, then I heard you two and thought I should make myself known."

"You very nearly gave me a heart attack," I said. "What are you doing out there? Have you come looking for food too?" It seemed unlikely.

"No, I came down to look at the body," said Siân simply. "I have to see if it's him."

"If it's who? And stop pointing that in my eyes." I sounded as cross as I felt.

Siân lowered the light and said quietly, "David Davies. I have to see if it's him. I couldn't believe it when Eirwen said his name."

"*I* told you the man's name," said Bud, sounding puzzled. "*I* told you it was David Davies. Cait even told me off for saying the guy's name the wrong way."

Siân smiled sadly. "She was the one who said 'Davies the Eyes,' you see. 'David Davies' could be anyone."

Bud held up his hands in confusion. "I don't get it."

"I knew four David Davieses growing up," I explained. "It's not an uncommon name in Wales."

"Aren't there enough names to go around?" replied Bud, bemused.

"Hmm, it's funny, isn't it? I also knew two John Joneses, a Thomas Thomas, an Owain Owens, and a Llewellyn Llewellyn. There is a reason, connected to sons taking fathers' names, to signify lineage, but I'll save the lecture, because I think we should focus on my sister. So, go on then, tell us what you're talking about, Siân."

She nodded. "When they said he was called Davies the Eyes earlier on, I couldn't believe it. I wondered if he was *my* Davies the Eyes, so I had to come and have a look. It's taken me forever to find this kitchen, but he's not here. I don't know where to look next."

"And who exactly is Davies the Eyes, and what is he to you?" I asked.

Siân clenched her hands into little fists and growled through her teeth. "Don't you ever remember the important stuff, Cait? I went out with him, back when I was seventeen, eighteen. Mum and Dad hated him, which, of course, made him all the more attractive."

I nodded. "You mentioned someone to me, once, on the phone, though only as 'David.' Mum told me more. Is he the one who dumped you before some big party or other?"

"Here's a great example of sisterly love for you, Bud," said Siân angrily. "Bluntly put, Cait left home for university when I was thirteen, so I was no more than a child to her then. A child with a very inferior academic ability to her older sister, so worse than nothing. Since then, we've had a relationship built solely on Cait's infrequent trips home when she was at university, phone calls, duty-visits, and, more recently, emails and photos."

Siân held up her hand to stop me responding. I thought it best to allow her to rant, which she did. "Cait's memory is a wonderful thing, if she's been paying attention. I'm pretty sure she took almost no notice of me at all until I hit my mid-twenties and married Todd. When she came to Wales for our wedding—yes, in case she hasn't told you, Todd and I came all the way from Australia to be married—she looked surprised to see an adult Siân, rather than a lanky kid. We hardly know each other. We just have childhood memories. Be honest, Cait, that's the truth, isn't it? If we were really more to each other than that, you'd know that David Davies was the man who broke my heart. In the worst possible way."

I wanted to say so much, and normally, I would have done. But one look at Siân told me it wasn't the right moment. So instead of biting back, or telling her how hurtful her words had been, I said, "I had no idea."

"Of course you didn't," spat Siân. She was exhibiting all the classic signs of distress, and stress.

My heart took another knock when I heard the unmistakable voice of Dilys Jones behind me. "What do you all think you're doing in my kitchen?" She seemed to be shouting, because we'd all been trying to keep our voices down. "No right to be down here, you haven't. No right at all. What do you think you're up to?"

Bud admitted, "I'm afraid we were drawn here by the thought of your delicious trifle, Dilys. I hope you don't mind that we ate some."

I'd suspected that we'd get a thorough scolding, but, almost immediately, Mrs. Jones's demeanor softened a little. She even almost smiled. "It's a very nice accent you've got there, Bud," she said sweetly, "but guests shouldn't be down here, by rights. The missus doesn't like it, nor does Idris. It's not proper. You should be upstairs, where you belong. Off you go now. It's the middle of the night. Noise carries in a place like this, you know. Wake the whole place you will. Go on now, back to bed with the lot of you."

"We were also looking for the body, Mrs. Jones," replied Bud in his no-nonsense voice. "Where is it, please?"

Dilys looked surprised—to be fair, she had every right. "Idris helped me move it. It was in my way, his body, right at the bottom of the up stairs like that."

"The 'upstairs'?" I echoed. "I thought the body was down here, downstairs."

Mrs. Jones looked me up and down, then rolled her eyes as she tutted, "A bit *twp* are you?"

I straightened my back as she used a word for "stupid" that I hadn't heard in years, and certainly not applied to myself.

Her thin lips pursed before she spoke. "There's stairs for going down, the down stairs, these ones behind me, which bring you into this end of the kitchen, and there's stairs for going up, the up stairs, which you use when you go out of the other end of the kitchen, and up to the dining room. Otherwise people going to and fro would always be bumping into each other. See?"

"I'm sorry, I don't think I understand," said Siân simply. She sounded tired.

Mrs. Jones shook her head as though she were sorry for us all. "Oh dear me. Let me explain." She began to speak more loudly, imagining it would help us better understand her, I supposed. "The stairs are the same, but we use them different. You've got to have a system, see? Otherwise everything goes to pot. Besides, the up stairs come out next to the dining room, so the food stays hot. The down stairs, these ones," she motioned behind her, "are at the other end of the little corridor under the main staircase. They come out over by the drawing room. No use to me when I've got hot food in my hands. Alright for clearing things away, though. I needed my up stairs cleared, so we moved the body, see?"

"Earlier on, you and Eirwen referred to the man who died as 'Davies the Eyes,' Mrs. Jones," said Siân, clearly wanting to get information about the body, rather than the layout of the place. "Why was that? Was he always known that way?"

The cook straightened her shoulders. As I noted her curlers and hairnet, I felt a little less intimidated by her presence.

"Always been called that, as far as I know," she said. "Always before and since he married my Rhian. Married six years, they've been. Never any children, mind you. Sad. I don't think it was Rhian's fault. To my mind it was him." She gave Siân a withering look. "So, yes, always called 'Davies the Eyes,' he was. Men and woman called him the same. Anyway, why d'you ask? Know him, did you?"

Mrs. Jones's eyes narrowed as, this time, she gave Siân a good looking over. Siân squirmed. "Tall, blond, slim. Just his type," assessed the cook. "Mind you, his type was any woman with a pulse," she added bitterly, "and maybe a bit of money in her pocket. Rhian was a pretty thing when she married him, but look at her now. Let herself go something terrible, she has. But that's enough about him. This is my kitchen, and you shouldn't be in it by rights. Even I have to wear a hairnet in here. Health and safety rubbish. You shouldn't be where the food is. Not till it's in front of you, on a plate anyway. So go on, off you all go."

"I want to see the body, Mrs. Jones," said Siân firmly.

"Alright, alright, don't get your knickers in a twist. It doesn't bother me one way or the other if you want to see it, my dear. So long as you're respectful with it. He was married to my Rhian, after all. Though why you'd want to, I don't know. Still meant something to you, did he, after all that time?"

"No, he did not," said Siân angrily.

"So you won't be sorry he's dead then?" said Dilys slyly.

"Why would I be?" Siân tried to sound unconcerned. It didn't work, which worried me.

Dilys pounced. "Did *you* do it? Did you push him to get your own back on him for something? I bet you wouldn't have minded doing it. Mind you, I think you'd be in a queue."

What an interesting comment.

Involuntarily my eyes followed Mrs. Jones's gaze toward Siân. "Kangaroo caught in headlights" came to mind as I saw her startled expression, but that seemed an unfair representation of my sister's choice to become an Australian.

"Of course I didn't," Siân spluttered. She was defensive when she continued, "I didn't even know he was here, at Castell Llwyd. And even if I had, why on earth would I want to kill him?"

"You tell me," said Mrs. Jones. "I bet it's a good story. Probably got a sad ending, if I know anything about him. Break your heart, and take your money, did he? You wouldn't be the only one. Settled down for a few years after he married my poor Rhian, he did, and I thought she'd tamed him, or at least that he'd changed. But I know what I knows. There, I've said it now."

I butted in. "You haven't said anything, Mrs. Jones, though you've implied that your son-in-law was an inveterate womanizer with sticky fingers to boot. Is that what you're saying, outright? That someone might have wanted to kill him for one, or both, of those reasons."

"Better ask her," said the cook, nodding at Siân. "I can tell by her face she knows what I mean."

As Bud and I looked at Siân, she blushed to the roots of her highlighted and perfectly bobbed hair. "I didn't know he was here," she bleated, her eyes downcast.

"Well, if you two believe that, you'll believe anything," the sharp-tongued cook let loose. "When this one drove into the grounds, she parked her car in the stable block. Am I right?"

Siân nodded.

"Those windows over there?" She waved an arm toward the row of shallow panes just above eye level in the wall, which were as black as the night beyond them. We all nodded. "This kitchen's in the original part of the castle, the medieval part they used as the foundations for the pretend-Norman monstrosity the first Cadwallader built. Those windows might only be small, but they are at ground level outside. No one notices them, but I can see out very well, all round, and I see what I sees. What do you think of that, then?"

"So what did you see?" I asked. The woman's oblique insinuations were getting on my nerves.

"That's for me to know." She tapped a finger on the side of her impressive nose. "Walls have ears," she added.

I tried to not let my exasperation show. "Mrs. Jones, are you saying you saw my sister Siân with David Davies earlier today?"

"No, she didn't," shouted Siân.

Successfully defusing an increasingly tense situation, Bud quietly demanded, "Could you tell me where to find the body of David Davies?"

Dilys Jones sniffed as she replied, "Go round the corner there, down the corridor, into the back kitchen. We put him up on the big table; you can't miss him. There's a light inside the door. Turn it off when you leave, then I suppose you'll all have to troop back through here again, because I won't have you going up the down stairs. You have to go up the up ones. Go on with you, I'm going back to bed. Got to be up at the crack of dawn to get the breakfast done. Turn off all the lights, right?"

We followed her grumpily delivered directions, and found ourselves in yet another black, massive room. Once again, ancient fluorescent tubes crackled to life when Bud flicked a switch. It was immediately evident that the space was used to house unwanted items of all sorts, from broken stepladders to buckets with no handles and mops with mere stumps for heads, as well as boxes filled with supplies for the kitchen. Mrs. Jones had been correct in her assertion that we wouldn't be able to miss the resting place for her son-in-law's body—it lay on an impressively large wooden table in the middle of the cluttered room. The outline of the corpse beneath a white sheet made me think of the old Frankenstein movies. It was a very eerie sight.

"Right," said Siân determinedly, "let's have a look at him," and she pulled back the sheet with a flourish.

As the dust from the table swirled about us, I heard Siân gasp. "It's him. He's hardly changed at all," she whispered. "Older, of course, but he's still . . . oh my God, it's really him. David is dead."

Siân began to shake. I could tell she was grappling with some very strong emotions. I realized that maybe she'd made a valid point when she'd said we hardly knew each other as adults. I didn't have a clue about the nature or the depth of relationship that had once existed between my sister—my own flesh and blood—and the lifeless corpse in front of us.

I tried to put an arm around Siân, but she pushed me away and moved to the end of the table where she gripped its edge. Having been rejected by my sibling, I thought it best to take in what I could about the body. An obviously broken neck; a badly scraped and cut chin; hands knocked about, maybe from trying to save himself as he toppled. I completely removed the sheet and took a look at the rest of his body. His clothes—a pair of old jeans and a polo-necked gray sweater—were grubby and dusty, but they also had what looked like coal dust on them. His jeans were very creased at the bottom, and rolled up to a couple of inches above his black dress shoes, which seemed an odd choice of footwear. Turning over his hands, I noted that both palms were rough to the touch and also bore traces of black dust. On closer examination I spotted what seemed to be a rust mark across his jeans. I bent forward and sniffed.

"Cait—stop it!" hissed Bud.

Siân seemed to snap out of her reverie. "What on earth are you doing?" she asked sharply.

I sighed as I explained, "I thought this was a rust mark, but it doesn't smell like iron. I wondered if . . ."

"What are you doing now, Cait?" Bud sounded puzzled, as I pulled at David Davies's jeans.

"Help me pull up the legs of these a bit farther, will you?" I asked Bud as I did my best alone. Rigor hadn't set in, but it still wasn't easy.

"What on earth for?" he asked. "I don't think you should be doing this. Just let the body be. This is nothing to do with us."

Bud was acting in a very un-Bud-like manner.

"Come on, Bud, I just want to check something. Please, give me a hand?"

Bud sighed and looked cross, but he helped anyway.

"Look!" I said, maybe a little too triumphantly. I pointed at a mark that ran across the front of both of the dead man's legs. "What do you think did that?" The mark was slightly pink, about half an inch wide, and appeared on each of his shins, a few inches above the top of his short, black dress socks.

"Oh no," said Bud, and he cursed under his breath.

"Strewth," exclaimed Siân. "It looks like something might have knocked across his shins. It could have made him fall down the stairs."

I nodded.

Siân looked thoughtful. "It's not my area really, but there might have been blood pumping around his body long enough for those marks to have formed. We did quite a lot of work on cadavers in training, and you'd be amazed how badly bruised up they can be, even when whatever caused the bruises happened very shortly prior to death." She looked at the grim expressions on our faces, and added, "Or maybe you two wouldn't be so surprised?"

All three of us were quiet for a moment.

"He might have got those marks weeks ago," said Bud half-heartedly.

I replied calmly, "They aren't old bruises, Bud, and you know it. There's none of the discoloration that comes with that age of injury. It's not my main area of knowledge either, but I, too, have done a fair bit of work with bodies, of the living and the dead, and these are fresh marks. Look—if you get close, you can just see where the skin is broken in a few places. That's raw. I know I'm no expert, but we must mention it when the authorities arrive, whenever that might be."

"You're right, of course," said Bud miserably.

"Now let's have a look at the rest of him," I said. "Come on, help me roll him, will you?"

Bud held back. *Weird.*

"I'll help," said Siân, and between us, we managed to lift his shoulders enough for me to see some more marks on the back of his sweater.

"They could be anything," said Bud. *Too quickly.*

Siân and I both glared at Bud as we lay the body back down. Siân gave me a sheepish look, and I knew I had to step up.

"Bud, those marks couldn't be 'anything.' They are, quite clearly, two handprints, in coal dust, on the man's back. On the back of a man we've all been thinking—hoping—accidentally fell down the stairs. What on earth are you playing at, Bud? A mark on the front of his shins, which might suggest he was tripped. Two handprints on his back, which might suggest a push. This man's body is almost screaming that foul play was involved. So why are you insisting that he fell?"

Bud sighed. "Because I *want* him to have fallen, Cait. You're right when you say I've been hoping he fell. I don't want this to be a suspicious death, or a possible murder. I just want it to be an accident, and nothing to do with us. I'm sorry, Siân. I don't know what this man once meant to you, but I am putting Cait first. It's our wedding weekend, and I *need* this to be just an accident."

I softened. Bud's entire life had been dedicated to seeking justice. I realized how hard this was for him, and I shared his anguish.

"I love you, Bud, and I, too, wish it could have been an accident. But I don't think it was. I don't believe any of us think it was—not anymore. And we must act on that. We all agree on that, don't we?"

Bud and Siân nodded.

The silence closed around us, broken only by the humming of the lights that shone on the remains of a man I had never met, but whose death, I suspected, was about to ruin my wedding.

Naw

I WAS FINISHED WITH THE body. It had told me all it could with its clothing on, so we respectfully replaced the sheet. The three of us made our way back into the working kitchen, which was marginally less cold than the abandoned one. Bud and I resumed our seated positions on the edge of the kitchen table, and Siân took the only chair in the room.

"This is bad," said Bud, echoing my own thoughts. "A man falls down a staircase and breaks his neck. It's very sad, but it might not be so very unusual. However, now that we've seen the marks on him, I'm concerned that moving the body might have contaminated a possible crime scene."

I replied thoughtfully, "I wonder if they'd have left the body where it fell if the authorities had been able to promise they'd be here in a timely manner. What do you think?"

Bud shrugged. "Everyone here is so bizarre it's hard to know."

I mused quietly, "We know that his not being 'officially' removed led to his relocation, and, to be fair, the table out there is a pretty good spot to choose, if you have to leave a body lying around overnight that is. It's out of the way, not posing a health hazard, and, as we know, it's as cold as a refrigerator out there."

"That's true," said my sister unhappily. "He should keep for a while in there at least."

Rather than dwell on the unpleasant effects of decomposition, I said, "We cannot ignore what we've seen. Give me five minutes, and I'll be back."

Bud quietly called, "Cait, where are you going?" but I ignored him.

I returned to the kitchen disappointed, and announced, "There are several things to consider. First, there is the coal dust on his hands, and on his jeans, which were rolled up. Then there's that mark on his legs. The coal-dust prints on his back were bigger than my hands, but smaller than yours, Bud, which might be an interesting fact. I would like to know where he'd been to get himself that grubby, and what it was that caused his broken skin. My initial thought was that some sort of rod hit his shins, but I couldn't see any marks on the up stairs—where Dilys said she found his body—to indicate that a stick, or a rod of any sort, had been wedged across the steps. There'd have been a mark visible somewhere on one of the two walls, I'm sure of that. The walls are painted in cream—a very impractical color for the purpose, I'll grant you, but useful for us on this occasion. The marks on his legs were too thick to have been made by string, twine, or even wire, which would have cut into his flesh more. In any case, something like that would have had to have been affixed to each side of the stairway somehow. But there aren't any stair rails; there are just those ropes looped along the walls, so there isn't anything to attach a string, or something like it, to. Oh—what about those rope-loops?"

"Hmmm," said Bud thoughtfully. "Maybe one of those . . . No. No, it wouldn't work. If one had hung down and caught his ankle, or something like that, then maybe. But that's not where the marks are." I nodded, still thinking things through. "Of course," Bud continued, "he could have been hit across the legs, rather than walking into something, but the marks made a straight line. How could a person get that low down to hit two legs in a straight line about six inches off the ground?"

Siân was sitting in silence, chewing her nails. She seemed more than a little distracted. She didn't even take any notice when Bud jumped down from the table and crouched, waving his arm across his body at the height he had specified.

"To hit someone across both legs, in a straight line, at this height," he said, "you'd certainly have to be positioned to one side of the person you were hitting, which would allow a stick, or a weapon of some sort, to make a straight line, as David had on his legs." His motions made that much clear. "Otherwise, the thing in your hand wouldn't make contact with both legs equally."

"But that would be impossible, Bud," I replied, since Siân clearly wasn't interested. "The stairs have a wall on each side, and while they are wide, they aren't *that* wide. Besides, why would you run down a flight of stairs into someone crouching on one of them? You'd wait for them to move."

"He might not have seen someone crouching on a step. The light down here at the bottom might not have been turned on, and it was dark by then. That could make you miss things."

"Granted it might make you miss your footing, Bud, but I think you'd see a person as at least a lump of something on the step. Besides, like I said, the stairs aren't *that* wide—a person would have to be tiny to have been able to be on a step beside David as he descended. And invisible."

"So we're looking for a skinny ghost or an invisible leprechaun of some sort then?" mused Bud. He smiled in Siân's direction, and I could tell he was trying to get her to engage, but she didn't.

"As you know very well, leprechauns are Irish. In Wales we have the *bwca*," I said.

Bud smiled wanly. "Go on then, tell me, what's a *bwca*?"

I settled my shoulders. "It's like a brownie, or a sprite. It wants to be helpful, and it will be if you thank it for its work with a bowl of milk or cream, but if you annoy one, it'll become mischievous. It'll thrown stones and break things, or knock on the walls or doors to confuse you, or pinch you as you sleep, or steal your clothes. Maybe there's a *bwca* in the castle and it tripped David Davies." I grinned cheekily. "Mum used to call me a 'little *bwca*' when I was naughty. Siân too. Two 'naughty little *bwcas*,' we were. Remember, Siân?" *Nothing.*

Bud remained silent as I recalled my mum's face with a warm smile. I rallied. "A *bwca* is related to the *bucca* of Cornwall and Devon, or the American tommyknocker. The knocking association comes from mining, when men working underground would hear creaking before a cave-in. They came to think of a knocking sound as a forewarning of disaster. Stephen King wrote a book called *The Tommyknockers*, though that's really more of a science-fiction book. Very similar to *Quatermass and the Pit*, in fact, which happens to be one of my favorite movies. Made in 1967. Love it, though I've never seen the original TV series. Have you seen it? The movie, I mean."

Bud shook his head. "Quite how you manage to get from leprechauns to 1960s science-fiction movies in more or less one breath is beyond me. Your brain must get very hot, sometimes. But, putting all other information aside, I just wanted to point out to you how difficult, if not impossible, it would have been for a person to deliver a blow to the front of David Davies's legs, in the manner in which his body presents. There *must* have been a device he walked into, set at that height across his path, for him to have gotten that mark. Agreed?"

I nodded. "Or he might have done it before he was on the stairs," I added. "Maybe he just happened to walk into something, getting the marks, a couple of moments before he fell down the stairs, and we're giving too much significance to the stain on his jeans, and the mark on his legs."

"*We?*" said Bud. "*You're* the one doing that, Cait. I'm just helping you see it's not possible for a bar to have been hit across his legs while he was on the stairs. I think your new theory is much more likely."

I jumped down from the table to join Bud. "Okay then, so let's go back upstairs and see what he might have knocked against within a couple of minutes of his fall. He couldn't have covered much ground in that time, so we could go up the stairs he came down and hunt about at the top. Oh, wait a minute . . . let me think." I held up my hand as my mind whirred.

"I wasn't saying a word," whispered Bud.

"Ssh. Think about it, Bud. David Davies's body was at the bottom of the up stairs—Dilys said so—not at the bottom of the down stairs. Why would that be?"

Bud shrugged. "We just walked down the up stairs, Cait. Why wouldn't, or couldn't, he do the same thing?"

"Because we didn't know the difference, because we don't live here, and it's the middle of the night, so we weren't likely to be found out by the delightful Dilys. Besides, even if we had known, we're guests here and we leave in a few days, so what's the worst she can do to us? David lived here. He was her son-in-law, and I bet he'd get it in the neck from her if she ever found him using the wrong stairs. Also, it was the middle of the afternoon. It would have been very risky for him to use the wrong stairs."

Bud shook his head. "I know you have a brain the size of a planet, and you're a genius and belong to Mensa, and all that, but you really do overthink things sometimes, Cait. David Davies, if we're to believe what little we've heard, wasn't someone who was well liked by Dilys Jones, and maybe that's because he was habitually misusing her stairs. Just saying it sounds ridiculous, I realize that. Stairs are stairs, for heaven's sake. Of course I get that using the ones nearest the dining room means that the food gets there hotter, but, other than that, there really cannot be a good reason for her rules being observed. And this is me saying this, Cait, and you know what I'm like for obeying the rules."

"Except when it comes to stealing trifle in the wee hours." I smirked.

Bud shivered. "That aside, maybe when there was a huge staff of people running up and down with dishes and multiple servings, it would have made more sense to have an in-door and an out-door for the kitchen, like they do in modern restaurants, and associated up and down staircases. But these days? It seems to be just her carrying food from one place to another, so why all the fuss? She can't run into herself."

"Maybe Rhian, her daughter, usually helps?" I suggested. "Despite the fact that no one wanted to talk about the nature of David's death very much, there's no denying that tonight's dinner wasn't what had been planned. Delicious though it was."

Bud dropped his shoulders and admitted, "Yes, maybe you have a point there." Then he lifted his head and added, "But I still think that David Davies sounds like the kind of guy who'd quite happily jog down the up stairs if they got him where he wanted to go. And hang what his mother-in-law might say to him if she found him breaking her rules."

"Why was David Davies in the kitchen, or coming down the stairs to it, at least?"

"Oh come on, Cait. That's no great mystery. His wife might have been down here, or he might have had any of a number of other reasons to be coming here—you know, like being hungry and wanting to nibble on something? Or he might have been looking for someone he thought was down here—anyone who lives here. Well, not Alice, I guess, because there's no way she'd get down here because of her wheelchair. But anyone else. We just don't know." Bud sounded exasperated. *Not with me, I hope.*

I had to admit it. "You're right, Bud. In fact we hardly know anything about the whole matter. If I'm brutally honest, we don't even know if any foul play took place at all. And I don't like not knowing. I can't help it. It's my nature. I like to understand things. And this is a puzzle."

"A puzzle. A maybe-murder mystery? With treasure?" Siân had finally roused herself. "Sounds just like your cup of tea, doesn't it?" *Is she sneering?*

"If you like," I replied softly. She didn't look well. Beneath the glow of her suntan, I could see that her face was drained.

"How are you doing, Siân?" I asked.

Siân shook her head in despair. "Not good, sis, not good at all. I thought I'd put it all behind me. I honestly thought I'd got over what he did to me, how he made me feel at the time, and the anger that I allowed to grow inside me afterwards. But seeing him lying there, like that, it's all as fresh as it ever was. Oddly enough, I can even remember how very much I loved him. And why. I feel sorry for him." She rubbed her face with both hands. "I've got to pull myself together. I cannot allow him to win again. I will not become full of the same hate. We have to find out who killed him. However horrible he was to me, no one deserves to die before their time. Not even him. I was a nurse. I helped to save lives. Then I created two new lives, my children, and now I keep them safe. I owe it to him, as a human being I cared about, to help him now, the only way I can."

She stood, steadying herself against the chair. I reached up and put my arm around her shoulder. She's a good three inches taller than me, so I stood on tiptoe. This time she allowed me to comfort her.

"I'm so sorry, Siân, I know this must be difficult for you," I said.

"It's okay, Cait. I'll be fine. I just have to come to terms with how all this is making me feel. It's weird. I don't like it. But I'm really glad you're both here, because you can help me work out how he died and who killed him."

"Oh no, we're not doing anything like that," said Bud firmly.

Siân gave Bud a cold stare. "I don't know you well, Bud, nor, frankly, do I really know my sister—as an adult. But I do know what you two have done for complete strangers, when justice has needed serving. Cait's at least shared that with me in her emails. So, maybe, this time, you can help someone who's family."

It was clear that this was a critical moment for the future of my relationship with my sister. I chose my words carefully.

"I think we could at least make some inquiries, Bud," I said gently.

Bud and I locked eyes. Eventually, he nodded. "It's the moral thing to do, and the right thing to do, I know," he said quietly. I smiled my gratitude.

"Thank you, both," said Siân. "If someone meant to kill David, by whatever means, then I'd like to know who it was, and why they did it. I'll be honest and say I'm surprised at myself, because I didn't think I'd care if, or when, or how he died. But I do. And if we can find out who did it, then, I admit, I think I might be tempted to shake their hand. I know that causing someone's death is wrong. I do. Of course I do. Everyone does. But, frankly, for most of my adult life, I'd have fought off a crowd to be able to push him down the stairs myself."

She nibbled her lip as Bud and I stood in silence, then added, "I . . . I am finding it hard to believe that I'm so . . . that I feel so strongly about this."

Bud moved to stand behind me and gave my shoulders a squeeze. "It's decided then. I don't think we should say anything to anyone about what we've seen on the body, or our suspicions, agreed? We're guests, just guests. It wouldn't be a 'normal' thing, for us to get involved."

I nodded. "We don't know who might be a suspect, so everyone has to be considered as a possible pusher or tripper. So no cats out of bags, I agree."

"I agree too," said Siân sleepily.

I said, "Let's just hunt about upstairs for a few moments, please? I want to see if I can find something that might have hit him on the legs just moments before he fell. I won't rest at all until I do. And it would be difficult to do that when everyone's up and about, without letting on that we're looking into David's death."

About half an hour later we stood outside the door to Siân's bedroom. I was still puzzled about the mark on the dead man's legs—we hadn't been able to locate anything that might have hit him or that he might have inadvertently walked into. But we'd all agreed it was impossible to judge, moving slowly in the darkness, just how far a man confident in his own home surroundings could stride in a couple of minutes.

"We'll tackle that issue in the morning," whispered Bud sensibly, "when we can move like normal human beings, and not naughty schoolchildren."

I agreed. "I suspect we shouldn't be late for breakfast. Dilys said half past eight, so we'd better be in the dining room by 8:29 AM at the latest, okay?" We all said our goodnights.

Deg

BUD KNOCKED AT MY DOOR at exactly 8:23 AM the next morning. Luckily, I was ready, so we walked to Siân's room. I knocked, but there was no reply. I knocked again and called her name. I dared to open her door a crack, then stuck my head inside. There was no sign of my sister. Her bed was perfectly made, and her room was neat, though I could tell she'd unpacked. I could see right into her bathroom, so I was sure she'd left the room altogether.

"Maybe she went down early," I said to Bud.

Almost immediately, Siân appeared, running up the stairs looking flushed and out of breath. Her hair was wet, and her spandex-clad body was entirely soaked.

My expression, I suspected, spoke volumes, because she didn't so much greet us as shout at us, "You two go on down. I'll be there in five minutes. I had to have a run. Needed to clear my head."

I heard myself tut just like my mother. "Of course you did, Siân. Can't stop still for a minute, can you?"

"Ha!" she called as she swung past us and into her room. "Still as active as a bump on a log, is she, Bud?" Then she shut the door, and I fumed as Bud and I made our way down the stairs toward what I hoped would be a hearty breakfast.

"She seems a good deal more chipper this morning. But don't let what she said get to you," whispered Bud as we entered the dining room.

"I won't. I'll eat my way through it," I whispered back.

And, thank goodness, Dilys Jones's spread was obviously going to give me the chance to do just that. Mair was already seated at the table, nibbling toast, when we arrived. She greeted us warmly and informed us that Alice Cadwallader always breakfasted in her apartment, and that we should help ourselves from the dishes on the sideboards. She also warned us that Dilys cleared everything away promptly at 9:15 AM so we'd better have all we wanted before then.

A little hesitantly, Bud and I began to open silver-domed dishes to see what was on offer. I was pleased for Bud to see that scrambled eggs were available, and I was delighted for myself that the second lid I opened was to a warming dish laden with perfectly cooked, glistening black pudding and chunks of golden fried potato. I took a little of each, while Bud heaped creamy scrambled eggs on top of hot, buttered toast.

Grimacing at what I had on my plate, Bud said, "That's that blood sausage, right? I don't know how you can eat it. Just the thought is enough to make my stomach turn over. What's in that dish, there? I dread to think."

I lifted the lid on the next dish, and my nose told me what it held, even before my eyes could—cockles and laverbread.

"Good grief, what's that?" exclaimed Bud.

"It's seaweed that's been boiled for many hours, until it becomes this thick, green-black sludge. It's cooled, rolled with oats, sold that way, then prepared in your own kitchen by frying it with bacon, or certainly in bacon fat. Finally, the cockles are added so they warm through. They are like tiny little clams."

"It looks disgusting," Bud finally mustered, and I had to agree with him. "Does it taste better than it looks? It must do, or no one would eat it." He looked horrified, and I thought he might start to heave.

"Okay, calm down, I won't force you to taste any of it." I smiled nervously at Owain as he entered the room, greeted his sister, then us, and poured himself a cup of tea at the sideboard next to the one bearing the food. His appearance was rather alarming. The tired old suit he'd been wearing last night was obviously reserved for dinner wear, and he was now sporting a pair of vivid green tweed pants and a long-sleeved purple turtleneck sweater, over which he'd elected to don a V-necked, sleeveless, knitted mustard top. The garish ensemble was finished off with an incongruous pair of red rubber clogs, and the ultimate flourish of a large gold medallion, resting on, and occasionally bouncing off, his little pot of a tummy. I could tell it was engraved with something, but couldn't make out what. The chain upon which it hung was heavy and long—the thickness of a watch chain. Luckily I hadn't drunk enough the night before to develop a hangover, or I'd have needed sunglasses.

Owain and Mair had adopted what I guessed to be their usual places to the right and left of the vacant space at the head of the table. I noted that the seat there seemed to have been removed permanently to accommodate Alice's wheelchair. It also meant that no one else could sit at the head of the table when she wasn't present. *Telling.*

Bud and I applied ourselves to our food. Mair was fixated on an e-reader, using her knuckle to move the pages along. I wondered what she was reading.

"Sounds like we were lucky that we didn't lose power last night," she said, to no one in particular. She didn't lift her head as she spoke, so I wasn't sure if a response was required. "Lines down all over the place, it says here," she added.

"Do you generate your own power here at the castle?" I asked.

Mair looked up and smiled. "That's quite a sore point hereabouts. Grandfather invested in bringing electricity to the Gower Peninsula very early on. Just so the castle could be hooked up. So we still get our electricity from the main grid. But we have our own generator ready to go as a backup, of course. If the lines on our property were to go down, we wouldn't be a priority for reconnection. Luckily they didn't last night, and the whole of the Gower seems to be fine as well."

"Newspaper?" I asked.

Mair smiled and blushed a little. "I'm sorry, it's very rude of me to read at the table, but it's usually only family, and it's nice to know what's going on in the world. This is the local one. *South Wales Evening Post*. Pretty good usually, they are. Of course, they've got a lot in here about that terrible business with the football supporters' coaches on the M4. Five dead, twenty or more with serious injuries, hundreds treated for cuts and bruises. Very sad. And they're still trying to clear all the wreckage. Down to one lane eastbound for a couple of days, they say. Then they've got lots of stories from people sending in photos on Facebook or Twitter about how the storms affected them."

"Why does everyone think we're interested in the minutiae of their lives, these days?" asked Owain pointedly. "I grant you there might well have been some inspiring tales of folks overcoming challenges caused by the weather, but I bet they aren't the people sending out Twit-things."

"It's Twitter, Owain, as you very well know," snapped Mair.

"Lowest common denominator pseudo-communication, that's what it is. I suppose they've filled their pages with photographs of broken branches, overflowing garden ponds, and drenched tabbies looking cute despite nearly drowning. It's all rubbish."

Mair rolled her eyes as she looked toward me. "Owain thinks that the time I spend communicating with friends on Facebook is all wasted. He cannot believe that I am able to have wonderful fun discussing knitting patterns with people who share my passion for them all over the world."

Siân bounded into the room, looking annoyingly slender in magenta sweats, just as Mair was talking about knitting. I braced myself. I could guess what was about to happen.

"Are you a knitter, Mair?" asked Siân brightly. I was taken aback by her cheeriness, given how upset she'd been when we'd left her the night before.

"Yes, I am," replied Mair defensively.

"Me too." My sister grinned. "Ever heard of a web community called 'Ravelry'?"

Mair glowed. "I'm on there a lot. I have a busy project page, and I belong to lots of groups; the Archers' group and the classical music and opera one are my favorites."

"Me too," exclaimed Siân. She walked around the table to Mair's seat and reached out her hand saying, "You're Mair from Wales, aren't you? I'm Siân from Perth. We've talked on forums."

Mair leapt up from her seat. "How silly of me, of course! I hadn't put two and two together. I saw that fabulous shawl you just made, on your project page. Beautiful colors. I can't believe it's you. I'm so very pleased to meet you in person. How wonderful to meet a fellow Raveler, and you of all people. That music forum's a bit quiet these days, isn't it?"

"You're right," replied Siân, "it is. Which is a great shame; I miss talking to knitters about opera—listening and knitting go together so well. You make those wonderful socks, don't you? You post a lot of patterns, and all your own original work."

I could feel the happy enthusiasm buzzing between them from across the table.

"I enjoy designing patterns. What a coincidence, us meeting like this, here in my very home. I've got some projects I'd love to show you," observed Mair, looking gleeful. I envisaged hours of pally knitting chats between the two of them. "Did you bring a project with you?"

Siân nodded. "I couldn't knit on the flight, of course, but I packed one. It's going to be a lace scarf for the winter. I got the yarn from a woman in Perth, lives down near the Swan River. She uses local soils and minerals to dye it. Mixture of wool and silk, lovely to work with."

Siân tutted as she peered down at my plate on her way to get some breakfast. She hovered at the sideboard, poured some hot water into a cup, dunked in a teabag for a millisecond, then plopped herself beside Mair. She'd put a half a slice of toast on her plate. *Dry toast, of course.*

Settled beside her yarn-buddy, Siân said brightly, "Well this is a super coincidence, Mair. Serendipity. It'll make my weekend so much more enjoyable."

My sister's words stung me. "Bud and I aren't big on coincidences," I said grumpily.

"Well, you two wouldn't be, would you? You work with people who do horrible things, so I expect you always think that there's some sort of plot being played out."

I couldn't believe Siân's dismissive words and tone. It threw me. Where was the Siân who'd wept for hours last night? The one who'd begged me to help her?

Bud shifted uncomfortably in his chair as he replied, "I'm not sure that's quite fair, Siân. Both Cait and I are trained to spot similarities and, of course, differences. You can't blame us for not believing in things falling into a pattern for no reason, because in the business of tracking down criminals there usually is a pattern, and one that's based upon a series of decisions taken by the person or persons involved. Often it's been created by people trying to cover their tracks. Cait's exceptionally good at finding such patterns in people's lives—the linkages, if you will, they have created as they live—and using those to assess their true natures."

I silently thanked Bud for rushing to my defense.

"You might have a point if you're looking at one person's life under a microscope," chimed in Owain, "but if you stand back and look at the broader picture, you can see patterns that cannot be explained. You moving from Swansea to live beside the Swan River, for example, Siân. I would call that a coincidence."

I replied, "Or it might be that Siân was drawn to a place that 'felt' familiar and welcoming because it had a name similar to where she grew up. It would have probably been an unconscious connection, but I believe it might have played a part in her decision making."

Siân glared at me across the table as she said, "So we're all just slaves to our psyches, are we? Incapable of breaking early-life patterns? So it's all our parents' faults? I don't believe it for a minute. Of course parenting is very important, the most important job in the world, but people can change, people can make a new path for themselves."

"If we all decide how to live our lives for ourselves, then why is parenting so important? You can't have it both ways, Siân." I sounded more cross than I'd meant to.

"Why not?" snapped Siân.

Owain seemed oblivious to the sniping taking place in front of him as he followed his own train of thought. "As I mentioned last night, I have been putting together a detailed genealogy for the Cadwalladers, and I discovered that there's a river in South America called Arinos, the same as Mother's maiden name, but her family didn't originate anywhere near the river—they migrated from Patagonia to Bolivia. See? A coincidence."

"Alice is Bolivian?" I couldn't place her red hair and pale skin in that part of the world at all.

Owain guffawed dismissively. "Not what I said, Cait. I said her *family* is from there, and it is. I have checked the Brazilian town of Arinos as well as the entire river area, and I can only find the roots of her paternal family in Bolivia, but nowhere near the river. It was a fascinating search."

"I thought she was from Philadelphia. Are you saying she was born in Bolivia? Or how many generations removed is she?"

Owain smiled. "To be fair to you, her grandfather was from Bolivia, but he married a Welsh girl in Patagonia—as you know there is a large Welsh population there"—I nodded—"and they had a son who moved to Philadelphia, who then married Alice's mother. Her mother's family pretty much ostracized her at that point. Alice's mother was a Grand Dame of America—a very pure lineage going back to the Founding Fathers, and those who built the United States of America. The son of a Bolivian salt miner and a Patagonian spinner

79

and weaver of wool wasn't who they wanted as a son-in-law."

"So Alice was 'Alicia Arinos' before she became Alice Cadwallader. That's quite a change," Bud observed.

"And there are some more coincidences," said Siân joyously. "Owain and Mair's great-grandparents, on their mother's side, were a miner and a weaver—and here's Mair a knitter and Owain interested in geology." She smiled triumphantly.

"Not coincidences," I said. "Owain's entire family seems to have always had an interest in rocks, geology, and mining, so he's been surrounded by it since he was a small child, and might have developed his interest as a way to impress and gain affection from his father. Mair lives in a country with a rich heritage of yarn-based crafts, as did her great-grandmother. Sheep are not a coincidence, they are a fact of life in Wales, Patagonia—and in Australia, Siân, another point of similarity between your old and new homes, which might well have made you feel comfortable when you moved there."

"Coincidences do exist," said Owain firmly. "It's the only way you can explain certain things."

"It's the only *obvious* way to connect certain things, Owain," I replied, just as firmly. "Further investigation usually reveals other more complex, decision-based reasons for connections."

"That would be like your plate then, Owain," said Mair flatly. "Though you've been investigating that for donkey's years, and you're still no closer to knowing what it all means."

Owain moved his shoulders in an uncomfortable shrug as he studiously sipped his tea. "It's not something I think we should discuss outside the family any further, Mair," he said quietly.

"Oh come off it, Owain," said Mair. "Siân here is my sister-in-yarn, and we Cadwalladers have always said we'll try to treat our guests like family—though in our case that's more of a threat than a promise." She grinned at Bud and me.

"Don't remind Cait that there's a puzzle, or a riddle, to solve here," said Siân stirring her tea. "Cait's view is that life itself is a puzzle that has to be solved. She thinks there's an answer to everything—that there's always a solution to a problem. She has no idea that life isn't a mystery; it's a journey. You don't sit around and think about it, you get on with living it. No one ever found happiness by doing nothing, you have to actively search it out."

I was pretty sure Bud had noticed that my knuckles had begun to turn white as I gripped my cutlery. He stepped in to defuse the explosive atmosphere that was beginning to encircle the breakfast table. He's good at that.

"Any idea what will happen with David Davies's body?" he asked. *Way to go, Bud!*

Un ar ddeg

"NO NEWS THAT I KNOW of," replied Mair, "but maybe Idris would be more likely to know. Or Rhian, of course. Though I don't expect we'll see much of her today."

Owain had lost interest in the rest of us humans and had escaped to his own little world again. I tucked into my food with relish, while Siân nibbled at her tiny piece of toast. I wondered why she was acting so belligerently toward me. I wasn't aware I'd done anything to deserve it. I'd been nothing but supportive and helpful the night before.

Finally Siân broke the silence and said, more to Mair than anyone else, "Sorry it all got a bit weird last night. It must have been the jetlag. To be honest, I should have stayed in my bed in the first place and not tried to keep going. But I wanted to make the effort."

Owain re-engaged. "No worries, Siân, as I said last night, I absolutely understand how taxing a journey it can be from Australia."

"Did you?" asked Siân. "Have you been there then?"

Owain looked mildly confused. "I believe I mentioned that I've been there to study some unique geological sites, which led you to explain that your husband is in mining. I'm guessing he's an engineer, rather than someone who works in the mines themselves?"

It was Siân's turn to look confused. "Oh, that's right, I remember the part about your liking geology, but not about visiting Australia, or about Todd being in mining. I told you that? I don't remember that at all. But I must have told you, because he is in mining, though he's not even in engineering any more. Management now. He's good at it, they say. Highly valued."

"You mentioned last night that Todd travels a lot," I said quietly.

Siân shrugged. "Yes, he does, but then he always has. It goes with the job. It's the norm for us."

It was interesting to note that Siân's angry and dismissive comments about her husband of the night before seemed not only to be forgotten, but to have been made due to jetlag. I suspected that she was hiding her true feelings at the breakfast table, and that we'd caught a glimpse of her real emotions the night before. I chose not to pursue the matter, and I could feel Bud become less tense as I said, "Well, that was last night, and that's over now. So, did you sleep well, sis?"

Siân smiled as she sipped what was, as far as I could see, little more than steaming water, then said, "I don't know. I suppose I must have done."

I nodded. I'd hoped we'd share a conspiratorial smile, but none was forthcoming.

My sister simply said, "And what were you up to when you came into my room?"

I was puzzled. "I didn't come into you room. You must have dreamed it."

Siân nibbled at a corner of her toast, swallowed, then said calmly, "No, I know I was awake, because we spoke to each other. When I asked you what you wanted you said it was a secret. You were wearing a black sweat suit. You had a flashlight."

It's very unusual for me to be lost for words, but, at that moment, I was. I knew what I wanted to say, and I knew what I should say, but what I decided to say was, "I really think you must have dreamed it, Siân. For a start, I don't own a black sweat suit, and I certainly didn't come into your room last night. Dreams can seem very real, especially when we're in an altered state. And jetlag can do that to you. The same type of thing can happen when you suffer with an elevated temperature, or are under the influence of certain opiates. It's a sort of hallucination, but it's a dream. It was probably your brain's way of filing away being here, seeing me again, and knowing there's a treasure hidden here."

Siân brightened. "And we're back to the Cadwallader Cache. A coincidence, Cait, or did you mean to return to the question of the clues painted on the plate so quickly?"

"Ha ha," I pantomimed across the table, just as we were joined by Eirwen and Idris, who rushed into the dining room and made a beeline for the food.

"I hope Uncle Owain isn't boring you to death with more of his stories about that plate," said Eirwen nervously as she spooned eggs onto a small plate. "None of us believe it's real, do we, Idris?"

"If only it were," said the young man heartily. "It would make life so much easier if we only had a big cash injection from . . . somewhere." He stopped short, encouraged to do so by a dagger stare from his wife.

I noticed that Eirwen was less stooped than she had been the night before. I wondered if that was because she knew that Alice wasn't due to join us. Whatever the reason, there was a slight spring in her step. It couldn't have been the weather, because we could all see, only too clearly through the tall windows that surrounded us, that the rain was pelting down, and the thick cloud cover didn't suggest it was going to stop anytime soon.

Dilys Jones marched into the dining room, set down two large hot water jugs, and refreshed the teapots and the coffee. "The police and an ambulance will be here by about ten, they said," she announced to the wall as she poured hot water. "Then he'll be gone. Rhian's having breakfast in her rooms, and Gwen is going to go with the body. Rhian's not up to it."

I wondered if, given the circumstances, I'd see Rhian before our wedding, or even during or after it. I dug into my black pudding as I began to wonder how everything we'd planned was going to be achieved, but I tried to not let the panic I could feel put me off my food.

"How will they get here?" asked Siân.

Dilys was just about to leave the dining room when she answered dismissively, "There's only one way onto this headland, if you don't count the path down the cliff to the beach. Over the bridge. The way you came in yesterday. You remember that, don't you?"

Siân paused with her last morsel of toast hovering in mid-air. "But the bridge has been washed over by the river. I was just up there, and it's all but collapsed. Didn't you know?"

Everyone, except Bud and me, responded the same way—using different levels of politeness—essentially telling Siân that she didn't know what she was talking about. Siân took it all in her stride.

"I understand that I'm only a visitor, but, unless you have two different bridges, all I can tell you is that there's a short, wide bridge, with crenellations, over which I drove yesterday to get here. Today it doesn't have crenellations any more. They've been washed away by the river, which is still running so high that it's rushing over the bridge itself."

"But it's a *Roman* bridge," said Idris in disbelief. "It's been there for almost two thousand years. It can't have collapsed. It's never collapsed before."

"Now that's not one hundred percent accurate," interjected Owain. "When my great-grandfather decided to build the first part of this castle, he significantly reinforced the bridge that was already in place—the bridge the Romans built to gain access to the headland and their temple to Neptune. He added the crenellations, to match those he built on the original castle. But it suffered under all the heavy traffic it took during the next fifty years or so that they spent building the original house, then the two additional wings. By the early 1900s the bridge was in danger of total collapse. My grandfather reinforced the sides, resurfaced it, and put some extra work into the anchors to the river banks."

Idris almost shouted, "We had it all thoroughly examined before they'd allow tourist coaches to drive over it. I can't believe it. How will we manage? It'll cost a fortune to repair. And we'll have to do it ourselves. It's on our land. It'll be all down to us." He was close to tears as Eirwen rubbed his back, trying to comfort him. "And you say the river is running so high it's actually inundating the road on the bridge, Siân?"

Siân nodded as she sipped her tea. The huge impact of what she'd told us didn't seem to have dawned on her at all, which annoyed me a great deal. She could see Idris's distress, and she should have been able to understand my own.

Bud must have sensed my growing concerns, which had even prevented me from clearing my plate, because he said quietly, but firmly, "How about you and I take a walk up to the bridge after breakfast, Idris, and we can see how it looks."

"I'd like to come too," I piped up.

"Why on earth do you want to go tramping about out there?" asked Siân sharply. "You're not exactly Little Miss Outdoors, are you?"

I did my best to ignore her manner and replied, as calmly as I could, "Because if no one can get over the bridge, then how are the registrars going to get here tomorrow morning to perform our wedding?"

Siân put down her cup and her expression showed me that the penny had finally dropped. "Right. Of course. Sorry, sis." To be fair, she looked genuinely concerned.

"And I'm due my deliveries for the lunch you ordered. And the cake. That's not here yet," added Dilys.

"And there are the floral arrangements," added a small voice from the doorway.

All heads turned. It was Rhian Davies. Red-faced, with greasy hair pulled into a ponytail, she'd pulled on a worn but serviceable navy pantsuit and a white shirt. It was tight on her flabby body. She looked as though she'd gained the twenty pounds I'd lost in the past few months, and it was obvious that she'd stopped having her hair highlighted some time ago—two inches of roots were much darker than the rest of her lank locks. Her mother's sharp features were softened on Rhian's face; despite her grief, hers was an expression of sensitivity, not spite.

Her mother stood beside her daughter and said, "What do you think you're doing out of bed? This is no place for you, child. Get back into your room."

There wasn't a shred of pity in Dilys's voice; she simply sounded annoyed. My heart went out to poor Rhian. She'd lost her husband and wasn't getting any sympathy from her one remaining parent.

I leapt to my feet and approached her. Although we'd met in October, and we'd communicated dozens of times by email, I didn't feel it appropriate to give her the hug I felt she deserved. I put my hand gently on her arm and said, "Your mum's right. You don't need to be here. And please, *please* don't give our wedding plans another thought. If we can just get the registrars here, somehow, that'll be enough. We don't need flowers, or food, or music to be married."

As I realized what I'd said, I could have kicked myself.

"That's lovely, mentioning music like that." Dilys's tone was cutting. "She doesn't need reminding."

I felt myself blush, even as I acknowledged that, for once, Dilys was doing something to defend and protect her daughter.

"But I *need* to be here, Mam. I smelled the food, and I'm starving. I know you said you'd bring me something upstairs later on, but I can't just sit about crying. That won't do anyone any good at all. So I've got myself cleaned up, and I told Gwen to do the same. She'll be here in a minute. So please don't fuss, Mam. I'll have something to eat here, we'll all be civil, and we'll wait to hear what the authorities say when they see the bridge."

Rhian glanced at the grandfather clock that stood beside the doorway, then said, "I don't know where they'll be coming from," she said. "Swansea, I expect. Singleton probably. So they might be on their way already. If they said they'd be here at ten, then I'd like to be up at the bridge myself at that time, and we can all see what's what."

I knew that Rhian was forty years old, because she'd told me, but at that moment she looked ten years older. She forced a smile, patted her mother on the arm, and headed for the food. I resumed my seat, because I didn't know what else to do. Idris and Eirwen seemed to be having something of a heated conversation—about how to pay for repairing an ancient bridge, I gathered from their whispers—and Mair sat eating toast in silence, staring at Rhian's back with a peculiar expression on her face. I wanted to believe it was pity, but it seemed closer to anger. *Odd.*

At that moment a little mouse of a woman rushed into the dining room. Not quite five feet tall, she wore brown, wooly everything. *Not another knitter?* She had poorly dyed brown hair arranged in a dreadful bubbly perm and wore not a scrap of makeup. She'd clearly spent the night crying. I put her age around the mid-forties. Her hands fluttered constantly, even when the rest of her body was still, and her little brown eyes darted about, her tongue constantly licking her lips.

"Good morning, everyone," she said. "Oh, no, it's not really 'good,' is it? I don't know why I said that. Sorry, Rhian, I didn't mean to say 'good.' Hello, everybody. For those of you who don't know me I'm Gwen. Gwen Thomas. David's accompanist. The choir's accompanist. Oh dear, I'm saying everything wrong. I'd better shut up now."

Instead of doing just that, she rushed toward Rhian and continued to fuss. "Can I help you to something, some food from there, Rhian?" I noted a North-Walian accent, which differs from that of South Wales. It's a very nasal accent, set at the back of the mouth. Once, while at university in Cardiff, I shared a flat with a girl for two weeks before I realized she wasn't from Liverpool, as I'd thought, but from a little village near Rhyl, in North Wales, and she hadn't even learned to speak English until she was sixteen.

"Thanks, Gwen, but I'm quite capable of serving myself. Introduce yourself properly to Cait, Bud, and Siân, alright?" Rhian didn't snap or dismiss the overly attentive Gwen, but I didn't get the impression that she felt warmly about her. I wondered why Gwen had been accepted as an overnight guest by the grieving widow, and why on earth Rhian would allow her to be the one to accompany her husband's remains when they were taken away.

I reasoned that maybe Rhian had simply had enough of the fussy little woman. I felt I had already, and I'd only been in her company for two minutes. Gwen Thomas had a constant air of panic about her, which I found immediately unsettling, and, frankly, I was quite unsettled enough.

Gwen dithered beside her companion, and distractedly poured herself a cup of coffee. She then, rather alarmingly, sat herself next to me.

"It's very nice to see you again, Cait," she said, "and to get to meet your fiancé, and your sister. Though, of course, it's a terrible tragedy—about David, you know."

I was confused, and I must have looked it. "Have we met before?" I asked.

Gwen laughed, too loudly. "Oh silly you. We were in school together. Llwyn-y-Bryn. You were my house captain. Caerleon House. Remember?"

I wracked my brain. Having a photographic memory means I don't have to do that very often. I was thrown.

"Of course, I looked a bit different in those days," added Gwen sulkily. "I was a big girl, and I had a difficult time with my skin. And I've had my eyes fixed now, so I don't need those thick old glasses all the time."

"Got it!" I exclaimed. "You had a lovely voice, very light. Didn't you turn the pages for the pianist when we competed in our inter-house *eisteddfod*?"

"Yes, that's right," replied Gwen, beaming. "I knew you'd remember me. Of course I was a few years younger than you, so I suppose I was just one of dozens of little girls who followed you around when you were our captain. You were wonderful." She was almost vibrating with excitement.

"Puppy," whispered Bud under his breath.

I glared at him for using the term we adopted to refer to the students who trail around after me at the university where I teach, then I returned my attention to Gwen, who was obviously eager to have a conversation with me. "I clearly recall you were a talented and very musical girl, Gwen. Though I don't remember you having a North Wales accent. How did you come by that?"

Gwen grinned. "I came to Swansea from Wrexham when I was ten, but my mum made me take elocution lessons so I'd fit in better. When I left college I got a job back in Wrexham, so it crept back in again. I moved back here about five years ago. I won't shake it now."

"Probably not," I agreed. "So, if you are the choral accompanist, does that mean you made a career out of your music?"

"Welsh College of Music and Drama in Cardiff after school, then teacher training, and I've taught ever since. Piano and voice are my things. I've been so lucky. And to get to work with David and the choir was just a joy. I don't know what will happen now. There aren't many conductors like him around." As Rhian joined us at the table, Gwen stopped talking and sipped her coffee.

Rhian sat beside Siân. They exchanged nods. Looking over her coffee, Rhian said, "By the way, Gwen, it seems that the bridge is out, so they probably won't be able to take the body away when they planned. Isn't that going to be fun for us all?"

I thought it was a very odd thing to say.

"Oh no! You're kidding," exclaimed Gwen, and she burst into tears. Blubbing, she added, "That's so unfair. He needs to be attended to properly. Oh Rhian, what's to be done? Oh, my poor, poor David."

Anyone would have thought she was his widow, rather than just his accompanist.

Looking around the table, I could tell I wasn't the only one thinking that this was very odd behavior, on the part of both women. I sat in silence for a moment and gave my thoughts to my memories of Gwen at school. I recalled tears at choir practice, a wobbly, spotty little girl who was always being shunned or bullied. I was pleased to see that she'd been able to make a living from her love of music. It had seemed to be her solace even then.

I pulled myself back to my present reality. I was beginning to wonder if I would, in fact, be married to Bud Anderson the next day, or if a collapsed bridge and a corpse would conspire to stop our wedding in its tracks. I determined that I wouldn't let that happen. *But how?*

Deuddeg

THE ENIGMATIC PREHISTORIC STONE CIRCLE looked right at home in the horrendous weather, as did the ruins of the Roman temple, both of which we had to pass as we headed toward the bridge. Although we didn't pass right by the half-timbered, Tudor-style stable block, I could tell, by looking back toward the castle, that Dilys Jones had been correct—the windows from her basement kitchen would have given her an excellent view of the stable block, which was now a garage, as well as the ruins. She'd also have seen anyone on the roadway to the drive and the main entrance, as the road swooped along the gradient of the hillside.

We crunched heavily across the pea gravel, and it was clear that all our spirits matched the weather—miserable. Bud walked ahead with Idris. I walked beside Rhian. For a few moments she was completely silent, then she said something that startled, intrigued, and worried me, in pretty much equal measure.

"You and Bud solve mysteries, don't you?" she asked. "At least, you've told me in some emails that you have done in the past. Right?"

I nodded, apprehensive about what she'd say next.

"Look, I'm just going to come out with it, Cait. I don't believe that David fell down those stairs. I don't think he could have. He must have been pushed, or tripped up somehow, and I want you to find out who did it. And why. I can't pay you anything, but I wondered if you'd do it for me, as a favor?"

I hesitated for only a second before I hugged her and said, "Of course I will." Bud had already agreed with me the night before that we'd do some snooping on behalf of my sister, so how could this make things any worse?

Her reaction surprised me. She hugged me back, but then pushed away and said, "Right then, what do you want to know? Ask anything and I'll tell you. Anything about his glad eye, his womanizing, his bad side, or his good side. Whatever anyone else might think, I knew David very well. He was a complicated person, but I loved him."

She paused and, through the sheets of rain, gave me a piercing look. "I know you're here to marry Bud tomorrow, and it's quite clear you're a very well-suited couple. But have you ever loved someone you shouldn't have? Have you ever known a person was bad for you, but you just couldn't stop loving them? Couldn't stop hoping they'd love you back the same way?"

I turned and began the climb up the hill again as I replied, "I suspect you know the answer to that question very well, Rhian." I sighed. "Is this a little test?"

Rhian shook her head as she fell into step with me. Drops of rain flew off the end of her nose. "I'm sorry, that was silly of me. Of course I know all about you and your ex-boyfriend. Gwen told me all about it. Then I did a bit of googling."

"Really?" I didn't know why I was surprised. The newspapers had made a real meal of Angus's death, and my arrest, at the time.

"Oh yes. She followed the whole story, it seems. She'd been on some sort of musical course in Cambridge just before . . . it happened, she said." Rhian turned her wet face to me and smiled. "I think Gwen worships you a bit—always has, since she was in school with you. She got very excited when I told her your name. I couldn't shut her up about how you inspired her to take up music, to follow her talent. She's a strange little woman, but a very good accompanist. David thought a lot of her abilities. Unfortunately, I think she had a bit of a crush on him too—which, of course, he exploited mercilessly."

"How d'you mean?" I asked.

Rhian almost smiled. "I think he palmed off a lot of the grunt work onto her. She sorts out all the music parts, gets to rehearsals early and leaves late, that sort of thing. And she does all the admin stuff—keeping in touch with all the members, organizing buses to get them here and there, you know?"

Ahead of us, Bud and Idris had already reached the bridge, and we could just see them through the curtain of rain as they bent down to examine the structure at its base. It didn't look promising. I sighed. I wasn't likely to be able to change the weather, or shift ancient bridge footings, but I could try to help Rhian. I decided to be direct.

"Rhian, I don't know exactly what Gwen told you, but I had a rough relationship with Angus. He was desperately good-looking—to me, anyway—and he used his charm on women and men alike. He usually got his way, and he had a terrible temper—he could blow up in a millisecond. I never quite knew which Angus I'd be sharing space with—the charming one, or the angry one. Triggers were utterly unpredictable; a look, a word, a shrug could set him off. But, when he felt like it, he could be the best possible company, the most romantic gentleman. Then he'd snap, and I'd be looking for cover. Is that how it was for you and David?"

Rhian looked horrified. "No, thank God. David never hit me," said Rhian. "Well, only once, and he apologized for months. It never happened again. Yes, he'd lose his temper with people, but he'd seethe silently, and then he'd plot his revenge. He always said that revenge was a dish best served cold, and I know he got his own back on people after years of waiting for the right moment."

"Did he have a challenging upbringing?" I asked. I wanted to try to understand the man. *It's what I do.*

Rhian shrugged. "Define challenging. Whatever we get it's normal to us, isn't it? I mean Mam's a right tartar, but I'm used to it. I know most people think she's an old witch, but she's my mam, and I give her a lot of rope. David's father was a drinker. He spent most of his time in the pub, or 'down the club,' by which he meant the working men's club—though I don't think he was much of a worker. On the sick for years. Sick 'cos of the drinking, he was. David's mother had a job at the Mettoy factory in Fforestfach. Worked shifts. David sort of brought himself up, I think."

I grinned. Rhian looked taken aback. "Sorry," I said quickly, "I wasn't smiling because of David's lack of parental oversight, but because of where his mother worked." Her quizzical look demanded a response. "I used to live in Manselton, grew up there. It's just down the hill from Fforestfach, so the Mettoy factory isn't unknown to me. Some of the children at school with me had parents who worked there, and they'd get cheap Corgi Toys sometimes. It's amazing to think how valuable some of those little cars and trucks are these days."

"I think they were lorries, not trucks." Rhian grinned. "You're very Canadian. You know, North American, when you talk."

"So your mother has mentioned, though not as kindly as you," I dared.

"Oh, just ignore her," said Rhian. "Her bark's worse than her bite." She cocked her head and smiled as she added, "Usually."

For a brief moment, we were just two women sharing a little joke in the rain, and I felt a difficult issue pick at my conscience. My sister was just a quarter of a mile away, and all we'd done since we'd been under the same roof was snipe at each other, or admit how little we each knew about the other. I wondered why that was, and why I felt a warmth toward Rhian I really couldn't find in my heart for my own flesh and blood.

I stopped climbing and pulled at Rhian's sleeve. Bud and Idris were standing up again and pointing and gesticulating at the bridge, which was awash with water, lumps of rubble lying across it. "Rhian, before we join the men, tell me, why do you think David was killed? Not 'what was the motive,' but what makes you think it wasn't an accident?"

"He was like a goat. As nimble as you like. Light and fast on his feet. Always was. Those feet of his were legendary. Bud told me you saw him conduct the choir, so you'll know what he was like. It was as though he was dancing. And he was a very good dancer, when it came to it. He'd run up and down those stairs to the kitchen a thousand times, over the years. He wasn't in great shape, but he wasn't a plodder. I can't believe he'd have fallen."

"Accidents happen, Rhian," I pressed. "He might have been nimble, but accidents are just that—unexpected happenings that catch us off guard. He might have been distracted, or something might have caught his attention and he simply missed his footing. It's possible, Rhian. It could have been 'just an accident,' you know. Not that there's any 'just' about it, of course."

Rhian nodded. "Alright, I'll give you that. But could you prove it? Could you prove somebody didn't kill him?"

I shook my head and wiped my face, thinking of my suspicions from the night before. "I have no idea. It's difficult to prove that something didn't happen. But . . ." I hesitated as I carefully selected my words. "I could do some poking about. If I ask the other question—what motive do you think someone might have had to kill him—what would you say?"

"Cait! Cait!" called Bud, beckoning for me to join him. I waved back and motioned I'd be with him in two minutes. He nodded. I had to give Rhian my attention for a moment longer. I knew he'd understand. At least, I knew he'd understand when I explained what I was doing.

"Two reasons come to mind," she said thoughtfully. "Women, and money. Loved them both, he did. But I'm struggling with this because I can't imagine anyone at the castle being a killer, you see. There could well be a few people who might have come to the castle especially to kill him. A few husbands here and there, to start with. But given the way the weather was, and the fact that the front door was locked against the storm all afternoon, I don't know how they'd have got to him to do it. I mean, how would anyone from outside, or inside for that matter, know he'd be on the stairs at that moment, see? Unless they were following him, and just pushed him down."

I gave the matter some thought. Rhian made a very good point about how difficult it would have been for someone to happen upon David conveniently at the top of a staircase.

"Would David ever go down the up stairs? Your mother seems quite keen on enforcing her rules, and he was apparently found at the bottom of the up stairs, which doesn't make much sense, unless he was planning to use them to descend."

Rhian swallowed a smile. "Ah yes, Mam's system. A hangover from the old days, that is. To be honest, she's scolded us all about it so many times over the years it's sort of automatic to go down and up the correct stairs. I know I do, anyway, but then I've lived there all my life. David and Mam used to argue about it all the time when he first moved in, and I know he used to use the wrong stairs just to goad her. But I think even he got used to using the right ones in the end. Besides, he didn't usually mean to annoy Mam. Not anymore. They sort of called a truce when she realized I wasn't going to give him up just because she didn't think he was good enough for me. I won't say they ever got on, but they did at least stop nagging at each other. It gets very wearing when people do that, doesn't it? And there's no point to it—it doesn't make anyone any happier, after all. So—would he go down the up stairs? I can't say he wouldn't, but I don't think it's something he did habitually. Maybe if he was in such a rush that he didn't want to go to the other door he would, but that would mean he'd set off from the dining room side of the house to go down. Then it would all depend on where he wanted to end up, and there's not much downstairs."

"What's down there, other than the two kitchens?"

"There's them, the boiler room, the laundry area, oh—and the cellar."

"Wine cellar?" I asked, perking up at the thought.

Rhian smiled and shook her head. "No, the coal cellar, of course. All the fires in the house were coal once upon a time. Not now, of course. We only really have two fires any more—the ones in the drawing room and the dining room, logs now, and they're as much for show as anything. Oil-fueled central heating—those dreadful radiators, you know? The bane of David's life, they were. Having to go about fixing them at all hours he was, all over the place."

"So he wouldn't need to go to the coal cellar?"

"No." She sounded very certain.

"Why not?" I asked, thinking of the coal dust on David's jeans.

"Well there's nothing there except a few bits of old coal left over from when it was used around the house. I can't imagine anyone wanting to go in there at all. It would be filthy, to start with, and it's just a cellar—you know, a big old room with no windows. Probably an old dungeon in medieval times, I'd say." She looked puzzled. "Anyway, why do you ask?"

I didn't have a chance to answer, because we'd finally reached the top of the road and the bridge itself. The sorry sight put a stop to our conversation, but I gave Rhian a reassuring wink. "I'll get on it, right away," I said quietly.

Tri ar ddeg

"HERE THEY COME," ANNOUNCED IDRIS. He waved his dripping arm toward a dark, unmarked panel van that was making its way, slowly, along the road to the bridge, followed by a Range Rover bedecked in police colors. "I wonder what they'll have to say about all this."

He sounded deflated as he continued. "Bud and I have had a good look at it, and there's no way a vehicle should cross this bridge. The footings are only just hanging on to the far bank. I think it might take the weight of people walking across it, but not vehicles. Even then it could just wash away at any moment. It would be very risky. I'm so sorry—for all of you. Obviously for very different reasons. Eirwen and I wouldn't have had this happen to any of you. Rhian—all this to deal with on top of David's death. And you—you two are supposed to be the Happy Couple. I can't imagine you're feeling the least little bit happy about any of it."

He wiped rain from his face, which looked haggard. It seemed that the collapse of the bridge had hit him harder than the death of David Davies, which made me wonder about the relationship between the two men.

Digging into relationships would have to wait, however, because the vehicles had ground to a halt on their side of the raging river, thanks to Idris's frantic waving. I gave my attention to the structure of the bridge. As Siân had said, the raging river was washing over the bridge deck, through gaps in the stone wall that had been tall and secure when Bud and I had driven over it the previous afternoon. Many of the rocks, which had been dislodged by the torrent, were still lying on the roadway, unable to escape the confines of the bridge, because the wall farthest from the direction of flow was more intact than the one facing it, which had taken the brunt of the force of the swollen stream and collapsed almost completely. It was also easy to see that the footings of the bridge had been undermined on the far bank. It looked as though it was the bank itself that had given way, so the foundations had little to cling to and were crumbling.

Several moments of unproductive gesticulating and shouting followed. The rain beating on our hoods and hats, plus the roar of the river, made it impossible for voices to carry and be comprehensible. I had an idea.

"Have you got a cellphone with you, Idris?" I shouted.

"You mean my mobile?" he asked.

I smiled. "Yes, your 'mobile,' sorry. Sometimes I forget the differences in terminology back here in Wales."

Idris nodded.

Eventually, by way of making "call me" gestures and pointing like a madwoman, I managed to make myself understood by one of the policemen, who disappeared into his car for a moment, then popped out holding a makeshift sign bearing his phone number.

Idris punched the numbers into his own phone and briefly explained the events as he saw them. As it was Sunday, it would be unlikely that anyone would come to assess the reliability of the structure of the bridge until the next day, and it was finally agreed that Idris would liaise with the police about the bridge, the body, and the issue of accessibility. Neither the police nor the driver and his mate in the van from the coroner's office seemed keen to test the safety of the bridge. They seemed resigned to waiting a day to collect the corpse, having all been up all night working at the crash site on the M4.

With the matter settled, they began to reverse along the roadway until they disappeared behind the curtain of rain. As I stood there wondering how on earth it would be possible for Bud and me to be married the next day if the registrars couldn't reach us, my wonderful fiancé walked to my side and gave me a big wet hug. We squelched.

He must have known what I was thinking. "Come on, Cait,

we'll sort something out," he said softly, right next to my ear. "I'm not without a few good ideas of my own, you know. So don't panic yet, right?"

Idris and Rhian stomped off ahead of us, and I took the chance to talk with Bud. I thought it best to be direct. Bud's good at absorbing facts and information.

After I'd caught him up with the conversation between Rhian and myself, Bud cursed loudly. "I know we said we'd investigate a bit, to help out Siân, but this? Now we're committed to helping a grieving widow. Don't you think we've got our hands full enough with the wedding plans, Cait?"

"*What* wedding plans, Bud? I think we should call the register office in the morning and find out what our options are. I never looked into what's involved with getting a new license, because it didn't occur to me we'd need one. Bud, I do want to be married tomorrow, but not with the ghost of David Davies in the room. And that's that."

Bud stood stock still, rain dripping off him in too many places to count. Finally he nodded. "Right. So we need a plan. I suggest that you concentrate on finding out all you can about David Davies and his death. Of course I want to be in on that—I'll do all I can to help you, but it's obvious that you've hit it off with Rhian, and, of course, Siân's your sister. I know very well that your natural desire will be to help them in their time of need, so why don't you take the lead on that?"

"Okay, you do the bridge and the registrars, I'll do death."

"You know what?"

I shook my head, spraying Bud with droplets of water as I did so.

"Cait Morgan, you have an extraordinary mind. A wonderful ability for understanding why people do what they do, or don't do what they don't do, and for allowing your desire to see justice done to focus your talents. So let's do it."

"'The Choir That Didn't Sing,'" I said wistfully.

"Eh?"

"You know, like 'The Dog That Didn't Bark,'" I replied.

"You mean someone might have killed David to stop the choral performance we'd planned for tomorrow? It seems a bit far-fetched, but I suppose it's one line of inquiry." Bud didn't sound convinced.

"I didn't mean that." I smiled. "What I mean is that we must treat this as a proper inquiry. Let's get back and have a sit-down with Rhian. It might be helpful if I could have a look at their apartment. Maybe she'd let me have a poke about. She seemed quite keen on our being involved."

A gust of wind shoved me down the hill more quickly than I had planned, and I skidded on the roadway, where pea gravel was being washed into little heaps by the downpour.

"Careful, Cait," called Bud, grabbing at my arm.

I was annoyed with my clumsiness, but decided to ignore it. "What about Siân? What on earth am I going to do about Siân, Bud? I'm at a loss. She seemed so upset last night, but it's as though she's had a personality transplant this morning. And she seems very confused about some things that happened at dinner last night. Forgetting a whole conversation with Owain, and thinking she saw me in her bedroom? It's very strange."

Bud gripped my slimy hand. "It's probably a mixture of jetlag and shock. Look, it's not going as well with her as you'd hoped this morning, I can tell. You two just don't seem to be able to exchange three words without one of you snapping at the other. I have no idea why. You haven't seen each other since your parents' funeral, so you'd think you guys would have a lot to catch up on. You know, sister stuff. But, if what Siân said yesterday is correct, you two don't have what I'd call a truly close, personal relationship, and I'll grant you you're similar in some ways—you're both as stubborn as each other, for example, which might be fun, but more likely not. But then so different in other ways. I don't know what to suggest. Either you suck it up and start being as polite to her as you would be to a stranger, or you distract her. What about the treasure thing? She seemed pretty keen on that. Could you tell her we'll concentrate on David, and try to sidetrack her with the puzzle plate a bit?"

I gave it a moment's thought. I couldn't come up with anything else.

"Good thinking, Bud. I don't really want to offload her, but she and Mair seem to be getting on like a house on fire. Why don't I encourage the two of them to focus on that? I could poke into it a bit myself, of course," I added, not wanting to miss out on a chance to solve a riddle. "Not too much, just enough so I can see what Dilys might have meant when she said David was hunting for the treasure. Oh—that reminds me—Rhian said there's a coal cellar in the basement, thought that seems like an inadequate term for what was a medieval dungeon."

"Really? I'm surprised," said Bud. "Not so much about the dungeon part, more about the coal cellar. Do you think that's where David's pants picked up the traces of coal dust we saw on them?"

"I think it's likely," I replied. "Rhian also told me there aren't any coal fires in the castle anymore, so I cannot imagine there'd be any coal dust anywhere else than in the coal cellar. So I'll take a look down there too."

Bud paused, then said, "You are not to go taking any chances. So, listen, this is the plan: me—registrars and bridge tomorrow; Siân and Mair—treasure; you and me, and whomever else we need to talk to, or poke with a stick, to get information—David Davies's death, starting right away. Got it? You *and* me, Cait. I'm serious."

Just as we entered the prehistoric stone circle and began to skirt the Roman ruins, Rhian and Idris began to sprint toward the front doors, which I could see were wide open. Idris paused and beckoned to us, pointing toward the private wing, looking panic-stricken.

Bud and I exchanged a glance, but neither of us bothered to say "What now?" because we each knew the other was thinking it.

I picked up my pace to a trot, and we got to the doors pretty quickly. Even before we entered I could hear the wailing—it was loud and primal. *Bonechilling.*

Pedwar ar ddeg

WHEN A SOUND MAKES THE hairs on the back of your neck stand up, it tends to be a sign that nothing good is going to happen in your immediate future. Reaching the doors, neither Bud nor I stopped to get rid of our wet clothes. We just ran inside, which was one of my less good ideas. I skidded on the Victorian tile floor and ended up coming down hard on my bottom. Of course I put my arm out to save myself—the arm I've already broken twice—but, luckily, I was so well padded with layers of clothes, and my own natural fleshy parts, that when Bud pulled me gently to my feet, we were both relieved to discover that I hadn't broken or sprained anything. For me, that in itself was a minor victory.

"You alright?" asked Bud.

I nodded. "I seem to have cut my arm a bit," I noted, as blood joined one of the little rivers of rainwater running down my arm. Bud pulled a wet paper tissue from his pocket and dabbed at the blood.

"You have to take more care of yourself, Cait," he said almost angrily.

"My bottom's a bit sore too," I mentioned quietly, seeking sympathy.

He hugged me to him, and I pressed the wet hanky to my bleeding wrist. After a moment we headed toward the drawing room, where, thankfully, the wailing had stopped. Upon entering, all I could tell was that there were no bodies strewn about the place, and that everyone present seemed to have all their limbs, if not all their wits.

Alice Cadwallader was in the center of the room in her wheelchair, much as she had been the night before, but now the portrait of her that had hung above the fireplace was propped up against two occasional chairs. It had been slashed to shreds. It was clear that the damage wasn't the result of an accident—unless it's possible to "accidentally" cut into an object about twenty times, in different directions, and over the whole piece. The canvas clung to the frame in tatters. Although she'd stopped wailing, Alice was still visibly distraught, and the people crowding around her were all shocked, but trying to pacify the old woman. The whole scene was chaotic.

Bud and I stood just inside the room, dripping. I quickly realized we couldn't do anything practical to help, so I suggested we at least dump our outer clothes in the entryway, thereby saving the wooden floorboards and rugs from a further soaking. It looked as though Idris and Rhian had already caused quite a few stains, though Dilys was ignoring them for the moment, fussing over her employer as though she were the only person in the world.

As Bud and I pulled off our borrowed wellington boots and rain slickers in the hall, Rhian appeared with a few towels. As we mopped at ourselves, she said, "Alice is in a right state. I'm sorry if Idris and I alarmed you when we called you in, but we had no idea what was going on—all we could hear was that ungodly screaming. Then we came in and found her moaning at her lost portrait. I'm just glad there isn't an actual person hurt. There'll be hell to pay over this. What do you two make of it?"

Bud was finished with his hair before I was with mine—he has a bit less than I do—and he replied, "There's no question it was deliberate. And it looks like the work of a very angry, spiteful person. Any candidates?"

With the ball firmly back in her court Rhian shook her head. "We might seem like a strange group to outsiders, but we all rub along quite well, usually. But with this coming on top of David's death, I'm not feeling as comfortable as I usually do here. It's such a big place. Someone could be hiding out here, or even living here I suppose, and we wouldn't necessarily know. There are parts of the castle no one ever goes to. It's *got* to be an outsider. It *can't* be one of us."

I wondered whether Rhian was trying to convince us, or herself. Either way, I wasn't going to be persuaded by a "passing tramp" theory.

She looked worried as she added, "I don't think either Owain or Mair would ever do that to their mother, nor would Idris or Eirwen. Gwen's a bit clingy, and she can be a bit, you know, over the top, but that's just her way. She means well. Always doing little things for me and David. Nurse Janet? I don't know her that well, though she seems to cope with Alice pretty adequately. She and I don't really see a lot of each other, because of our different duties. Got the patience of a saint, Mam says, and I can't argue with her on that one. So that only leaves Mam, who, as I said, has a bark that promises much, but she hasn't got the real anger it would take to do that."

Rhian paused and a strange look of doubt crossed her face. "I know I've asked you to look into David's death, and I suppose you'll have to consider whether this incident is somehow linked to it too. Nothing like this has ever happened before. You know, not before you three arrived. But none of you three even knew David before this weekend, so I don't see how there'd be any reason for you to hurt him. It's why I felt confident about asking you, in fact."

I cleared my throat as I said, rather sheepishly, "By way of full disclosure, Rhian, my sister, Siân, did know David before this weekend. In fact they were boyfriend and girlfriend when she was a teenager. I'm telling you this because the topic came up in front of your mother, in the early hours of this morning, when we examined David's body. Maybe she's told you already, but I thought I'd better mention it."

Rhian sat down, hard, on a carved oak settle that stood just inside the doorway, beneath the head of a stuffed ibex. She looked as though all the wind had been knocked out of her. She dropped her head. "Mam never said. I had no idea," she said.

The silence that followed lasted for a few moments.

The next time she looked at me, Rhian's eyes were ablaze. "So let me get this straight. I've just asked a woman who was once arrested for killing her ex-boyfriend to investigate the possible murder of my husband, who, it turns out, is her sister's ex-boyfriend. Lovely!"

I was at a bit of a loss for words because she was right. It didn't sound good.

"Rhian, listen to me for a minute, eh?" Bud was using his calming, professional voice. I hoped it worked. "This is a very difficult time for you, Rhian, I know that. Cait knows it too. And that's why she's been very open with you about her sister's connection to David. But you need to understand that it was a very old, long-dead connection. It was a teenaged fling. Siân's married with children, and happily living the perfect life in Australia nowadays. She had no idea that David was even here, until she found out about his passing. But even if she had known, she wouldn't have had a reason to do him harm. Besides, I don't believe she's the type to kill a person, whatever the circumstances. And Cait? You told her you'd looked her up online, and that Gwen told you all about what she went through at the time, so you know she was exonerated of any blame whatsoever in the death of Angus, her ex-boyfriend. It's just . . . a coincidence, that's all."

As Bud used his least favorite word I knew how much it must have cost him to do so. Even as he said it I could hear his mantra about connections not being coincidental, but, on this occasion, I chose to back him up.

"Bud's right," I said. "And you've done a very sensible thing, asking us to look into David's death, because, between us, we have a range of skills and abilities that we can put to good use on your behalf."

Rhian was crying, wiping away her tears with a towel. Eventually she nodded. "I'm sorry. I didn't mean to imply that your family had anything to do with David's death. I don't know what came over me."

"Stress and grief," I said. "It's perfectly understandable. And this business with the portrait must be adding to your concerns, worry, and maybe even anger."

"Whoever's doing this, I don't like it," said Rhian, sounding worried again. "It's unsettling, and sad, and a bit creepy. Alice loved that painting of herself. The way she went on and on about it was a bit strange. She was very *connected* to it. I only have vague memories of the other one. She took it down when I was little. But this one? Mad for it, she was."

I'd felt it appropriate to give my hair a final rub, and wondered if I'd missed something. "Are you saying there were two portraits of Alice?"

Rhian looked tired. "No, no, that's not what I meant, though it might well have been what I said. What I meant was that, originally, there was the portrait you saw last night, and that was on the wall in the alcove to the right of the fireplace, then there was one of Alice's husband, Gryffudd Cadwallader, done by the same artist at the same time, hung on the wall in the alcove to the left of the fireplace. A sort of matching pair."

"So what happened to the painting of Alice's late husband? Did she remove it?" I asked. It seemed an obvious question, but it drew a less than expected response from Rhian.

She drew close to Bud and me and whispered, "She had it taken down a couple of days after he died, and hid it goodness knows where, Mam said." Rhian looked over her shoulder toward the drawing room, but it was clear from the hubbub that we were the last people anyone was thinking about.

"*Why* did she do that?" asked Bud.

Rhian shrugged. "Mam said that Alice never liked it. She also said that Mr. Gryffudd was a bit weird about the painting of Alice. She said he used to sit in the drawing room talking to it, but he'd completely ignore Alice herself. He'd sit, drink, smoke, and talk—then Alice would come into the room and chase him out. See? Weird."

Bud and I agreed with her, and it gave me pause for thought, though Alice's husband having a strange relationship with a painting of his wife hardly explained why it was now cut to ribbons.

"And when was that—that he died, and she moved the portrait?" I asked.

"Well, I was very little. Maybe four or five, so mid to late 1970s, I'd say. Mam would know."

"And Alice's portrait has hung in its central position, over the fireplace, ever since?" I pushed.

Rhian looked thoughtful. "As far as I know, though, again, Mam would be the better person to ask. All I can tell you is that I only have a very vague memory of there being a man on one side of the fire and a lady on the other. For as long as I can properly remember, there's just been Alice, above the fire. Why?"

Rhian seemed suddenly curious about why I was asking so many questions about the portrait, and I could tell by his expression that Bud was equally puzzled.

"No particular reason," I lied.

Pymtheg

THAT SOME SORT OF NORMALITY was returning to the castle was signaled by Dilys Jones rushing from the drawing room in search of mops to clear up the pooling water that had dripped all over the floor. She shooed Idris into the hall ahead of her, where he almost skidded in the same way I had.

Alice, who shot out of the drawing room in her wheelchair at a dangerously high speed, was followed by Janet. I was seeing her in her uniform for the first time. Alice completely ignored our little group at the door and went screeching across the wet hallway toward a door in the wall beyond the drawing room.

As she flew by she called to Janet, "Keep up, girl. Come and open the door to the lift for me and help me turn."

The chances of anyone being as fast on their feet as Alice was on her wheels were very slim, unless they were an Olympic sprinter. So Alice had to wait for Janet to catch up.

In her haste, Janet dropped something from her pocket as she rushed past me, so I bent, picked it up, and followed. At the door of the lift, Janet dutifully helped Alice reverse into a little booth, which was only slightly larger than the dimensions of her chair. Janet tried to close the door gently, but it seemed that Alice hadn't reversed quite enough, so she pulled at her little control stick, hit the back of the lift, and Janet allowed the door to shut. It still banged on the footrests at the front of the wheelchair, and I noticed the transfer of paint from the interior of the door to the little footrests. I suspected that the device hadn't been built to cope with the new machine that Alice was driving around the castle as though it were a race track.

"I'll see you up there," called Alice as she pushed a button beside her and the miniscule lift jerked into silent motion. It moved very slowly, but the action seemed smooth.

"You dropped this as you passed me," I said, holding out the crumpled piece of paper that I'd picked up.

Janet took it from me without looking at it, and said, "Thanks, but I can't stop, I have to race her up. It's a game we play." She grinned and took off up the stairs.

"Ah, the litheness of youth," said Siân close to my ear.

"What?" I spluttered, startled. For no apparent reason I'd started to cough.

Siân sighed. "Sorry, forgot I was talking to you, sis. Litheness is not something you were ever overly familiar with, is it?" She spoke as though she weren't insulting me. "So, what do you think about that picture being slashed? Pretty spiteful. Nasty thing for someone to do. Seems as though someone's got it in for the arts. I'd better guard my knitting." She grinned.

"What *are* you talking about?" I hadn't meant to sound irritated, it just came out that way. I wasn't feeling my best. I even thought I might be coming down with something because my throat felt a bit scratchy and sore. Getting soaked to the skin hadn't helped on that score, I suspected.

"First a choirmaster, now a painting? There's someone here who doesn't appreciate art," said Siân sulkily. "Mair's been filling me in on what David had been doing with his life. Seems he was quite famous hereabouts for his skill as a teacher and conductor. So that's what he was now, an artist. And now there's the damaged painting. You do think the two things are connected, right? I mean, they must be."

Bud arrived, breathing heavily. "Don't do that, Cait. You just went dashing off and then you completely disappeared. I had no idea where you were. I don't like it when I lose sight of you."

I decided to answer Bud, not Siân, so I said, "I picked up something that Janet dropped and came over here to give it back to her."

"What was it?" asked Bud.

"Just a piece of paper," I replied.

"You sound distracted," observed Bud.

"Hmmm?"

Siân butted in. "She's not listening, Bud. She's thinking. Strewth, she's always been the same. Just tunes people out. What is it, Cait? Cat got your tongue?"

By way of a response I held my palm toward Bud. "Coal dust," I said.

Siân laughed. "Oh, and that's typical too. Silence, then some stupid cryptic remark. You're priceless, Cait. I'd forgotten how annoying you can be. Right, I'm off to find out what Mair thinks about all this. Her mum's pretty upset about that portrait."

I snapped out of my thoughts. "Yes, I wouldn't mind a word with Mair too, if that's alright, Siân? I wanted to talk to her about the puzzle plate and the hidden treasure. Could we do that, do you think?"

Siân snapped, "I don't know why you're asking me if it's alright to talk to Mair, but yes, why don't we do that? You coming, Bud?" Siân looked at her watch. "We've still got an hour before lunch, so there's lots of time. And as we hunt down Mair, you two can tell me all about the bridge. It's out, right? Like I said?"

Bud nodded as the three of us wandered back to the drawing room to look for Mair. "Yes. Too dangerous for vehicles, certainly, but it might be okay for pedestrians. We won't know until tomorrow, at the earliest."

"So no one's coming or going by that route then," noted Siân. "Sorry, sis." She shook her head. "I apologize for being a bit crotchety. I don't know what's up with me. Everyone seems to be so cutting toward each other here, and it's like an infection. I do understand, sis. You must be worried about the wedding."

I nodded.

Siân put her arm around my shoulders. "Come on, buck up, it'll work out alright. No point brooding on it. Let's do what we can to find out about David's death, like we agreed last night. Have you done anything about it yet? I was pumping Mair about him, but then there was all this kerfuffle about the painting. And what about the riddle on the puzzle plate that his mother-in-law said he was fascinated by? I've been thinking about that, and I've been wondering if the two things could be linked in some way. Should we follow up on that?"

It seemed as though Siân had returned to her old self. She was bright and energetic, and I couldn't imagine what was going on with all the mood swings. She interrupted my thought process by grabbing my arm and hissing, "Look, there's Mair. Okay, I'm going to get everything she knows out of her—it should be easy enough . . ."

I was about to tell her that she should take things gently, but she was gone.

"Mair—there you are, we wanted a word," Siân called toward Mair's back as the woman was disappearing through a door that led off the drawing room toward the back of the castle.

Mair stopped, holding the doorknob. "Hullo, Siân. I wondered where you'd got to, though I often don't know where anyone is in this place. I'm just going to sit in the music room and knit for a while. The light's better there—such as it is with this horrendous weather. Mother has gone for a lie down, which is the best thing for her, so I thought I'd get on with the socks I'm working on. Want to join me?"

Siân looked gleeful. "Absolutely yes. I've got another shawl I'm working on. We can knit together. We all wanted to talk to you about something else too—but I'd love to see the music room. That piano you talked about earlier must be quite something."

Mair walked through the door and ushered us in. "Welcome to the music room," she announced. We all thanked her politely, then marveled, in chorus, at the sights that met our eyes.

The room was gold. The carpeting shone with gold thread; the walls were upholstered with gold brocade; the windows, which ran from floor to ceiling, were framed with gold and decorated with gold ormolu swags and crests; and gold-framed mirrors all but covered the wall that faced the windows, and bounced the light around. It meant that even on such an exceptionally dark day, the room felt light and airy. Several upholstered chairs dotting the room looked as though they'd been imported to this magical land from a much dourer place, because they weren't gold at all, but dark wood, and a bit knocked around the edges. Each was paired with an occasional table. As I wandered around the room I also noticed that it wasn't just the furniture that had seen better days—the mirror frames, the woodwork at the windows, even the ormolu, were all marked, scratched, and worn in places.

At the far end of the room, close to a wall with no windows and just one small door, sat the undoubted star of the room: an ornate rosewood piano, with turned legs and a highly decorative fretted music desk. It was open and ready to be played.

"It's beautiful," cooed Siân.

"It's a Blüthner, isn't it?" I said.

Mair nodded. "You know pianos?" She sounded surprised.

I couldn't resist. "It looks like a Blüthner style 7 grand. The lyre-shaped pedal suggests it's an early one. About 1887? Before 1900, I'd say. Do you play, Mair?"

Mair shook her head. "I had lessons, for years, but I never found it easy, so I let others do that for me nowadays. David would play for me sometimes. Gwen came here yesterday to tune it for the performance on Monday. Tomorrow. Oh dear . . . your wedding. It's not sounding too hopeful, is it? Idris was telling me about the bridge. I'm so sorry for you both. Well, all three of you, of course. You've come such a long way for this, Siân, and you've left your poor children behind, and everything. What will you do? Do you know yet?"

I jumped right in. "In all honesty, Mair, we don't think there's anything we can do until tomorrow at the earliest, so we thought we'd try to ignore it, and just throw ourselves into life at the castle. Of course, we didn't expect to return to such an unpleasant occurrence. Your mother must have had a nasty shock. Was she the one who first discovered the damage to the portrait?"

"Yes," replied Mair. "Mother very rarely comes down from her apartment until dinner time, but today she insisted upon coming down early. As I said, Gwen was here to tune the piano yesterday, and she kindly offered to play for Mother before lunch today. Mother used to play, you see, but she can't anymore because her hands are in such a terrible state, so it's always a special treat for her when there's someone here who can play for her. Mother would always ask her to play the same piece, 'Trois Gymnopédies' by Satie, and Gwen would do it for her. Happily. She is really very good. Even I could tell she had a lovely touch. Good control."

"So your mother was heading here when she found the painting?" asked Bud.

Mair nodded sadly. "Yes. Of course it shocked her. It shocked us all. Mother's always been very fond of that painting. As you saw last night, Cait, she's very proud of her youthful self. In fact, I'd go so far as to say that, as she's aged, the painting has become even more important to her. But there, I suppose it's the same for all of us when we see photos of our younger selves, isn't it? We don't all have larger than life oil paintings of ourselves hung about the place, though, do we?"

I smiled and recalled the photo of me holding my baby sister. I looked across the room at Siân and struggled with my feelings toward her. Surely feeling affection for your little sister shouldn't be so difficult?

"It begs the question, who do you think might have done such a thing?" I said quietly.

Mair shook her head. "I can't think that it could be one of us," she said flatly.

So there we were again. *Not one of us.*

Despite my natural reluctance to countenance a nomadic stranger as being a possible culprit, I allowed myself to consider whether there might, in fact, be someone secreted in the castle after all. Then I wondered if I could come up with an excuse to have a good hunt about.

Un ar bymtheg

"THE STYLE AND ATMOSPHERE OF this wing is very different to the wing housing my bridal boudoir and the dining room." I wanted to begin to build a better mental map of the castle, so I thought I'd take advantage of Mair's knowledge.

"Very much so," replied Mair. "Don't tell Owain, but I actually find the history of this place fascinating," she whispered. "If I let on, he'd never shut up about it. Besides, I'm interested more in the artistic aspects than the historical ones. I mean, given that we've got a prehistoric stone circle and a Roman temple in the middle of our driveway, and a medieval basement, this building is so new, by comparison."

I knew I had her, so I allowed myself to settle into a surprisingly comfortable battered old armchair. "I've read what's on the website, about your great-grandfather and your grandfather building the place, but it would be so much more fun to hear it from a family member. How's the place to live in? Did you grow up here, hunting through secret passages and so forth?"

We'd all taken seats, and, if you'd peeped through the window into the music room at that moment, you'd have been forgiven for thinking we were a nonchalant group of friends idling away the time, with Mair and Siân both knitting almost absentmindedly. I, however, knew I was investigating, so I was on full alert. I felt safe in the assumption that Bud would have the same perspective.

Mair looked wistful. "I'll be honest and admit that my childhood here was anything but happy. Mother decided I should be homeschooled, so with Owain and my late brother, Teilo, away at boarding school, I was the only child in the house. I had my very own tutor, who also pretty much parented me. You see, although Father didn't die until I was sixteen, he was seventy when I was born, so I didn't mix much with him."

"Your father was seventy when you were born?" exclaimed Siân in disbelief.

Mair nodded. "Yes. When Mother goes on about the fact that I was a late baby and I nearly killed her, she has a point. She's told me the story over and over again, though, to be honest, I only have her word for it all. Of course, Dilys backs her up. But then she always does. Dilys was about ten when I was born, and I think she always was a little girl who listened at doors and so forth, so I suppose she'd know. Mother says she didn't even know she was pregnant with me until she was about five months gone. At forty she thought her 'symptoms,' as she refers to them, as though I were some sort of illness, were just signs that her body was changing."

"Was it a difficult birth?" asked Siân. "At that age they can be tough."

"Who knows," replied Mair. "Mother speaks of near-death experiences and thirty hours of labor, but I believe she's exaggerating for effect. In any case, I was born healthy, which they were relieved about, and they decided to keep me, for which I suppose I should be grateful. No, that's not fair, I am grateful, because however odd my so-called 'family life' has been, I am sure it was a lot better than it would have been if I'd been handed off for adoption."

"Why on earth do you think they might have put you up for adoption?" asked Siân. I'd been about to ask that myself.

Mair looked evasive, then made an internal decision and told us, "It's another one of Mother's little weapons. She frequently mentioned it when I was a child—that she and my father were far too old to have a baby about the place, and that they should have handed me off to someone for them to raise. I was constantly made to feel as though I was in the way. Sometimes Mother isn't aware of how hurtful she can be."

I suspected that Alice Cadwallader had a very good idea about the effect her words had, and chose to use them anyway. Once again

I began to wonder at how we human beings can be so disconnected from those we are supposed to love.

We all held our silence and allowed Mair a moment or two, which she took. As she dwelt on the fortune of her upbringing I wondered about Dilys Jones's early life.

When a smile crossed Mair's face, I judged it time to prompt her more. "Did you and Dilys mix as children?" I asked.

Mair laughed. "Ten years is a big gap, Cait. By the time I was running about and more than a baby, she was a teen. Besides, I wasn't allowed to mix with the servants. There were many more of them in those days, of course. There were Dilys's parents—Mrs. Jones did what Dilys does now, she was the cook; her husband did what David has been doing, you know, general stuff around the place. But we had a chauffeur, a housekeeper, three women—or girls probably—who cleaned and waited on us, four gardeners, and, of course, there was Miss Williams, my tutor."

A shadow darkened Mair's expression. I read regret and sadness there as she spoke again. "She died a few years ago. She was only sixty. So young. It wasn't until I was grown up that I realized we were so close to each other in age. We'd kept in touch all that time. I suppose you could say she was my only real friend. I miss her terribly."

"It's such a different upbringing to the one we had, isn't it, Cait?" said Siân thoughtfully. "You just take it all for granted. The normality of your childhood. But who's to say what 'normal' is?"

I sensed a maudlin moment that I wanted to avoid. "Did you use the castle as a playground, Mair? I've got some idea of the layout, but there must have been lots of places to have as hidey-holes and so forth." I wondered if Mair might give us an insight into places where an interloper might be hiding.

Mair rallied. "I wasn't encouraged to run about the place. The only time I had fun was when Owain and Teilo came home for the holidays. As boys, they were expected to go clambering about the place, but Teilo was seven years older than me, and Owain is five years my senior, so they sometimes allowed their baby sister to tag along, but they largely ignored me."

"Like you ignored me when we were growing up, Cait," said Siân wistfully. "I suppose it was to be expected, given our age difference, but I always felt as though I was being left out of something exciting."

"There you go," said Mair, jumping on Siân's point, "that's it exactly. I'm not sure how much fun the boys really had, but I always imagined it was lots. I think that was when Owain decided he wanted to find out all about the castle's ancient history. Teilo once got lost for a day and a night, and I remember the panic. After that, he and Owain used to go off on secret exploring trips. They wouldn't let me join them then. It was like being invisible. To everyone. Except Miss Williams, of course. She would always play with me. Up on the floor above your rooms, that's where I used to have my room, with Miss Williams next door. This wing is very elegant, very smart, as you can see," she waved at the golden womb about us, "but the Gothic wing is a bit gloomy, I've always thought."

"What's through that door?" I asked, pointing to the surprisingly small door beside the piano.

"That's the library," replied Mair. "It's in the original part of the castle that my great-grandfather built—the Norman-style part, modeled after the Norman Keep at Cardiff Castle, but made of the stones that gave this castle its name, Castell Llwyd—Gray Castle. Of course, with browner stones having been used for the Gothic wing, and sandstone and terracotta for this wing—the 'Jacobethan' wing, as I'm sure our late poet laureate John Betjeman would have referred to it—the name seems a bit silly, but they never changed it. If you go through there, you go down a couple of steps to the library, which faces the sea. The original castle structure was built in the shape of an open arrow, pointing out to sea, so they just added one wing onto each side. Grandfather built the Gothic one because he so admired the new buildings at Cardiff Castle and wanted to outdo the Marquess of Bute who built it."

"Did they know each other?" I asked.

Mair nodded. "Huge rivals. John Bute was the man who enlarged the docks in Cardiff, making that city a much bigger port than Swansea. Powell Cadwallader was a Swansea champion, and he'd managed to ensure that its place at the center of the world of copper would go down in history. The two men were fierce competitors in terms of commerce, civic pride, and, of course, castle building."

All three of us nodded. "Cait made sure we went to Cardiff Castle during our October visit," replied Bud. "It's quite something. The Norman Keep on the hill is a wonderful thing, so very old, and the Victorian castle is like something out of a movie."

"Well that's it, you see," said Mair. "There wasn't any Norman building here, only the medieval ruins. So Great-grandfather, Hywel, built it himself. Then Grandfather saw what was happening at Castell Coch, which Bute was building outside Cardiff, and decided he could do it better, and faster. They finished building the Gothic wing you're in, in record time. Then he met my grandmother, Iris, and she was just nuts about Hatfield House, so he added this wing, in a similar style to her object of desire, just for her. Even so the construction here was finished around the same time as construction at Castell Coch, in 1899. It's said they had an amazing party here to welcome in the twentieth century, but I imagine it was still a bit of a mess really, because a lot of the tile work, and many of the murals and so forth, weren't finished properly until just before the First World War."

"Is there much of the original medieval castle left?" I pressed, keen to hear about the coal cellar.

"Now that's where Owain would be your man," admitted Mair. "I like the new parts, the Victorian parts, but as for the stone circle, the Roman temple, and the medieval castle parts, he'd know a lot more than me. That's his passion—the old bits, and, of course, the lay lines. Get him going on those and—well, let's just say you've been warned. He's obsessed with a line that runs through our stone circle and the Neolithic burial chamber over at Parc le Breos, in Parkmill.

Do you know it?" Siân and I nodded. Bud looked puzzled.

"I'm not very interested in rocks," continued Mair, "and that's all those parts are, to me. Old, I'll grant you, and wonderful because of that, but I find it difficult to get excited about what happened here two, three, or four thousand years ago, despite the fact that I'm surrounded by the leftovers from those times. I love the décor, the design, the mood of the new parts, you see. I think it's thrilling that almost everything in this castle is handmade, in some way, shape, or form. It's not mass-produced stuff. The china we eat off every day, the silverware, that piano, these rugs, the enameled gold tiles inside the fireplaces—everything was made by an artisan or an artist. But people don't seem to see the value in that. You must find that with your knitting, Siân. Not a lot of people understand that handmade is good."

I asked, "Would it be possible to see the library, Mair?"

Mair consulted her wristwatch. "Owain will be in there, and he's very protective of his privacy. But it's been a disturbed enough day that I'm sure he'll put up with a few visitors. Let's go now; soon it'll be time for lunch."

We all stood, and Mair led the way through the little door. I wondered why it was so small, but then saw there'd have been no point in making it any wider. The few steps to which it led were just as narrow.

Mair called out to her brother as we followed her down the three steps. She turned left into the vast expanse of the shelf-lined library, which had very small windows overlooking the sea—not that you could see the sea through the rain—and a good number of iron chandeliers running the length of the chevron-shaped room. The angle at the center of the room wasn't acute, but we couldn't see around it from where we all stood.

I heard it before I saw anything. Sobbing. Quiet and miserable, it sounded like the unhappy sobs of a child.

"Owain? Is that you?" Mair rushed forward, and we all followed.

As we rounded the slight bend we were met by a strange sight. Owain Cadwallader was sitting cross-legged on the floor, his whole body shaking, head down. He was distraught.

Hearing his sister's voice he lifted his head. His red eyes blinked through his thick spectacles.

"Look," he said, pathetically. He held up his hands, which were filled with shards of pottery. "It's broken. Shattered. Someone's been in here and broken the puzzle plate. Why would anyone do that, Mair? It's a family treasure, and now it's gone. We've been robbed of another piece of our history, and this one's much more important than that disgusting painting of Mother."

"When did this happen?" asked Mair.

"It must have been this morning. Just within the last couple of hours, because I brought it in here after breakfast. I . . ." he looked at me and blushed as he hesitated, "I didn't want it to be talked about by everyone any more. I wanted it to be private again. I put it there, on that stand. When I came in here after all that business with Mother, it was on the floor, broken."

"Could a window have blown open this morning and disturbed it?" I thought I should be the voice of reason, for once.

Owain shook his head. "None of these windows open. Never designed too. So it can't have been the wind. It must have been a person." He sounded shocked as he said the words aloud.

"Or maybe there really is a *bwca* in the castle," said Mair, smiling as brightly as she could at her brother.

"A *bwca* that shreds paintings and breaks plates?" asked Bud, sounding proud that he knew what was being referred to.

"And knocks," added Mair. "Knocking though the night, keeping people awake," she said blackly. "Though I didn't hear it over the storm last night, at least."

"A *bwca* knocking?" Owain looked terrified.

Mair nodded. "Mother's heard it too."

Dau ar bymtheg

MAIR REACHED DOWN TO HER brother and took the shards from his hands. "Here, give me those. You get up and sort yourself out, Owain. Let's all look around for all the pieces we can find and put them here on the table, then we can see what's what."

We ended up with a pile of crockery that looked less than promising.

"Smashed to smithereens, it is," said Mair sadly. She patted her brother on the back. "I tell you what, Owain, you know I was always good with jigsaws, and I also happen to know that Siân's pretty good at spotting a pattern too—so why don't you let us two do the best we can to get it back into some sort of shape, then you can see if anything's missing. There's no way we can tell from this mound if it's all here or not. How about that? To make up for me being nasty to you, eh?"

Owain mumbled his acceptance, though I didn't note any words of thanks.

Siân spoke brightly when she said, "Yes, Owain, it'll be fun for me, and I'll feel as though I'm doing something useful. Thanks for letting me help." *She's up again.*

Owain wiped his wet spectacles on a bit of his sweater as he replied, blinking. "You're welcome. I mean, thank you. You're very kind. I know it's very silly of me, but that plate and I have spent many years together. It's like an old friend. Whatever you might have said about it, Cait."

I tried to stifle a deep sigh.

"You felt the same way about that plate as Mother felt about her portrait," said Mair as she started to pick out the larger pieces of the plate and work out where they might go.

"They are very different," replied Owain, sniffing.

"They might be very different," I said, "but Mair makes a good point, because the way they made two people feel was very much the same. Each of you has lost something that meant a great deal to you. Something with which you had a strong emotional bond." A thought occurred to me. "Mair, has anything like this happened to you recently? Has something that meant a great deal to you been damaged, broken, or lost?"

"You told me your Ravelry account was hacked, and that lots of nasty messages were posted in your name a couple of weeks back," said Siân.

Mair nodded uncertainly. "True, but that's hardly the same as this, is it?"

"Does your reputation on Ravelry matter to you a great deal?" I asked. "Did you have to work hard to repair bonds with people who matter to you in your virtual world?"

Mair nodded vigorously. "Oh yes, it took forever, and it was very upsetting for some people. They thought I'd really said those things, you see. But I hadn't. So it took a lot more than just changing my passwords and so on. I know there are a few people on the Archers' forum who'll never acknowledge my existence again; in fact, I suspect they are still trying to get me booted off the site. Something I hope won't happen, because then I'd lose something very precious to me—" She paused, and a look of great concern made her eyes grow round.

"Someone's got it in for you lot," said Siân simply. "And they're not being very subtle about it. If hacking Mair's Ravelry account was the first act of vandalism, a couple of weeks ago, why did they wait until now to do what they've done to these objects, here at the castle?"

Bud was raking his hand though his hair as he said, "It's a significant change in modus operandi—a completely different type of crime. Hacking an internet life is a crime that's impersonal, it takes place at a safe distance, and allows for total anonymity. I'm sure it didn't cross your mind to hire anyone to trace who did the hacking, did it, Mair?"

Mair shook her head. "No, it didn't occur to me to do that. Besides, I wouldn't know who to ask."

I watched Bud as his thought processes developed, and decided to let him run with it. He did. "You see, that's the difference. With a slashed painting and a smashed plate, we're seeing two very destructive acts—anger-fueled, I'd say, with a high risk of discovery. It's almost reckless. So we have a carefully planned, virtual attack on the one hand, and two aggressive, and possibly opportunistic, acts on the other. It's odd. It almost sounds like two different people."

Owain was now on his feet and almost back to his normal self. "I say, Bud, I think that's highly unlikely. I mean, it's one thing to believe there's a lunatic running around smashing things up, because I'm sure that's what's happened—someone has gained entry to our home and is hiding out here, bent on destroying our family's precious possessions. It's quite another to suggest that there's more than one person planning to do harm to the Cadwalladers. A conspiracy, in other words. It *cannot* be."

Bud still looked concerned. "If you all don't mind, I'd like to track down Idris and Eirwen. Anyone know where I might find them?" He looked at his watch. "It's almost noon, where might they be?"

"Dining room," replied Mair and Owain in chorus. They shared a smile.

"Lunch is at noon," said Mair, "so they'll either be there, or heading there. We should join them. Mother lunches in her apartment, but Dilys likes us to be prompt. Right, Owain? If you miss it, it's gone?"

Owain's beard smiled. "That's what Dilys always says about food here—'If you miss it, it's gone'—though she never tells us where it's gone to. I suspect it all gets recycled into a future meal," he mused.

Mair replied, "Maybe, but it all always tastes good, and none of us look like we're suffering from malnutrition, so I dare say she's doing a good job on a pretty tight budget. But, look, let's not hang about here. Siân—let's come back and work on this plate after lunch?"

Siân nodded, and we all took one last look at the broken pottery.

"Let's go round this way." Mair led the way toward the end of the library farthest from the door through which we'd entered. "Going this way we can cut through the morning room, then right into the dining room, okay? Follow me," and she was off.

Bud grabbed my arm as we walked. "We need to talk to Idris and Eirwen. I need, *we* need, to find out if anything bad has happened to them recently—because, if it hasn't, it might soon. And, I hate to say it, but we should also check about their children. If someone is undertaking a campaign of spite against the Cadwalladers, then we need to know what's what."

"Do you think that David Davies's death might be connected in some way?" I asked, knowing the answer I'd give myself.

Bud nodded. "He might have seen something he shouldn't have, or just got in the way. And if we're dealing with someone who has already killed once, who knows how much more damaging and dangerous their actions might become."

I squeezed Bud's hand as we passed through the vividly decorated morning room. I hadn't expected carved wooden ceiling panels and leaf green walls to be so uplifting, but they were. I hardly had time to admire yet another golden tiled fireplace before Bud dragged me into the dining room.

Deunaw

"MOTHER, WHAT ARE YOU DOING here?" Owain sounded surprised to see Alice Cadwallader seated at the head of the dining table. Idris and Eirwen had also taken their places, and it was clear that Gwen was now being treated as a "proper" guest, because she, too, was seated at the luncheon table. "You don't usually join us for lunch. To what do we owe this pleasure?"

"Don't patronize me, Owain, just sit down and let Dilys serve you. She's been hovering for at least three minutes, poor woman. You're late. You're all late."

"We're sorry, Mother," said Mair, who entered the dining room just ahead of Bud and me. "We got a bit caught up with Owain. His puzzle plate has been smashed to bits."

"*My* puzzle plate," said Alice imperiously. No one responded. "My portrait destroyed, and now my puzzle plate smashed. I am very concerned that someone in my home means me ill will."

Just as Alice spoke, a window blew open. Immediately the cast iron chandelier above the center of the dining table began to sway and creak alarmingly. Everyone already seated at the table leapt up from their seats, and Janet rushed to pull Alice back from the table, only to be run into by Alice's wheelchair. Alice had pushed the little stick that sent the chair into reverse, and had gained a fair amount of momentum before she smacked Janet in the side. Janet went down with a yelp. Alice screeched to a halt and began to wave her arms, trying to turn around to see what had happened.

Bud ran to close the window; the rest of us helped Janet.

Once she was seated, Janet assured us she would be just fine. "I haven't broken anything, though I dare say I'll bruise up lovely by the morning. Are you alright, Alice?"

Alice was flustered. "Why don't you have lunch in your room, Janet?"

"I'll be fine right here, thank you very much, Alice," replied Janet firmly. "Though I'll feel a lot better when that thing up there stops swinging about."

We all followed her gaze to the chandelier, which was still swaying. It took Dilys's arrival to snap us back to reality.

"What on earth are you all up to? And what's wrong with that then?" Her steely glare pierced our defenses, and we all rushed to our seats and tucked into our luncheon as quickly as we could.

As I bit into the thick, yielding topping of grated cheese mixed with cream, pepper, mustard, stout beer, and Worcestershire sauce, and the crunchy toast beneath, I was back in our old house in Manselton and it was Saturday teatime. I tried to wipe away a tear before anyone else could see it.

I cleared my lunch plate—salad and all—as quickly as I could, because I could see Dilys and Rhian hovering in the great hall out of the corner of my eye. It seemed I'd been correct in my assumption that Rhian helped her mother serve food, and I was pleased to see her doing so for this meal. She was following through with her stated preference to be doing something, rather than sitting about and dwelling on her husband's demise.

"We're ready now, Dilys," called Alice when she'd had enough. "Very good rabbit," she added as Dilys collected her plate, "as always." Alice turned her attention to Bud, Siân, and me. "It's our traditional Sunday lunch," she announced. "There'll be a full roast at five o'clock, on the dot. What is it today, Dilys? Lamb?"

Dilys shook her head, passing off plates to her daughter. "We're having lamb tomorrow for the wedding lunch, so I thought we'd have beef today, and yes, before you ask, I'll be doing Yorkshire pudding too, Owain." Owain glowed.

Bud leaned into me and whispered, "Why did Alice say it was

good rabbit? That was cheese on toast—well, very fancy, tasty cheese on toast—right? Or did she get something different?"

I kept my voice down as I replied, "Welsh rarebit is also often called Welsh rabbit. Either is correct. The name refers to the fact that the Welsh were so poor they couldn't afford any meat, not even rabbit, so they had to make do with cheese. I've made you Welsh rarebit before, at home, you know I have. It's the same thing."

Bud nodded. "Thanks. There always seems to be something I don't understand."

"Like the death and destruction around here?" I said bleakly.

Bud nodded, his face grim.

"There's *teisen lap*, some mince pies, and tea in the drawing room. You can help yourselves," announced Dilys as she left, following Rhian, who was carrying away the used dishes.

"I'll catch up with you," said Bud as he pecked me on the cheek. "I just want a private word with Idris—about our concerns, you know?" I nodded and left the dining room.

Striding across the great hall I noticed that Janet, who was following Alice's wheelchair ahead of me, was limping. I scurried after her, touching her on the arm as I caught up.

"Are you really alright?" I asked. "You seem to be limping."

Janet smiled. "That's not today, that's from when I fell off a horse when I was little. You just haven't noticed it till now, I suppose. It does come on a bit more when I'm tired. But, usually, it's not a problem. I've got one leg a bit shorter than the other because of the fall, that's all. Doesn't stop me from running around this place all day."

"Does it affect you when you're lifting?" I nodded toward Alice. "You know, when you have to move Alice about?"

The effortlessly cheery Janet smiled again. "No, light as a feather she is. You should see some of them I have to hump about the place. Well, it's not their fault—sitting down all day and people trying to tempt you with this and that, you're bound to get a bit heavy, right?

But Alice is on the way down now; she won't be putting on any weight to speak of any more. Eats well, mind you, and likes a tipple or two. But at her age, it's smaller they get."

We both watched as Alice maneuvered her chair to what appeared to be her favorite spot right in the middle of the drawing room. I dawdled a little and said, "She seems to have got over the distress of earlier on, I see. Does she seem okay to you?"

Janet whispered, "I put a little something in a drop of warm whiskey milk for her. She always refuses tablets when she knows about them, so I sneak them into something where she won't notice them. I just gave her something to calm her down a bit and put a smile back on her face. She'll be fine. It's funny, what you said about her weight," she added.

"How do you mean?"

"Well, there she is wasting away from that beautiful woman she was in the painting, and now she weighs less than the frame it was in. It took both Rhian *and* Dilys to move it out of the room, they said."

"Yes, that is funny," I replied, lost in thought, "or odd, at least, that she now weighs less than her own portrait." But Janet was gone, and I found I was talking to myself.

Pedwar ar bymtheg

WHEN BUD ENTERED THE DRAWING room, he didn't come to sit to have a cup of tea. Instead he started gesticulating and nodding his head. I knew very well that he was trying to call me away, without doing so aloud, but he looked so funny that I let him carry on for about thirty seconds.

"Are you quite well, Bud?" called Alice, noticing his antics.

Bud grudgingly walked farther into the room. "Yes, thanks, Alice. I was just trying to get Cait to come outside for a private word or two about something."

"I would say something about 'young love,' but you're neither of you that young, so I won't," said Alice. Rather unnecessarily, I thought.

Idris and Eirwen appeared behind Bud, each a picture of flat out panic. "Alice, they don't want a private word about anything to do with their wedding, it's about us."

"What do you mean, 'us'?" replied Alice haughtily.

Dilys and Rhian trooped into the room next, each bearing a hot water jug, so we were all present and correct. I knew it was time to step up, so I put down my tea, gave Bud a significant look, and began.

"Everyone's here, so I think this should be talked about. I know there's a popular phrase about 'addressing the elephant in the room.' Well this isn't about an elephant, it's about a possible murder and some very destructive actions that have taken place here recently."

"What murder? There's been no murder here—just a nasty accident," shouted Alice, sloshing her tea into her saucer. "That's a wicked thing to say, Cait. Why would you say such a thing?"

"I don't believe that David's death was an accident," said Rhian bluntly. "I know, and many of you are also aware, that David was exceptionally good on his feet. The idea that he would fall down those stairs is ludicrous."

Rhian's words, and their meaning, hung in the air. The fire crackled in the grate, and the usually comforting sound of settling logs took on a menacing edge. I felt as though the balance of life in the castle was about to tilt off its axis forever.

"My plate—the Cadwallader Puzzle Plate—was smashed deliberately," added Owain, breaking the heavy silence.

"And then there's Mother's portrait," added Mair, "and me being hacked online." A few puzzled faces met her last statement, but Mair chose to not elaborate.

"Bud's just been talking to us about it all," said Idris, "and I am thinking about a couple of recent incidents in a new light. Last night, for example, those glass decorations on the Christmas tree in the great hall were all smashed."

"The glass balls, you mean?" asked Siân.

"Exactly," said Idris. "They've been in the family for about sixty years. Eleri and little Hywel know all their stories, and it's their big treat to be able to place them on the tree themselves. Each one of them, and only those particular decorations, were smashed on the floor. They were a devil to clear up, weren't they, Dilys?"

"Yes, glass and glitter everywhere, there was. Horrendous job to get it all up," she sniffed.

That explained why I'd managed to cut myself when I fell in the hall earlier in the day.

"The children will be very upset about it," added Eirwen. "It was a very spiteful thing to do."

"And that's what seems to be linking all these things," said Bud. "They are very spiteful, personal attacks against the members of the Cadwallader family. And I really think it's in everyone's interests for us to try to get to the bottom of this."

"Young man," called Alice—*I bet Bud loved being called that*—"do you think that David Davies's death is somehow connected to these attacks? That the same person has done all these things, including killing David?"

"It's a reasonable assumption," replied Bud carefully.

Again, silence followed, as everyone in the room let the significance of Bud's words sink in.

"My suggestion is that we search this whole place from top to bottom," said Idris. "And that's because I cannot imagine that anyone in this room has done any of these things. So it stands to reason that someone else is here, or at least coming and going at will. I believe we should all throw out any ideas about maintaining our privacy, and allow a full search to be made of the place. Starting with all the places that aren't lived in or used on a regular basis, of course, but not excluding our own apartments."

"That's a very bold suggestion, Idris," said Alice. She gave the idea some thought. "I agree. You should organize search parties. I suggest you start at the top of each wing, and work your way down."

"You want to let people search our rooms? Where we *live*?" said Dilys, shocked to the core. "I'm not sure that's very nice," she added. "It doesn't say much for trust, does it?"

Alice's face softened, as did her tone. "Dilys, I've known you since you were no more than a bump under your mother's apron, and I trust you with my life every day by eating the food you prepare for me. But this is one occasion where I believe that only complete thoroughness will work, to allow us all to sleep soundly in our beds tonight. So, yes, I do want everyone to allow their rooms to be searched, but, out of deference to our long acquaintance, I will suggest that Bud searches yours."

"But he's a complete stranger," exclaimed Dilys, looking at Bud as though he were Jack the Ripper.

"Exactly, Dilys," said Bud, "so when I leave here on Tuesday you'll never have to look me in the eye knowing that I've searched your rooms. And I *have* been trained to conduct searches, as a professional, so there'll be no snooping, just hunting with a purpose."

"And that purpose is?" asked Owain haughtily.

"To find signs of entry or egress not formerly known; to discover signs of someone having been in a part of the house you all believe to be unused; to check for signs of someone maybe even staying here for long periods of time; and, of course, to generally be on the lookout for items that have been hidden away in unexpected places."

"What sort of items?" asked Gwen, who'd been very quiet all through lunch, and afterwards. It was almost as though she was trying to be as little bother as possible as a guest.

"Anything out of the ordinary. Something in a place where it shouldn't be. Or something that should be somewhere, not being there anymore. In our search we are all trying to spot things that are curious or out of the ordinary," said Bud.

"There are probably pretty odd things in every room in this castle," said Rhian. "Those of us who live here would know about things being out of place, those of you visiting wouldn't. So can I suggest that the visitors—Bud, Cait, Siân, and Gwen—take the parts of the buildings that are supposed to be unused, because you're as likely to find something odd as we all would be. That means that those of us who live here can focus on a part of the castle we know well. Other than Bud doing Mam's rooms, of course. And you can do mine with Cait, if you want. Well, anyone can. It doesn't bother me. I just want to find out if anyone's been messing about with our home, and, if they have, if they might have pushed my husband down the stairs to his death." Her mouth set itself in a grim line as she finished speaking.

"Yes," I said—*maybe a little too quickly*, "let's do that. Bud and I will start on the top floor of the private wing, so we'll tackle your quarters first, then we'll go down to the cellar and kitchen areas, because there's nothing personal there. Maybe you can all agree who will search whose apartments. I suggest you all just swap. Of course, you don't need to get involved, Alice."

"But I want to," she replied sharply. "Janet can come with me through the music room and the morning room, and we can scan the hall as well."

"Good idea, Mother," said Mair. Her mother looked surprised and more than a little pleased by her daughter's reaction.

We all agreed on the pairings—Janet and Alice, Gwen and Siân, Idris and Owain, Eirwen and Mair, Rhian and Dilys, Bud and Cait—and on who would tackle which areas of the castle. Of course Owain insisted that only he and Idris would be allowed to touch anything in his library, but, other than that caveat, and having overcome Dilys's misgivings, we were all pretty much set to go.

Bud and I headed up the staircase toward the Davies and Jones apartments. I wondered what we'd find there—if anything.

Ugain

ONCE WE'D REACHED THE FIRST landing, where the grand staircase ceased to exist, Bud and I followed our instructions and walked toward where the private wing was joined to the original castle. There we found another set of wooden, carpeted stairs, this time much less grand, which led to the next floor. Having heaved my way up those, we then had to walk through a door beside the stairs to get to the smallest staircase, which led up to the top floor, as well as going all the way back down to the basement.

"It hadn't occurred to me that there'd be an alternative route from the kitchen level to the other floors," noted Bud as I clambered up the stairs behind him, panting.

"It's not direct, because you can only get to it on the second floor, but you're right. I suppose it makes sense." I stopped for a moment to catch my breath, and noted that this final set of steps was as steep as the one that led down to the kitchen. "It looks like the expectation was that all servants had the constitution of an ox and the climbing ability of a mountain sheep," I puffed.

Bud grinned down at me. "Think how much worse it would be if you hadn't quit smoking a couple of months ago, right?"

"Let it go, Bud. I think the piece of gum I'm chewing right now didn't get its shot of nicotine, so just be careful, or the dam might break and the torrent that is my foul temper might wash you away."

Bud puffed out his cheeks in mock terror, then continued up the stairs.

I gathered my strength and continued my climb. By the time I reached the top I was red in the face and lathered with sweat. "Maybe it's just as well I didn't bother to change my clothes before lunch. As soon as we've finished grubbing about the place I want to wash my hair, have a hot bath, and get into some clean, dry, un-stinky clothes."

"I agree that is exactly what you need to do," said Bud, opening a door and peering in.

I didn't respond to his observation, but I too opened a door.

"I think this must be Dilys's," I said, looking at the old-fashioned furnishings and the trappings of an older person.

Bud joined me and peered in. "I agree. So I'll take this one, you take the other?"

I nodded. "I want a good hunt about in David's place, to get a sense of the man, but I really want to get down to those cellars. Let's be as quick as we can, but take as long as we need—agreed?"

"Wish me luck," said Bud staring into what appeared to be a very orderly apartment.

"Me too," I replied, panicking a little as the total disarray in the Davieses' rooms greeted me.

I plunged in and got to work. I quickly realized that my first impression—that the apartment was in a state of utter chaos—was not a fair one. It was just very full of furniture. First of all I got the lie of the land. A total of three rooms had been given over to living quarters for Rhian and David, with an archway connecting two separate rooms. The archway was narrow and covered with a heavy brown velvet curtain, but did the job of allowing access, while maintaining a division of space.

The door I'd entered by delivered me into what was obviously the sitting room: it contained a television, overstuffed armchairs, and a sofa, plus a sideboard. Bedding was neatly folded on the sofa, and a large bag sat on the floor beside it, the type people carry on to aircraft. I reasoned that this was where Gwen had spent the night. The room held nothing remarkable; the furnishings looked as though they had all come from a store where flat-packs were sold, and they were all well used. Where it existed, the upholstery was dark brown.

I moved into the next room, where a double bed was positioned beneath the window. I noticed that the rain had eased a little, though the storm clouds were still sufficiently pendulous to promise more before they were done with us.

The bed itself was in disarray, with pillows bearing the marks of tears and a frustrating night lying stained and dimpled on top of the bedclothes. There were two old-fashioned dark brown, flame-veneered wardrobes set against the wall at the foot of the bed. I opened the one on the right. Neatly hung shirts, pants, and jackets told me it was David's. Although the wood of the wardrobe smelled old, the clothes smelled like fabric softener and a man's cologne or aftershave. I sniffed, trying to differentiate between the two. It wasn't difficult, as David's choice of aftershave was well known to me—Old Spice, the original fragrance. It took me back to my childhood—our family doctor, Doctor Jenkins, used to wear it, and quite a lot of it at that. For me it would always be the fragrance I associated with the pain of tonsillitis, from which I suffered frequently as a child.

Rubbing my immediately sore throat, I took time to examine David Davies's clothing and accessories. His choices were relatively conservative—dark pants, an array of blue shirts, white shirts, and a couple of lilac ones. Work-wear clothing hung at one side, but only the sort of thing a man might wear to perform light duties, rather than heavy work. Beside them at the other end hung two evening suits covered by protective clothes bags. I unzipped the bags to find that one suit was much newer than the other, and each was accompanied by three sets of bow ties, cummerbunds, and wing-collared evening shirts. The conductor obviously took his concert-wear very seriously. There was also a highly polished pair of evening shoes in a cloth bag hanging with the newer of the two suits. I wondered if they were the ones he'd been wearing when I'd watched him conducting the choir in October. There didn't seem to be another pair, and, pulling them out, I could see that these were not new, but certainly not old. He also had two brown pairs—one dress, one casual—and three black. There were no work-shoes or boots to be seen. A drawer at the base of the wardrobe, which was awkward to open, contained underwear, socks, belts, and a few tees, all of which were neatly rolled.

I wondered if the neatness was one of David's attributes, or whether his wife was responsible. Opening the second wardrobe told me it wasn't Rhian who was careful with their clothes. Rhian's clothes were hung higgledy-piggledy, barely clinging to cheap wire hangers. Shoes lay jumbled in the bottom of the wardrobe—dozens of pairs of cheap navy, black, and brown shoes in a heap. All showed considerable signs of wear; some were even losing their soles or had stitching breaking apart. It made me wonder how poorly matched the couple's other habits might have been. The drawer at the base of Rhian's wardrobe contained a nest of underwear, tights, socks, gloves, and mittens.

Next, I ventured into the bathroom, which felt claustrophobic, but was sparklingly clean and smelled of bleach. I pulled open the mirrored door of a medicine cabinet that hung above the washbasin. There being no real surfaces in the bathroom, this was where I found shampoo and conditioner, a couple of bottles of painkillers, a bottle of eye drops, toothpaste, toothbrushes, and face-cleansing wipes. I wondered where these people kept all the "stuff" with which my own bathroom always seems to be cluttered, and reasoned they must just be better at editing their needs.

Re-entering the bedroom I investigated the contents of the two bedside cabinets. Bearing in mind the different levels of neatness displayed in the closets, it wasn't difficult for me to work out which side of the bed "belonged" to David, and which to Rhian. Rhian's little cupboard contained a couple of romance novels, a pair of reading glasses, some hand cream, and a pair of socks. David's contained two flashlights, neither of which worked, and a pamphlet about Roman mythology.

Finally back in the living room I noted the lack of any personal items to speak of, save one wedding photograph of the Happy Couple on their Big Day.

My overall impression of the apartment was that it didn't have a true "lived in" feel to it. It looked and felt as though two very different people were roommates, and that was it. There was no sense of a shared life there. Before I moved on to my next area of inquiry I allowed myself a final scan. Having just pared down my own belongings and moved my stuff into our new home, I understood how the belongings of two separate people who had just decided to share a space would highlight two different personalities. But I also knew, from my profiling experience, that these distinguishing features are gradually tempered over time, with possessions, taste, and space gradually taking on the personality of the pair, the new unit. That didn't seem to have happened in the case of Mr. and Mrs. Davies—not even after six years of co-habitation. It was certainly food for thought.

Just before I closed the door, a thought occurred to me—Gwen's large overnight bag had been sitting next to the sofa, and I hadn't looked in it. I retraced my steps, bent down, and flipped open the unzipped cover of the bag. I poked around a bit. There wasn't anything surprising to be found, just the standard overnight stuff: a toiletry bag, a change of clothes, a giant sweatshirt—which I assumed was what she'd worn to sleep in. Everything was folded neatly and placed in the bag just so, with a pair of slippers on the top.

It was only as I joined Bud, who was already back in the hallway outside the apartment, that a little niggle crept into the back of my mind. Why did Gwen arrive the previous day to tune the piano *with* an overnight bag? I'd have to find a chance to ask her.

Un ar hugain

"CAN WE EXCHANGE NOTES AS we go?" I asked Bud, eager to get to the basement.

Bud nodded and we set off down the narrow staircase that had obviously been designed to give servants living on the top floor of the castle direct access to the kitchen and basement areas. I walked carefully, because the stairs were steep.

"Let me go first," said Bud, "then at least if you fall you'll have a soft landing."

I followed Bud and said, "You tell me your news first," as I came to terms with the rake of the stairs.

"Okay—here goes. Mrs. Dilys Jones likes photographs, that's point number one. Every surface is covered with them. Mostly of Rhian, but some of her with, I am assuming, the late Mr. Jones—who was as round as she is slim—and just one wedding photo of Rhian and our victim. Her choice of artwork other than that is minimal and runs to children with large eyes, cats, and a few prints of Welsh castles, which I found bizarre, given that she lives in one. She has three rooms: a sitting room, a bedroom, and a bathroom."

"Same as Rhian and David," I said.

"Good. So you have the layout. The sitting room isn't anything out of the ordinary, except for all the photographs. A TV, a sofa, a couple of chairs, a small table, a few magazines, and a lot of cookbooks piled on a bookshelf. It looks like she reads romance novels and paperbacks. They're all in poor shape, so either she buys them used or she wears them out by reading them over and over."

"Interesting," I said.

"I thought you'd like that," replied Bud. "What does it tell you?"

"The first thing that comes to mind is that the stall in Swansea Market where my grandmother used to swap used romance novels seems to still be in business."

Bud sounded disappointed as he continued. "Her bedroom was neat and tidy, in fact the whole place was. She doesn't seem to have a lot of stuff—though I did find a collection of those pinafore things she wears hanging in her closet. Looks like she's got about twenty of them, all very well worn, but neatly hung. She's also got a few more of those uniform type dresses, like the one she wore when she was serving in the dining room. The bathroom? Small—compact, as those realtors we've seen too much of over the past few months might call it—and very, very clean. The place smelled of bleach."

"Rhian's bathroom was the same," I said.

"Clean freaks, or hiding something?"

"I suspect just being clean, Bud. So nothing of any note is what you're saying."

"Other than the photos, not a thing. It's clear that there wouldn't be anywhere for someone to hide out there, and no easy access from outside—too high, and the windows are very small. She looks out over the sea, which wouldn't be a bad view, if the windows weren't so high up. Come on, we're there." Bud brightened.

I took the last few steps slowly, then paused to allow my head to stop spinning. I took in our surroundings. "We're in the basement again, but we're at the back of it this time, near the back kitchen where they stored the body, rather than at the front of the castle, where the stairs come down from the main hall. A very *Upstairs, Downstairs* layout, don't you think?"

Bud nodded. "Where next? Try to find the coal cellar?" he suggested.

I strained my ears for sounds of anyone close by, but could hear nothing. "I wouldn't mind taking another quick look at the body, since we're so close to it," I whispered. I darted off before Bud could stop me.

The day outside the castle had never been bright, and the windowless back kitchen needed the lights turned on. Even then, the stone walls were as forbidding as they had been the night before, and seeing David Davies's body lying on the table was, once again, a sobering sight. However, I knew that I needed to examine him one more time, so I pulled back the cloth. I got close—I wanted to be close enough that I could see the pores on his skin, so I could examine the way that the stone of the steps had deeply grazed his chin, though I didn't plan on touching the body, now that Bud and I were pretty certain that foul play was to blame for his demise. Even though the poor dead man had been hauled about the place, I was well aware that there might still be trace evidence on the body that could prove useful once the police arrived. And not just the obvious smudges of coal dust. I wanted to re-examine the marks on his pants. But they were gone.

"He's changed his clothes," I said, quite loudly as it turned out. "These aren't the pants he was wearing when we saw him last night. Then he was wearing jeans. Now he's wearing brown dress pants. And he's wearing different shoes. These are brown; the others were black. But these are the same socks."

Bud looked as puzzled as I felt. "Why would someone change his clothes? And only his bottom half, at that. I'm remembering correctly, aren't I? This is how he was dressed above the waist? That is the sweater that had handprints on it?" asked Bud.

I nodded. "Yes, the top half hasn't changed, only the bottom half. Hang on, let's have a look at his back again."

"No, no more rolling him about," said Bud sternly.

I tutted, knowing he was right, then had a thought. I darted to the corner of the room, where I'd seen a box of kitchen supplies the night before. I rustled about and finally pulled out a couple of pairs of Marigold kitchen gloves, still in their wrappers.

Once we'd pulled on the gloves, Bud and I rolled the body far enough for me to be able to see that the grubby handprints on his back had disappeared.

"Maybe someone brushed them off?" mused Bud.

"Maybe," I replied thoughtfully.

"But why change only half his clothes?"

"Exactly," I replied. "Why indeed?"

As I mentally ran through the several reasons I could think of for someone changing only some of David Davies's clothes, Bud said, "Are you done with him now?"

I nodded, and we let him roll back into his original position, then replaced the sheet.

"What did you learn about him from his rooms?" asked Bud, carefully tucking the sheet around the edge of the body.

Pulling the yellow gloves off my hands, I looked at what had become of David Davies and said, "He was neat, very keen on looking his best in all ways. Rhian was either too busy to keep herself and her belongings in good condition, or she'd stopped caring. Her mother said that she'd let herself go—I saw signs of that. But David? No, he was clean, neat, tidy. His concert-wear was immaculate. He wanted to make a good personal impression."

Bud nodded sagely. "So, your assessment?"

"Taking the evidence of their living quarters together with what I've seen of Rhian, and judging by our interactions with her, I would say that David was keeping himself looking good for someone other than his wife, whereas she felt abandoned, yet still in love with the man. One thing that puzzled me was that I found nothing to do with music there. Yes, there were the clothes he'd wear to conduct the choir, but that was it. I'd have thought that a choral director would have a large amount of music—you know sheet music, different accompanist parts, maybe even orchestral parts—close at hand. I also didn't find any work clothes to speak of. He had some clothing there that suggested light DIY duties, but nothing that looked like it had been knocked about in a garden or while doing anything very dirty or involving manual labor, like fixing problematic radiators. Yet his hands suggested he did do work like that, and Rhian told me he did. So I believe that David had at least one other location where he kept belongings. We need to find that, I think."

"Unlikely to be the coal cellar," said Bud glumly.

I nodded. "True, but I want to look at it anyway. Let's find it and check it out, however dirty we might get. Hopefully, we'll discover why there's so much coal dust involved with this mystery."

We left the confines of the dank, abandoned back kitchen, and moved toward the wonderful smells coming from the working one. I couldn't help myself, my saliva glands kicked in and I drooled at the thought of the roast beef dinner to come. Judging by the aromas wafting about us, Dilys was well ahead with the cooking of the meat. I poked my head into the kitchen, which looked quite different now that pots and pans were in use on the stovetop and Dilys herself was bustling around the large central table.

As she noticed us, her head snapped up and she glared at us both. "Finished poking about in all my stuff, have you?" She sounded angry.

"Thank you very much for your patience, and your understanding," said Bud smoothly. "As a retired police officer who has, sadly, had to conduct many such searches, may I say what a beautiful home you have? I was very respectful of your property, Dilys, and I hope I haven't disturbed anything. I'd hate to have left things less than perfect for you, as you clearly take such good care of your personal space."

Dilys glowed with pride. She grew at least an inch, and her eyes softened. For the first time since I'd met her I saw a genuine smile flood her face with a warmth I couldn't have believed possible of the woman.

"Oh, go on with you now." She smiled coquettishly at Bud. "Saying nice things like that about me? It's just a few rooms, and not much to show for my life in them. But I do like to keep things tidy, see. Important that is, especially when you haven't got a lot of space. I don't know how that Rhian of mine can't see it. Terrible mess her place gets in sometimes, and I'm the one who has to go in and clean it all up."

"Well you do an excellent job, Dilys. And I wanted to thank you for letting me into your place." *Bud is very good at this.*

"I know that Cait was just as respectful of your daughter's living quarters," he added, "but we did just have a couple of questions."

Dilys beamed at him. "Ask away, go on, just ask away."

"We wondered if you knew of another area where David might have kept other personal effects. There didn't seem to be much music, or anything much associated with his work as a musician. Do you know where that might be?"

As Dilys wiped imaginary crumbs from the table, she said lightly, "Yes, he keeps a lot of his bits and bobs out in the old stable building. It's where they park the cars, you know?" Bud nodded and she continued, "He spends a lot of his time there, or spent it I should say. Liked to skulk about, he did. I know you shouldn't speak ill of the dead, but I thought Rhian could have done better, and she should have done, but he was a charmer, that one. Sly with it too. And he drank."

Dilys stopped wiping and looked at Bud. "One thing I can tell you is that the stable block is where he used to say he was going, but I don't know how he ever got as dirty as he did when he was there. I've seen him walking upstairs looking a right mess, and I've seen him stuffing things in the washing machine out the back here that he didn't know I saw."

"For example?" I asked, determined that I wouldn't be ignored.

Dilys gave me a withering look—it seemed that her warmth was reserved solely for Bud—and replied, "I can't remember specifics, but trousers, shirts, and things like that. Things it was his wife's job to keep clean for him. Mind you, keeping house isn't Rhian's strong point, I'm sorry to say."

Once again Dilys had managed to talk a lot but say very little. The only grains of insight I'd gleaned from our conversation was that David sometimes did his own laundry, and that Bud and I should probably brave the elements once again and traipse over to the stable block to try to discover more about the dead man's life.

"If you'd be kind enough to point us in the direction of the coal cellar, the laundry area, and maybe the boiler room and so forth, then Cait and I can hunt about in those areas. Also, if we're going to do that, would we need flashlights?"

"Flashlights? Oh, you mean torches," said Dilys. "Well, you won't because there's lights everywhere you've just mentioned, but you can have this one just in case." She reached into a cupboard beneath her capacious sink and pulling out something that looked like a small cannon. As Bud took it from her I noted the surprise on his face as he felt its weight.

Dilys walked us to the end of the kitchen. "Go in the opposite direction to the back kitchen and go alongside the stairs, and there's another little corridor behind there, and then it opens out into my room for doing the laundry. Farther along is another door into the boiler room. For the coal cellar you'll have to go right through; the cellar's on the other side of the house. You can't miss it. Like I said, there are lights everywhere, even if it's just a bulb hanging, but please turn everything off as you leave."

It seemed that the woman was dismissing us because she turned to the oven, looked at her wristwatch, and said, "That's that then."

I looked at my own watch. It was only just two o'clock, so the roast beef, which we were due to eat at five o'clock, couldn't be ready. I wondered what she had in the oven if it wasn't the beef, but I didn't get to find out because Bud all but dragged me out into the corridor on the side of the coal cellar. It seemed I was going to find out why David had been so grubby after all—*at least, I hoped I was.*

Dau ar hugain

FOLLOWING DILYS'S INSTRUCTIONS WAS A lot easier than she'd made it sound. The laundry room had been painted white, so the lights in there made the walls glare, and it was as clean as I imagined Dilys could manage, given its great age and location. The two washing machines and two dryers had seen better days. Beyond the laundry room was a grubbier area, full of heating equipment, which whirred and roared, and then we finally stood in front of what had to be the door to the coal cellar. It was very large, made of thick, rough-hewn planks of wood, and extremely dirty. A giant iron bolt was all that held it closed, and it slipped open easily in Bud's hand. *Interesting.*

Looking at his hand already covered with coal dust, Bud remarked, "Keeping those rubber gloves on might have been a bright idea."

He shrugged, pulled open the door, and reached around inside the room for a light switch.

"Flashlight?" I suggested. Bud clicked it on and immediately located the switch for a series of three light bulbs hanging from wires. I hadn't known quite what to expect of a medieval dungeon that had been transformed into a Victorian coal cellar, but the sight that met our eyes was definitely underwhelming.

Large stones had been mortared together, and were thick with decades of coal dust. The floor was uneven and strewn with the detritus of the thousands of tons of coal that had been delivered over the years, then carted out, presumably in buckets, to fill the fireplaces once used in every room of the castle.

"I wonder how they got the coal into here?" My words echoed in the ancient chamber. It was a deeply unsettling sound.

Bud turned the flashlight beam toward the ceiling of the room. "Doesn't seem to be any sort of an opening up there," he noted. "We must be under the great hall here. I can't imagine they'd deliver the coal into the house to get it down here. Have you any knowledge about coal deliveries in that giant memory of yours?"

I smiled sweetly as I replied, "I'm old enough to remember the coalman delivering coal to our very own home, you know." Bud chuckled. "The coalman would come to the front door and you'd say how much you wanted—the bags weighed a hundredweight. That's the imperial version, weighing one hundred and twelve pounds, not the one used in North America, which is one hundred pounds. So the coalman was always a strong man, because he'd carry the bag to the coalhouse. We didn't have a cellar at our home, but a big cupboard thing outside the back of the house. In our case, it was next to the toilet."

"Whoa! You had a toilet outside your house?" Bud sounded incredulous. "But you had other ones inside, right?"

I shook my head. "Not until I turned twenty, when Mum and Dad managed to get some money from the government to update the house and install a toilet indoors. It was upstairs, in the bathroom. I remember when I came home one Christmas to visit from university, how proud they were as they opened the door to the bathroom to show it off to me. It was a big surprise. Now maybe my telling you that it's ridiculous that we have four bathrooms in our new house makes a little more sense?"

Bud shrugged.

I continued, "By the way, you've just covered your face with coal dust. But, as I was saying, when the coalman came, he had to walk right through our house to get to the coal shed, so Mum would put newspaper on the floor for him to walk on. As you can imagine, his boots were filthy, and he'd shed dust as he walked. One of our grandmothers lived in a semi-detached house, unlike ours, which was terraced, so the coalman didn't have to walk through her home with his big, filthy sack, he'd just walk around the side path and to her coal house that way. Hers was her old air-raid shelter, dug up from the garden where it had been buried through the war, and repurposed."

Bud looked thoughtful as he said, "You've never really talked to me about all this family history of yours, Cait. And it's so very different from my own. We should do this more often—but maybe not while standing in a filthy place like this."

"You're right," I replied. "I have to admit that I love the smell of coal—it makes me feel safe." I took a deep breath, and Bud threw me a glance that suggested I was losing my mind. "But, no, coal wouldn't be delivered into the great hall above us, it would make far too much mess. I do have a thought though. If the original Norman-style structure was built on top of the even older medieval structure that was here, then, of course, what is now the great hall didn't exist at that time. The great hall floor and staircase were constructed between the two new wings, and that stained glass roof was stretched across it, creating the wonderful space that someone then decided to clutter up with all manner of ancient armor and stuffed beasts from around the world."

"And if it didn't exist when the original Castell Llwyd was built," said Bud proudly, but badly mangling the pronunciation, "then there might, indeed, have been a chute in the original driveway, or courtyard, or whatever they had there at that time, where they could bring the coal in a truck and dump it right in here. Good thinking, Cait. Then, when they built the great hall, they must have constructed some other way to get the coal down here. From the new driveway, I guess? A longer chute?"

I nodded. "But the question remains, where's that entry point?"

We moved farther inside the room, being careful about where we put our feet, and examined each of the four walls and the ceiling. Bud continued into the cellar, moving his light about as he did so.

"Stop!" I shouted, but it was too late, the beam of light had moved.

"What is it?" asked Bud, sounding alarmed.

"There—just when the light was there, on the far wall, I saw something that looked metallic. Can I take the flashlight?"

Bud handed it over and I played the light on the spot I'd noticed.

"I see it," said Bud excitedly, and he moved forward, trying to not slip on the rubble of coal that covered the floor. I followed, trying to keep the beam steady.

"It's a hook," he said as he raised his arm and grabbed at something. I saw him pull, then there was a clicking, grinding, and whirring sound and two whole sections of the wall opened like the shutters on a window. I shone the light into the blackness beyond them. About three feet off the ground was a square tunnel, the length of which exceeded the penetration of the flashlight. Bud and I looked at each other with wonderment on our faces.

Our expressions quickly creased into smiles when I hissed, "It's like a secret passage—how thrilling. Hey—what's that?"

I shone the light onto a large, dark, lumpy backpack that was wedged just inside the passageway. Bud reached in and pulled it out. It was filthy. He opened the flap on the top and pulled out two sets of coveralls, one smaller than the other, both made of bright green, heavy-weave nylon. The pack also contained a tub of baby wipes, several pairs of heavy-duty rubberized gloves, and two hardhats with flashlight attachments.

I could tell we were both thinking the same thing when Bud took the flashlight from me and played its beam around the inside of the passage. He reached in again and pulled out two pairs of wellington boots, sizes 11 and 7.

"These would pretty much fit us," said Bud tellingly.

"A man and a woman, covering themselves so they can get along that tunnel, no doubt about it," I replied. "The boots explain David's jeans being crumpled and turned up at the bottom—that's how your jeans get when you stuff them into wellingtons. And the baby wipes explain the general cleanliness, with a hint of remaining grubbiness. So that explains the coal dust. And, of course, all of this explains why the bolt to the main door slid back so easily; someone's been in and out of here frequently, and very recently. We should get in there ourselves."

Bud looked at me in a way he does sometimes and simply said, "No, Cait. Not right now, and probably not ever."

"You know I don't care for small spaces very much, and I wouldn't suggest it unless I thought it were important." I used my "pretty please" voice as best I could.

"It could be dangerous. I'll do it on my own, but you're not doing it with me." Bud countered my cajoling with his commanding voice.

It was an impasse with which we were both familiar, and I decided to use stealth tactics.

"How about you just reach in with the light as far as you can, and tell me if you can see anything?" I suggested.

"Fair enough."

I spread the larger of the two sets of coveralls across the lip of the opening and Bud lay forward and stretched out his arm. I could see the dancing light articulate the four sides of the passage, but nothing else.

"Tell me what you can see," I pressed.

Bud stood up again and said, "It slopes upward. Not very much, but there's a definite incline. I'd say it's about four feet square. But I can't see anything except blackness at the end of it."

I was disappointed.

"The only other point worth noting," continued Bud, "is that people have definitely been moving through it. I spotted scuff marks on all four of the surfaces, but mostly on the floor. It's lined with bricks, or more likely some sort of tiles, because I can see light reflecting where there are scuff marks."

"That explains the rubber boots," I said. "They'd give better traction against fired tiles. And fired tiles would provide better long-term slippage of coal down a chute. We've obviously found the way they got the coal in here. If they built this at the same time they erected the new wings, when they knew there'd be a hall built above here, then it's likely they constructed it to have an opening in what is now the main courtyard."

"It figures," mused Bud. "But that doesn't explain why David Davies, and whoever his sidekick might have been, would want to go climbing it. Not if it just leads to some sort of trap door arrangement out in the driveway. What would be the point?"

"Exactly."

We both stood still for a moment, coal dust settling silently around us. We could almost hear the echoes of our own thoughts.

"Well," I said finally, "we'll never know unless we follow in their footsteps, will we?"

"And that's where we came in, Cait. No way are you going in there."

I grinned. "How about we come back with a very long rope, I hold onto it here, and you go up into the chute and see what you can find? Would that be a good way to find out why this was so important to David Davies?"

Bud shook his head and allowed his shoulders to fall. "You're not going to take 'no' for an answer, are you?"

Tri ar hugain

BUD AND I USED THE baby wipes to clean up as best we could, then, having worked out how to open the hidden door to the coal chute, we shut it again.

"It's gone half past two, Bud, and we're all due to be meeting up in the drawing room at three o'clock to discuss our findings. We can't possibly go there looking like this, so come on, we'd better get back to our rooms and clean up pretty sharpish if we're not going to arouse suspicion."

Bud caught my arm as I began to make a dash for the door to the cellar. "Hang on there you, just a minute. There's no need to panic. We haven't been hunting about in secret—it was one of our duties to check out this whole basement area, so being dirty isn't going to be 'suspicious' at all."

I stopped in my tracks. "Of course, you're right. Why didn't I see that?"

Bud glared at me. "You're talking about something else now, aren't you?"

"Yes, I'm talking about the stables. Come on, Bud—you're right, no one will care if we're dirty when we show up to meet them, but we don't want to get clean until we've finished getting dirty. And we'll probably get very dirty at the stables. Come on . . ." I scampered out of the cellar, shouting, "Don't forget to turn off the lights when you follow me."

I made my way back along the side of the kitchen, which was now smelling even better than it had done earlier, and started up the stairs.

"Those are the down stairs," called Dilys from her all-seeing position in the kitchen. "I'll thank you to use the up ones."

I felt like a naughty schoolgirl. "Sorry, Dilys," I called back. "May I walk through your kitchen to get to the up stairs?"

By this time Bud had caught up with me, and I saw Dilys's demeanor change.

"You're very welcome to come through my kitchen, and thank you for being so kind as to respect our systems here," she added politely.

I rushed through as quickly as I could without running—*I suspect that would be against her rules*—and Bud followed with a cheery, "No, thank *you* very much, Dilys, we've really appreciated all your help."

I labored up the stone steps and, as I emerged into the great hall, was struck by the fact that, once again, the grandeur of the stained glass roof was beginning to disappear against an already almost dark sky.

"It looks like it'll be completely dark in a little while," I said, huffing and puffing as I began to encase myself in the rainwear I'd need to survive in the lashing rain. "How depressing is that?"

"It could be worse," said Bud brightly, "it could still be blowing like it was yesterday." He pulled on the waterproofs he'd worn earlier, which were still dripping onto the tile floor near the front doors.

Finally ready to brave the elements, I triumphantly held up the flashlight. "I didn't give it back to Dilys, so we still have it if we need it."

"You never know," said Bud as he pulled open the front door, and the noise of the beating rain drowned out whatever he might have said next.

We made sure the door was firmly closed behind us. I shouted into Bud's ear, "Let's see if we can find anything that looks like a hatch leading to that coal chute. It must be quite close to the building, and when I came out of the cellar I tried to run up the down stairs, so it must be on the side of the non-Gothic wing." Bud nodded and we moved in that direction.

I didn't know what I was looking for, but I was pretty sure I'd know it when I saw it. We moved with our heads down, and I tried to make sure that my rain hat steered the river of water running off it straight onto the ground.

"Here," called Bud. I joined him. Bud pointed to a large, square metal plate set into the driveway. He'd cleared the pea gravel with his boot to reveal it. It wasn't dissimilar to a manhole cover. We both stood and lined up what we believed to be the trajectory of the channel beneath it.

"That's quite a tunnel," observed Bud close to my ear. "At least we know where it comes up now, though I still don't understand why anyone would want to climb it."

I looked behind us and could see we were closer to the stone circle than I'd imagined. "Let's discuss it when we're out of the rain," I replied.

Bud nodded, and we headed off toward the stable block. We were both drenched by the time we got there. Luckily the door at the gable end of the block was unlocked, so we walked inside and had dumped our dripping outerwear in a matter of moments.

We were in what was obviously a small office. A paper-strewn desk suggested that whoever used the office didn't bother much with computers, and the wear on all the furnishings suggested they'd been there since long before the dawn of the digital age. Metal filing cabinets lined one wall, a giant clock, which would have been more at home in a Victorian railway waiting room, tocked ominously on another, and there was a door in the third. It was locked.

"That's the first locked door I've come across since we got here," I noted.

"In that case, we *must* go through it," said Bud. "See any keys anywhere?"

I looked around but didn't see anything obvious. I shoved a few papers on the desk and something clattered onto the tiled floor. I bent to pick it up.

"Look at this," I said.

Bud looked and took the object from my hand.

I took the chance to have a good look at the little metal cylinder he held, but I couldn't guess what it did. Its thickest section had a gouge cut out of it, then there was a narrower middle section then, finally, an even narrower section. It was blunt at both ends and looked dirty, and maybe even a little greasy.

"What is it?" We didn't really have time for a guessing game.

"It's a firing pin," said Bud rather smugly.

"A firing pin from a gun?"

"Uh huh," nodded Bud. "I'm going to suggest it's from a shotgun, but I don't know which one. You Brits have makes and models we just don't get our hands on in Canada."

"So there are guns involved in all this now?" I heard the stress creep into my voice as I spoke.

"Cait, even in the Welsh countryside people must have shotguns. Sure, it's not the States, but there are legal ways for a farmer to have a gun or two."

"What farmers, Bud? This is a castle. A castle that hosts weddings and other events. It's hardly overrun with livestock or the sort of creatures that would need to be shot. Maybe there's the odd bunny or two hopping about, but that would probably be it."

"We did have rabbit pâté yesterday, Cait. Maybe it was a Cadwallader Estate rabbit yesterday, and a Dilys Jones 'rabbit/rarebit' today, eh?"

"Oh right, culinary jokes now, Bud Anderson?" I pushed him playfully, and we each cracked a much-needed grin.

Beyond the locked door we both heard the clattering of metal onto a stony floor, and we froze, but it was too late, because whoever was inside the stables had heard our laughter and began to bang on the door and rattle the handle.

We heard a key being used and the next instant the door flew open.

The first thing I saw was the gun. The next thing I saw was an unexpected face.

Pedwar ar hugain

"I DON'T THINK YOU NEED that gun, Idris," said Bud evenly. "Why don't you put it down?"

There are few things more terrifying in this world than the realization that the person pointing a gun at you is more frightened than you are. Idris Cadwallader's hand was slick with rain and shaking almost uncontrollably. The ancient-looking shotgun that he'd tried to wedge against his shoulder kept slipping on his soaked Barbour jacket. His face was a dreadful mask of fear.

He closed his eyes tight, and for a split second I thought he was going to pull the trigger. Instead, he lowered the gun until it pointed at the floor.

"Thanks heavens it's you two," he almost wept. "I was in the drawing room and I saw a light bobbing about out here in the dusk, and I thought it was the person we've all been looking for. I couldn't find you two anywhere, so I pulled on some clothes and came up here. You didn't have this place on your list of areas to search. When I heard someone clattering about in the office I pulled this out of the old gun cupboard." He lay the gun on top of the piles of papers on the desk. He looked relieved to not be touching it any longer.

Bud sounded concerned when he spoke to the still-shaking man. "Are you okay, Idris?"

Idris shook his head. "Not really. I hate guns, and I don't even know what to do with them, but it suddenly dawned on me that I might find myself looking into the face of a maniac, bent on targeting my family with malicious acts, so I reckoned it was better than nothing."

Idris wiped his wet hands together, then across his face. I was almost as shaken as he was. Bud seemed to be the only cool one. Years of training do pay off, it seems.

"I didn't use the flashlight when we were walking up here," I said bluntly. "Nor did Bud, so I don't know what that light was, but it wasn't us." Bud threw me a sideways glance that showed me he was on full alert. I took the hint and pricked up my ears.

Idris took off his hat and shook his head. Water poured onto the floor of the little office, making a river along the gaps between the flagstones.

"I don't know how much more of this I can take," he said. His voice was heavy, his face drawn. "Maybe I imagined the light, I don't know any more."

"We're doing all we can to try to sort out this mess," Bud reassured. "Cait and I have made some real progress, but we need to finish checking the place. So, listen, since you're here, and you've opened that locked door, maybe you can help Cait and me scout out the stables? Then we can all get back to the castle and change into some clean, dry clothes." Bud's voice was soothing, almost cooing. It seemed to do the trick, because Idris began to think more logically.

"How did you get in?" Idris sounded puzzled.

I answered. "Only the door from here into the stables was locked. The one we used to come in, from outside, wasn't. Is that unusual?"

Idris shrugged. "We don't really lock anything much around here. My family cannot get it into their heads that they are surrounded by some very valuable items, which any number of people might like to steal. They just don't get it. I've spent money getting locks fitted all over the place, but nobody ever uses them. That's why I think that someone is lurking about Castell Llwyd and doing all these dreadful things. They'd have no problem getting into the place at all."

"Well someone seems to have used this lock at least," I remarked. "Whose office is this?"

"It's Rhian's," said Idris, finally sounding calm. "She does all the event stuff in here, and David has—had—his space inside the stable block. One of the old stalls is set up for him."

"There's no computer here, Idris, yet I know I've communicated with Rhian by email a great deal, so where does she do that part of her job?"

Idris looked around. "Her laptop isn't here. It's usually on the desk." He reached out to push the gun to one side, then lifted papers, searching for the laptop I knew wasn't there. "No idea where it could be. You should ask her, she'll know. It's critical to running the business. She brings it with her when we have meetings in my apartment. Alice won't let me take another room in the castle as an office, so everything is in the space that should be our sitting room. You know, maybe, with the weather the way it has been, she took it to her apartment with her so she wouldn't have to keep running out here in the rain." I hadn't seen a laptop there, either.

"Maybe," replied Bud. "We can check that when we get back. But for now, could Cait and I see 'David's space,' as you referred to it?"

"Absolutely," replied a now confident Idris. "Follow me. Oh—hang on a minute, I should lock that outer door before we leave, then everything will be secure here and we can leave by the door from the stables."

As Idris locked up, I said, "Shouldn't we put that gun back into the gun cupboard?"

Idris replied, "Absolutely. Maybe Bud could do it?" It was clear from the man's expression that he didn't care for the idea of picking up the gun again, and he expressed his thanks when Bud replaced it in what looked to be a very inadequate gun locker hanging on the stable wall.

The office secure, Idris showed us David Davies's space. And what a space it was.

The apartment he shared with his wife had shown me how two people with very different temperaments had managed to rub along in a relatively small physical area. Rhian's office had consolidated my opinion of her as a messy person who probably had a good sense of order in her mind—good enough to overcome the disarray in front of her eyes.

Her husband, the neat and tidy one in the apartment, had let loose in his own space, with a huge amount of perfectly stacked, boxed, and labeled material. The area was no more than a brick wall with two wooden partitions and nothing to divide it from the walkway that ran the entire length of the stable building. His was the only stall that remained—the rest of the space had been gutted. Parked in it were two compact Vauxhalls—one was ours, and I guessed the other was Siân's—along with a battered old brown Mini, a newer silver Renault Clio, an older model Range Rover, and something low and probably sleek covered with a very dusty tarpaulin. Against the wooden divider, facing the car-parking area, were shelves covered with a strange mix of tools and a makeshift workbench holding a good number of filthy rags. The smell of petroleum and oil filled the air.

The lighting came from fluorescent tubes hung high above our heads, so I took advantage and poked about on the workbench. I paid particular attention to a pad of order forms, the type that have a pink carbon copy underneath the original white sheet. I ran my fingers over the paper, which was very thin and almost rough.

"Do you know what this is?" I asked Idris.

He peered at the book. "They are the chits David filled out to tell me what he was ordering and buying for the upkeep of the vehicles owned by the business. The Range Rover 'belongs' to the castle, as does the old Aston Martin over there." He waved in the direction of the tarp-covered vehicle. "He's doing it up so we can display it. It's a sort of hobby-cum-ongoing project for him. I don't know what'll happen to it now. It's taking longer than he'd hoped, he said."

"May I take one of these forms?" I asked.

Idris, and Bud, looked puzzled. "If you like," replied Idris, almost absentmindedly.

"And so to David's area," said Bud, looking at his watch. "Cait, maybe you could take a look, then tell me about it when we get back to the castle? Time's pushing on."

I nodded and did my thing. I'm good at taking in a lot of information and being able to store it for future retrieval. So, instead of taking my time, I went to work at quite a pace. I opened boxes, drawers, files, folders, turned on an electronic keyboard and played a few notes, and, finally, asked Idris if he might have a key for the one locked drawer in David's desk. He didn't.

"Rhian might have one," he suggested. "Or maybe he had some keys on him when he . . . died."

I'd felt the pockets of David's jeans and he hadn't had any keys on him at the time, but I didn't tell Idris that.

Bud stood beside me and looked at the drawer. "It's a pretty old desk, Cait," he said, inserting himself between Idris and the item, "maybe the drawer is just stuck. Here, let me have a go. I'm a good bit stronger than you, and I have a way with these things."

A couple of seconds later the drawer flew open. "There you go," he said triumphantly, "just stuck. You can see what's in it now, Cait, but don't be too long about it, eh?"

I resolved to ask Bud about where and when he'd learned to pick a lock as soon as I could. In the meantime, I rooted around in the drawer, then pulled everything out onto the top of the desk so I could get a better look at what David had seen fit to hide from the world.

It was an eclectic and puzzling mix of items. A small book about the history of Bletchley Park and its role in the breaking of the Enigma Code was well thumbed. There was a black-and-white pamphlet about the Neolithic ruins at Parc le Breos. A lariat with a compass attached was being used as a bookmark in a copy of *The Myths and Legends of Ancient Greece and Rome* bound in blue linen, written by E. M. Berens in 1880, though I noted this was the tenth edition. The page marked was one of seven that dealt with Poseidon and Neptune. There was a pack of white blackboard chalk, with only one and a half sticks remaining; two large, horseshoe-shaped magnets; a flat, rectangular piece of some sort of black-colored stone; and a couple of little plastic bottles with a clear liquid inside. The final item was a large-scale topographic map of the Gower Peninsula, folded in such a way that the Cadwallader Estate was on display. The map had been marked with four red lines, which all crossed each other in the center of the ancient stone circle in the courtyard of the castle.

"I'd like to take this map back to the castle with me," I said, "but, other than that, I'm done here." I gave Bud a significant look. "We need to go."

We made our way back toward the castle as quickly as we could. The rain was so heavy that the light from our flashlights bounced back at us. By the time we entered the great hall, dripping and stamping our feet, it was almost as dark as night, though it was still, properly speaking, the afternoon.

"Is that you, Cait?" called Rhian from the drawing room. She rushed out to greet us. I was about to explain that I really needed to clean myself up, but Rhian's face stopped me in my tracks.

"What's happened?" I asked. I was afraid to hear the answer.

"It's your sister—you should really go and see to her. She's . . . well, she's had a bit of turn and she's locked herself in one of the rooms on the top floor of the Gothic wing. She won't let anyone in. She says she'll only talk to you."

Dilys joined her daughter and said bluntly, "That sister of yours has been having the screaming ab-dabs upstairs for the last ten minutes, though she's stopped now. Went up there with Gwen, she did, and never come down. Shut herself in, she has, and you'd better get her out."

"Where is she exactly?" I asked, throwing my wet outerwear at Bud as I started up the staircase.

Dilys shouted, "Go up there. Turn right, not left for your room. There's a door at the end, and more stairs behind it. Go up. Gwen said she's in the second room along. Threw Gwen out and locked the door, she did. Go on with you now. She's upset the missus already, and I won't have that."

As I reached the first landing I glanced down at Bud and called, "I'll go to Siân, you go in and find out what everyone has to say about their searches. I'll be back as quick as I can."

Bud raised his arm to wave, then I was gone.

Pump ar hugain

THE TOPMOST CORRIDOR OF THE castle was less grand than the one for the first floor, and the dust and the smell of damp suggested it hadn't been used in many years. The lighting was poor, though I could make out the doors easily enough. I gave myself only a moment to catch my breath, then I knocked on the second door along.

"It's me, Cait. Can I come in?"

Nothing.

"Siân, are you alright? It's me. Come on now, let me in. *Siân?*" I knocked again.

I heard a bolt slide, then the door opened. A pale, drawn face, streaked with dirt and tears, poked out. I hardly recognized my own sister. I heard myself gasp.

"It's just you, isn't it?" she said. I nodded. "Alright then, you can come in." She stood back as she allowed the door to creak and whine its way open.

The room was dimly lit by one very tattered old standard lamp. Dusty sheets covered formless items against all four walls. On the floor in the center of the room was an old-fashioned three-story dollhouse, its front open, displaying the little rooms inside. The light from the lamp seemed to shine into the little house, and I could see it was fully furnished. Siân slowly settled herself onto the floor beside it, weeping into a couple of sodden tissues. I didn't have anything else to offer her, so I let her sniffle into them.

I looked around for a chair, but plumped for a footstool. I've never been good at sitting on the floor—I'm just not bendy enough.

I thought it best to wait for Siân to speak, so I sat in silence. I'm not the world's most patient person, so after a couple of minutes I revised my approach and said, "Come on, Siân, you've got to tell me what's going on. Dilys said you were very upset." I thought it best not to use the woman's exact words. "What's up?"

"I don't know where to start," said Siân. Her body language, her tone of voice, her entire demeanor communicated helplessness.

"Well, start somewhere, or we won't get anywhere," I said, immediately wishing I could make myself sound calm, like Bud does.

"It's Todd, it's my life, it's my children, it's David, it's Mum and Dad, it's Wales, it's you, it's here, and it's that." She pointed at the dollhouse.

"Could you be more specific?" I thought I did quite well with that one.

"You're the flaming brain-box in the family, can't you work it out for yourself?" Siân's helplessness had morphed into anger. Directed at me, it seemed.

I put my psychologist's head on and gave what she'd said a moment's thought. Siân was my sister, so I thought she deserved the real me.

"Don't forget you asked for this," I said before I began. "I think you came into this room to do some hunting about, and found this dollhouse. There's nothing very special about it, except in terms of what it represents. A perfect home. And it set you off, because it became a focus for the frustrations, doubts, and worries that you have about your own life."

"Go on then, big sis, what's wrong with my life?" Siân looked almost feral.

I puffed out my cheeks and went for it. "Your husband travels more than you'd like, and you don't find you have much more in common with each other than the children. Most of the parenting falls to you. I know from your emails that a lot of your time is spent ferrying Mattie and Beccie from your home in Como in your 'Ute' to their golf lessons, to the Perth Zoo—where you also volunteer—to the beaches at Cottesloe and Trigg. You've told me how you all go to barrack for the West Coast

Eagles when they play footie, and how you haul them to and from their friends' homes for various activities. You do all the motherly and housewifely things you should, and you fill the rest of your time with meditation, yoga, exercise, and parading from one health-food store to another, it seems to me. You follow the opera, the symphony, you knit, you have an online life, you mix with virtual people who share your interests and, I'm sure, some real ones too. What does that tell me?"

"What?"

"You're trying to fill up the space that's empty because your husband isn't a constant and important part of your life anymore."

"Mattie and Beccie need me to get them about the place. That's a fact of modern life, Cait, and something you'd understand if you were a parent."

"I get that bit, Siân, but the rest of it? The dollhouse is a symbol of the perfection for which you are striving, but which is unattainable. Own the fact you'll never be the perfect wife and mother. Own the fact that someone broke your heart decades ago and that it's alright for that to still hurt. Own the fact that you went to Australia for all the wrong reasons. Own the fact that no marriage is perfect."

"Says my sister who's getting married in the morning."

"Possibly."

"Marriage is a trap, Cait. A trap you build for yourself, and then go leaping into wearing a really expensive frock and a stupid, naïve grin. Kids? Even more of a trap. And one you can't ever get out of, not even if you want to. At least you don't have that to face."

"A trap?" I knew I sounded exasperated as I spoke. "You might think that marriage is a trap, but people make traps for themselves all the time, in all sorts of ways. Of course, they don't know what they've done until it's too late, then they spend the greater part of their energy trying to work out how to escape the trap. I see it all the time in criminal psychopathy, but non-criminals do it too. It's surprisingly normal human behavior."

Siân sighed. "Not a lecture, Cait, I'm in no mood for it. Just get to the point, if there is one, please?"

"We're in exactly the right place to talk about being trapped. We're trapped at Castell Llwyd along with everyone else. *We'll* be able to get out when the bridge is sorted. But the others? It's too late for most of them, I think.

"You know what, Cait? You're right about this place. It gives me the creeps. You can feel the poison here. I haven't felt right since I got here. I thought I'd feel different, coming back to Wales. Back *home*. But it's not home anymore. It's just a place."

"Of course this isn't home, Siân. Home was a three up, three down in Manselton with an outside toilet and a diet of homework and cheap, filling foods, and an inculcation of a work ethic that taught us both that we could do better than our parents. We were their escape. We were their reason for doing all they did. Look at what we did. You and I live about as far away from Wales, and each other, as we could get, at almost opposite sides of the world. We left. We escaped."

"So you're saying that it's natural to feel trapped, and to focus on getting out, but when you get out, you're still trapped, or you just build yourself another trap you then have to try to escape from? That's flaming depressing. Thanks."

"Tell me about David. Why did you fall for him? And how hard did you fall?"

Siân had stopped crying, which was a good sign. She glared at me. "He was handsome, charming, witty, talented, funny, and he liked me. He liked me as me. I was gawky and quite clever but not very. I had a middling talent as a singer and didn't excel at anything, and I was a largely unnoticed person, whom he noticed. He was my first boyfriend, my first *everything*. I thought we would get married and have beautiful and talented children, but once he'd got what he wanted he dumped me and moved on to his next conquest. What really hurt was that he told everyone about us, so people would point and giggle. Thank heavens there wasn't Facebook, or any of the things my kids use these days. You must understand. You went through it with Angus, right?"

"I don't want to go there, Siân," I said quietly.

"It's alright for me to open up, but not you?"

I sighed. "David might have hurt you emotionally, but Angus hurt me physically *and* emotionally. The bruises and the cuts healed, even if some of them left physical scars."

"Like the one above your nose? How d'you get that one?"

I didn't know she'd noticed it. "He smashed my face into a mirror. I was very lucky. The big chunk I pulled out of my forehead missed my eyes and just left this little mark." I smiled ruefully. "I kept that piece of glass in a drawer for months, thinking I might one night use it on him while he lay beside me, unconscious from the booze. But I was a criminologist. I knew I'd get caught. So I threw it away. As I did, I noticed how my blood had crept in between the glass and the silvering on the back. Funny the things you remember, eh?"

"It's not funny the things *you* remember, Cait. You remember everything. Do you remember how it felt to be used up inside?"

I nodded. "And I remember how hard it was to break it off with him, which sounds ridiculous given what he put me through. It was his instability that led him to seek stability through power over me. And, talking about instability, you've been displaying some pretty ripe symptoms of that since 'Davies the Eyes' was mentioned. Why do you think that is?"

"Doing the shrink thing on me now are you, sis? Ask questions, don't make suggestions? Okay, I'll play. Overwhelmed by remembered unhappiness, and powerlessness, on the one hand; realizing that I feel some of that unhappiness in my current circumstances on the other; and then feeling guilty that I feel that way on . . . you know, the third hand." She managed a smile.

"You can't change the past, but you can learn from it. If you don't? You're an idiot. And you're not an idiot, Siân."

"But you'd let Angus back into your home the night he died, Cait. After you'd already thrown him out. You'd gone through all the tough stuff, kicking him out of your life. Why that night? I never, ever understood that."

"You deserve an explanation, Siân. I told the police at the time, of course, because they gave me no choice when they arrested me for his murder. Despite the fact that I was the one who called the ambulance and the police, what else could they think had happened? He was dead on my bathroom floor, and I was alive. I've told Bud too, of course. Angus was passed out drunk when the guys from the pub carried him into what they thought was still his home. He hadn't told anyone that I'd kicked him out. Didn't want to lose face. Once he'd passed out, he was never a problem. Of course, what I didn't know was that he wasn't just drunk, but that an injury from a pub fight several days earlier was already killing him because he'd ruptured his spleen. The police only found that out later on."

"So, if you hadn't felt sorry for Angus, you'd never have ended up being arrested?"

I nodded. "I made what I thought was the right decision at the time, but it turned out to be a bad one."

Siân sighed. "And now Davies the Eyes is dead, and I never got to tell him that if it hadn't been for him hurting me as he did I'd never have emigrated, or met Todd, or had Beccie and Mattie. I think it might have helped me a lot if I'd been able to tell him that, to his face. That the awful thing he did to me ended up making me happy. Fulfilled."

"What he did didn't end up making you happy, you made decisions to allow yourself to be happy. But, if it makes you feel better, you can still tell him how well you've done without him. He's just downstairs."

Siân shook her head. "It's too late. But I've told him in my heart. And I do love Todd, Cait. I just miss him. A lot. And I love my children. They are just such a huge responsibility. And I don't miss working at all. Standing for hours and hours on end and being treated badly by megalomaniac surgeons isn't all it's cracked up to be, you know. And I enjoy all my activities. They aren't my escape, they are a part of the life I enjoy living. I've just been railing against the world, Cait. I'm so very, very tired, and my back is so bad after the flight."

"Your back?"

"I have spinal osteoarthritis. It's why I exercise so much, eat healthily, and generally take good care of myself. I have to, or I can hardly move because of the pain. I take some pretty strong pills to help me cope with it, and when I don't take them I can get a bit irritable. There again, when I take too many the same thing happens. My mood can be all over the place if I'm not careful. Back pain is difficult to cope with—no one knows you've got it, they just think you're being grumpy and difficult. It's a chronic disease, and it'll only get worse. All I can do is try to be as healthy and flexible as I can be, to stave it off for as long as possible. But I'm afraid that by the time the kids are gone, and Todd can retire, I'll be a cripple, and he won't want to look after me. It's what Alice Cadwallader has, and you've seen how she is. Janet helps her exercise every day, but it's tough."

"I'm sorry, I had no idea. Why haven't you ever told me?"

"You're my sister, not my keeper. It's not really anything to do with you. Oh—what's that noise?"

I stood up from the stool, my own back beginning to ache, and strained my ears. I could hear Dilys, calling in the hallway outside the door. I opened the door to let her in, but there was no one there. I checked along the landing, in both directions, but there wasn't a soul in sight.

As I walked back into the dusty room, I said, "Did you hear that?" I had to be sure I wasn't imagining things.

Siân nodded. "I thought it was Dilys, just outside the door."

"So did I, but there's nobody there."

We both said "Weird," at the same time. We grinned. Siân stood, with some difficulty, and we hugged.

"Are you alright now?" I asked as kindly as I could.

Siân nodded. There was a glint in her eye. "I'm going to be just fine, sis. But you've just thought of something, haven't you? Is it something to do with David's death?"

I nodded absentmindedly. "I can almost taste it. I can almost see it. I need to think."

"Of course you do. Go on, I'll be fine."

"Did you find a portrait of Alice's husband up here? The one that matches hers?"

"You mean the one you've been sitting in front of all this time?"

I turned and saw it propped against a wall, behind me. The painting of Alice had shown me she was a vibrant, beautiful young woman. This one told me that Gryffudd Cadwallader had been a robust and pleasant-looking man with a ruddy complexion and a penchant for tweed. The background of the portrait showed Castell Llwyd in all its glory on an imagined horizon. The man himself filled about two thirds of the foreground, and his hands were overly large, it seemed. One hand held a scroll of paper, which bore a map showing South America; his other pointed down and to his left. His eyes twinkled with a wicked light. To one side of him was a table laden with exotic foods and piles of some sort of white crystalline substance. The Cadwallader Puzzle Plate stood upright on the table, his body obliterating most of the verse. But that didn't matter, nor did the fact that the plate itself had been smashed. I was pretty sure I knew what it meant, but couldn't work out how it was linked to David Davies's death. I needed a few more facts to crack the mystery of the puzzle plate.

Chwech ar hugain

I WENT DOWN THE STAIRS to the great hall as fast as I could. Once there I listened for a moment. Over the rain beating down on the glass above my head I could hear voices in the drawing room. I looked at my watch. It was gone three o'clock, so I was pretty sure that everyone would be in there, meeting to discuss their findings. I took a deep breath and launched myself at what I knew would be a critical encounter.

When I entered the room, I was struck by how bleak and dead the place seemed without the dancing flames of a fire in the grate. Quite a few people looked taken aback by my appearance, which, given how very grimy and damp I was, wasn't surprising. I didn't hesitate. I marched to the fireplace and poked about in the empty grate. I stuck my head into the opening beneath the chimney, which drew a few throat-clearings from the assembled group, then peered closely at the gold-backed glass tiles that surrounded every fireplace I'd seen, so far, in the castle. Even though the wind had died down, I could still hear whistling from the chimney.

I stood and spoke directly to a worried-looking Alice. "When you moved back into Castell Llwyd after the war, had all the flues and fireplaces been renovated? I could see from outside that all the chimneys seem to be original features, but what about the tile work, the mantles, and the flues?" I didn't exactly snap at the old woman, but I was trying to be businesslike. I noticed Bud's reaction out of the corner of my eye, and I was confident he'd pick up on the fact that I was nose-down on the trail.

Alice adjusted her shoulders. Clearly she wasn't used to being addressed in such a manner. She looked injured as she responded, "They'd all been redone. Gryffudd said that the ministry people had made a right mess of them. Although the fireplaces should have been mainly decorative, because all the heating had been put in before we moved out—which in itself caused a massive upheaval—they'd seen fit to use them all."

"And which ministry was it that took over your home?" I was terse.

Alice looked flummoxed. "I don't know. I don't remember, or I never knew. They were rather cagey about it all. Even Gryffudd."

I pressed on. "Owain, is everything that's been written about the layout of the Roman temple to Neptune in your courtyard accurate, as far as you know?"

It was Owain's turn to look strangely at me. "Yes, as far as I have been able to establish. It was built in the tholos style, so round, which is very unusual, though it might be accounted for by the fact that it sits within a stone circle. It is located in an unusual position—yes, it's close to the sea, of course, but temples were usually built as a part of a city, often close to the main forum. There was no city here, just the temple."

"It's never been excavated. Is that correct?" I tried not to snap.

"Heavens, no," he exclaimed. "There was little appetite for that sort of thing before the Cadwalladers bought up the land, and my great-grandfather would never have allowed it, nor my grandfather, or father. I think it would be a sin. How could you dig about there without possibly disturbing something ancient, or even unfooting the stone circle? It could be a disaster." *Curious.*

"So the Cadwalladers built between it and the sea," I mused, "cutting through Neptune's sightlines to his element."

Owain's bushy beard twitched. "You could put it like that," he accepted.

"One more thing, maybe for you this time, Idris," I said quickly. "The bridge that's collapsing, do you know if it, too, was repaired after the war?"

"I do happen to know that," he said, looking pleased with himself, "there was even paperwork about it. I had to dig it all out when we had the thing examined. The major rebuilding and reinforcing was done right after the major construction was finished here, so around 1900, but there was more done in 1941, though the papers didn't say what, and even more in 1950. The 1950 work focused on the roadway as well as the bridge, and a new track to the main road was laid at the same time. That's when it was paved for the second time. The first paving took place in 1903."

Owain butted in. "My grandfather, Powell Cadwallader, knew Edgar Hooley quite well. Powell had slag to get rid of from his steelworks, and Hooley had a wonderful way to use it. Hooley was born in Swansea, and Grandfather Powell was keen to use his new invention of modern-day tarmacadam. The family archives show that my grandfather allowed Hooley to test out some equipment he was developing to facilitate the preparation of his new product, equipment he then patented in 1904. When the Hickman family took over Hooley's tarmac company in 1905, Grandfather set up with a couple of other chaps, and I happen to know they did quite well out of the demand that came during the Second World War, when airfields all over Britain were desperate for runways to be laid. As we all now know, Hooley's invention changed the way we all live, and, quite literally, paved the way for the motorized world we know today. You know, it's always struck me as odd that a man who invented a generic term used the world over, 'tarmac,' isn't boasted about more by those of us who also come from Swansea."

"Hooley used steamrollers as a part of his process, didn't he?" I asked, knowing the answer.

Owain looked gleeful. "Indeed he did, Cait, and the children of the locals, and, indeed, many of the locals themselves, rushed to see the one they used here as it made its way to our estate. It was a major undertaking, considering the state of the local roads at the time. I believe that some local preachers called the whole thing 'the work of the Devil,' and pointed to the fumes and the smell as an example of what people might expect if they were to find themselves suffering in the damnation of Hellfire."

As Owain trailed off into a world where, I was convinced, he could find links for most of the world's major developments to someone from Swansea, or at least from Wales, I noted that I was the only one interested in his eager discourse, which struck me as a good sign.

"Mair, where were you when David Davies died?" My question brought everyone's attention back into sharp focus.

Mair looked terrified. *Good.* She spluttered, "I . . . I don't know. When did he die? No one has said."

"Exactly," I replied. "Dilys—you found his body at what time?"

By now everyone was on full alert, and Dilys spoke with authority. "About five o'clock, it was. I went down to the kitchen to get the trays to clear after tea. As I came to bring them up, there he was, at the bottom of the stairs."

"The bottom of the up stairs, right?" I asked.

Dilys nodded.

"So who saw David before five o'clock, and where?"

In deference to her position as his widow, I supposed, all eyes turned to Rhian. She looked confused. "I . . . I hadn't seen David since after lunch. He was leaving our apartment just as I entered. It must have been about half past one, I think." She looked sad, and almost ashamed, as she added, "I didn't even say 'goodbye,' just 'see you later.' I didn't know it was the last thing I'd ever say to him."

Rhian paused and seemed to be struggling with her emotions, but she pulled herself together and continued. "After that, I was busy all afternoon, then I helped Mam bring the tea up. I had a quick cuppa with her in the kitchen, then I went over to the stable office to pick up my laptop. I could see the weather wasn't going to break, so I braved it and ran as fast as I could. When I got back, I helped Mam clear up after tea, then, when she went down to get the tray, I went up to our apartment. Gwen was there. Oh! That reminds me. I think

I left my laptop in the kitchen, Mam. I'm sorry if it got in your way."

"No problem, love. You've got a lot on your plate. I shoved it in the back room," replied Dilys.

That was one question answered in my mind. I hadn't been looking for a laptop amid the detritus in the back room, where David Davies's body lay, but at least now I knew where it was, and that it wasn't something that had been smashed or stolen.

"Anyone else?" I asked.

Mair cleared her throat and said, "I saw him after tea. I was going into the music room to do some knitting, and he was leaving it. Gwen was still in there. I think you'd been tuning the piano and having a run through for the wedding. Is that right?"

Gwen nodded. "We'd done all we needed to do—discussed the pieces, got our music in order—and he said he was going to, you know, use the loo."

That raised an interesting point.

"Where are the public washrooms, for people using the downstairs rooms who aren't staying here?" asked Bud, right on cue.

Eirwen finally perked up. "The gents' are just past Alice's little lift, under the grand staircase, the ladies' are on the other side, in the same spot. They're above the kitchens, because that's where the plumbing was. They aren't very big, but each one has a disabled access stall, which takes up a lot of room."

"So David would have been out in the great hall at what time, Mair? Gwen?" I made eye contact with each woman in turn.

The two women glanced at each other. "About half past four?" asked Gwen of Mair.

Mair nodded. "That's about right, I think."

"Did anyone see David alive after half past four?"

Everyone shook their head.

"Good. So now you can all tell me where you were between four thirty and five o'clock. I'll start—I was in my bridal boudoir talking with Siân." As I uttered her name, my sister entered the drawing room. She was still red-faced, but she looked a lot better than she had done when I'd left her. I patted the chair next to me, and she sat down.

Rhian sniffed as she said, "I suppose I was coming back from the stable office, and then helping Mam."

"I was in the music room the whole time," said Mair. "I was knitting and listening to a CD." She looked over at Siân and added excitedly, "It was the new Simon Rattle one—the concert performance of *Carmen*, with Jonas Kaufmann. It only came out a few months ago. Have you heard it yet?"

Siân nodded. "He sings a wonderful Don José," she said with a smile.

"Alone the whole time?" I asked, determined to not be sidetracked. Mair nodded.

"I went up to see Rhian when I left the music room," said Gwen, "but she wasn't in her apartment. I took the chance to make some notes on the running order for your wedding. So I was alone too, until Rhian came back around five." She looked somehow disappointed.

Janet spoke next. "Alice was taking her nap, and I was relaxing in my room. Alice usually naps after teatime, then gets up and dresses for drinks and dinner. It's my break time." She smiled broadly as she spoke, and Alice acknowledged her words kindly.

"From what time were you each alone in your respective rooms?" I pressed.

"It takes about five minutes for her to get me out of my chair and settled on my daybed," replied Alice, "and I like to be roused at 5:15 PM. It means I don't have to rush to get down by 6:45. Idris came in to tell me about David while I was getting dressed, so Janet and I were apart from about 4:40 until she woke me at 5:15. Is that sufficiently accurate for you, Cait?"

Her dismissive tone was now being directed at me, I noticed, but I chose to ignore it.

"I told Alice about David, as she said," volunteered Idris. "Dilys came to our apartment not long after five o'clock. Eirwen and I were both there at that time. We'd gone up after tea, so at about four thirty. I made the necessary phone calls, then went to tell Alice, then Owain. I checked the library for Owain after I'd seen Alice, because he hadn't joined us for tea, and Uncle Owain sometimes needs to be reminded what time of day it is, but the library was empty, and I found him in his apartment. By then, it must have been about a quarter to six."

"Where were you between 4:30 PM and five o'clock, Owain?" I asked.

"I think I was in my library all afternoon. I don't recollect being anywhere else. I remember it getting dark very early—or so it seemed—then I realized it was past teatime, so I went up to my room to put my feet up for a little while before I, too, changed for dinner. I don't remember talking to anyone all that time, and I couldn't say what time it was that Idris came to my door, though I know he did."

"Anyone else?" I asked.

"Only me," replied Bud.

"And where were you between 4:30 and 5:00 PM?" I asked pointedly.

"I was due to meet David Davies at half past four, so I was wandering about the place, trying to find him. I walked through the drawing room, the music room, the library, the morning room, and the dining room, but I was unable to locate him." Bud was using the delivery that had served him so well in courts of law over the years.

"And did you see anyone else during your exploration of Castell Llwyd?" I asked.

"Not a soul," he said calmly. "Until I encountered Dilys."

I noticed that Mair blushed, and Owain looked puzzled. No one else batted an eyelid. *Very telling.*

I didn't need to react to the fact that everyone now knew that Mair and Owain had been lying about their whereabouts. Alice did it for me.

"Typical of you two to be telling lies. Come on, out with it, where were you both really?"

Owain sounded childlike when he said, "I don't know, Mother. I thought I was in the library the whole time. I don't remember leaving it at all. But I cannot say for certain that I didn't, though where I might have gone, or why, is a mystery to me."

"What's above your library, Owain?" I asked.

"More library," replied Owain sounding puzzled. "The Norman-style structure here was essentially one very large, open hall, as you saw when you visited me earlier today, and above it were the living quarters. There's a spiral staircase at each end of the building, and a series of rooms that open off a corridor above. It was all rather basic, and Great-grandfather never finished it properly, so there wasn't much work involved for Grandfather to turn each room into a study-cum-library. Over the last forty years or so I have grown our collections to the point where I needed the lower level as well. Of course—" it looked as though Owain was having his very own eureka moment, "I went upstairs to get something I needed for the work I'm doing on the stone circle. Maybe that's where I was when you passed through, Bud?" He didn't sound too sure of himself, nor was I.

"Is there any way to access the new wings from the library building other than by walking through the morning room or the music room?" I asked.

Owain shifted uncomfortably. "The walls of that part of the castle are very thick. They accommodate a couple of staircases and passages that I know of." I had suspected as much.

"And where were you, Mair, if not in the music room?" Alice jutted her chin toward her daughter as she spoke.

Mair seemed to shrink. "Alright, Mother, you don't have to tell everyone, I'll do it for myself. I went out into the garden—yes, in weather like that—to have a smoke. I'm trying to give it up, but it's not easy. I only have one or two menthols a day now, Mother. I'm almost there. So I'd possibly stepped outside the doors from the music room to the garden when Bud walked through." She blushed again. "I haven't had one since—not even with all that's been going on here," she added grudgingly.

I stood. Bud tensed. "Thank you all very much, I need to clean myself up now," I announced. General puzzlement reigned. I chose to ignore it. "Will dinner be served at five o'clock as planned?" I asked Dilys.

She looked at her watch and blanched. "Oh dear me, would you look at the time. It'll take me at least an hour to get it all to the table, so no, it won't be. It'll be half past, on the dot." I noted that she didn't defer to Alice at all, but made her own decision.

"Good," I said. "I need a bath. Bud, would you walk with me?"

I left as quickly as I could, and when Bud caught up with me, I whispered, "Sorry to be so abrupt about all this, but I need to use my own process."

Bud nodded. "Know what's been happening yet? Because I'm still in the dark."

"I'm very close, but I need to do my thing. I need to allow my mind to drift free. A bath should help."

Bud held my arm. "A shallow bath, and make sure you can't slip under the water, right?"

"You haven't seen the size of the bath I've got," I replied. "It's tiny—short *and* narrow—and I'm pretty sure I'll be safely wedged in." I started up the stairs, then turned and looked at the man I loved. "Sorry I've become so preoccupied with all this, Bud. You know that I'm doing it because I don't want it hanging over us when we get married in the morning, don't you? If we get married in the morning, that is."

Bud smiled and winked. "Yes, I know why you're doing it, and I wouldn't expect any less of you. I'm giving it my own brand of thought too. And we will be married tomorrow—rest assured I've reserved the most active part of my brain for that little problem. Now go and get yourself sorted. I won't be far behind you. See you back here at 5:15 PM for a drink before a delayed dinner?"

I gave him the thumbs up and dragged my tired body up the stairs.

Saith ar hugain

AS I LAY WEDGED IN my bath, I knew where I wanted to start—with the map that was a part of the collection of items that David Davies had secreted away in a locked drawer in the stable block. I began to visualize it.

The wonderful thing about an eidetic memory, if you admit that such a thing exists, is that you can re-examine moments or things at your leisure. I think a lot of the work taking place in neuroscience might, one day, prove that most people possess the potential to do what I have always been able to do naturally. But it's early days yet, and the majority of the world would either dismiss my skill set or else want to put me in a laboratory and study me, which is why I keep quiet about it.

With my eyes screwed up to the point where everything goes fuzzy, and with a bit of humming—I have no idea why it helps, but it does—I am able to see things that are not physically in front of me anymore. I prepared myself and called to mind David's collection. I'd already worked out what everything had meant to David, but I wanted to analyze the map one more time.

I consider the feel of the map first. It's old. I can tell that from the feel of the paper in my hand and the numerous refoldings it has undergone. It's soft to the touch, almost like aged skin. I concentrate on where the red lines drawn on it begin, end, and intersect. They've been drawn with a straight edge. I notice calculations in pencil. They are very faint. Can I make them out? No, I cannot. The pencil has been rubbed off by the passing of fingers, rather than erased on purpose.

I can see the red lines clearly and, because it is a topological map, I can tell that one line begins at the highest point of the land on the Cadwallader Estate, and runs through the stable block and the center of the stone circle, past the end of the land into the sea. Another begins at the central point of the original Norman-style castle building and runs directly through the center of the stone circle, crossing the marked course of the river. The third runs from the point where the new Jacobethan wing joins the older block and runs through the center of the stone circle until it too runs off the end of the land, and the fourth and final line begins at the point where the Gothic-style wing joins the older building and runs to the Roman bridge. It's geometrically pleasing.

I notice one more line, a remnant of a pencil line. It is a continuation of the first line I'd noted, running from the high point of the estate through the stable block and the center of the stone circle. It continues over a fold in the map. I am cross with myself. Why didn't I notice that before, and why didn't I unfold the map? I take a deep, calming breath, and remind myself that the map is in my bedroom, and I can check where the line leads to when I get out of the bath. Considering the rest of the items David had hidden, I believe I know where it finishes, though I tell myself I must double-check.

Next I turn my mind to the portrait of Alice Cadwallader as it had been before it was slashed. I can see the light in the woman's eyes, and I can almost feel the firmness of her flesh. I marvel again at the skill with which the artist created a feeling of movement in her tumbling locks, and I examine, for the first time in fact, the scene around the woman. Having realized how critical the setting for Gryffudd had been in his portrait, I know I must understand the picture of Alice in the same way.

I recall the creatures depicted on the screen in her room. They are strange ones to see in a woman's bedroom. I see flamingoes, sloths, armadillos, anteaters, cougars, spectacled bears, condors, some sort of alpaca or llama, capybara, tapirs, and a maned wolf. The surreal landscape through the window is next for examination. Why does it look as though Dali has painted it? I see—it is white, flat, desolate, almost plastic looking, with those little islands. I know where I have seen this before, and I tie that in with what Owain had told me about her family background. Of course—South America. It makes sense.

I notice one more thing that I believe is important. The screen, dressing table, and window are on the right-hand side of the background. Alice herself, and the skirts of her flowing gown, fill the entire foreground. Almost hidden, on the left of the background, is a fireplace, crackling with a coal fire and glowing within its glass-on-gold tile surround. The mantle seems to be of carved white marble—*it's not a fireplace I've seen in the castle.*

I relaxed and squeezed warm water from a sponge down the back of my neck. "Wakeful dreaming" is a technique I've used with subjects, where I allow them to reach a state of physical relaxation, and encourage their mind to become active. I've utilized it myself on many occasions, and I knew it was just what I needed to do. I needed to allow my brain to gather together the facts, my own knowledge, everything I had learned about the people and the place involved, and see what linkages I might discover. For this process no humming was required, nor any fuzziness of vision, so I closed my eyes and let it all begin.

Alarmingly, the first thing I see is Angus's angry face screaming at me that no way am I going to leave him to marry a pig. He pulls on a British policeman's helmet, which keeps growing until it swallows his head. I can hear him screaming inside the helmet, then he disappears and explodes into a bunch of fat, pink peonies. Next I see Siân. She is, unsurprisingly, bouncing like a kangaroo across an Australian-rules football oval. Behind her she is dragging dozens of little wallabies, all screaming at her for more attention. She is crying and singing, simultaneously, and seems to be shrinking as she runs. Bud runs after her, shouting that she shouldn't despair, that he has a whole troop of topless dancers just waiting to take the wallabies off her hands for the right price. Bud stops chasing Siân and turns his attention to the wobbling mass that I know is Angus, and he stomps all over it, flattening it into the ground. I look around and see Castell Llwyd in the distance, sitting on top of a glittering temple, with a halo of lightning surrounding it. I try to move toward it, but I am rooted in the ground, with only my top half able to move. I try to wriggle, but I cannot move. A group of children wielding golf clubs surround me, and then cover me with a massive Welsh flag. I cannot breathe, I flail my arms, and try harder to release myself, but to no avail.

"Cait! Cait? Are you alright in there?"

I pulled myself back to reality at the sound of Bud's voice at my bathroom door.

"What's going on in there? I could hear you from my room. Are you alright? Why did you lock this door? Let me in! Answer me, Cait!"

"I'm fine, don't panic," I replied. "Just give me a minute." I hauled myself out of the bath, which took more effort than I would have imagined, and sloshed through the mess on the bathroom floor. I'd apparently been doing a lot of splashing. Gathering a large towel about myself I unlocked the door—which I didn't recall locking in the first place—and poked out my head.

Bud's relieved expression was almost immediately replaced by one of impatience laced with anger. "What on earth were you doing in there? It sounded as though you were being attacked by a gang of washerwomen."

I smiled. "I was doing my wakeful dreaming thing, and it seems I got a bit carried away. I'm sorry, I didn't mean to worry you."

Bud's shoulders relaxed and he looked relieved again. "You're sure you're okay?"

I nodded and tried to look as appealing as I could under the circumstances. "I was trying to focus on everything that's going on here—but it seems that my mind decided I had a few other issues to deal with first. I didn't end up achieving what I'd hoped for. I'm cross with myself. I can usually manage to do it when I need to, the way I want. But this time? I seem to be grappling with a lot more personal stuff than I usually have to."

"It'll come to you—you'll get there. You always do. Maybe this time you have to tackle things a different way, you know? As in life, maybe you need to take a new path? Like we're about to do."

He hugged me, sopping wet towel and all. I gave in and allowed myself to enjoy the moment. *I don't often do that, usually my brain's a whirl.*

I pulled back. "A new path! Of course. That's what they did. When they used the steamrollers for the tarmacadam, they must have created an entirely new path."

Bud shook his head. "I have no idea what you're talking about, but I guess you do."

I nodded. The failing river bank, the talk of Neptune on the Cadwallader Puzzle Plate, the new chute to the coal cellar, the lines drawn on David's map, they all made sense. That breakthrough, plus the portraits of Alice and Gryffudd Cadwallader, meant I'd solved the riddle at last. I was pretty sure it would allow Idris and Eirwen's children to have a bright future and the current Cadwallader clan to live a life of indulgence.

"I've got it, I've solved the puzzle," I said aloud. "If my assumption about the roadway is correct. But I still cannot fathom the link to David's death, or the destructive acts that have been taking place here. That part needs more thought."

Bud walked across my room to leave. "Right—well, now that I know you're safe, and you know your brain is back to normal, I'm going to get ready for dinner. You'd better get a move on, Cait, there'll be a G&T with your name on it in the drawing room in fifteen minutes." And he was gone.

Wyth ar hugain

I BOUNCED DOWN THE GRAND staircase as quickly and as lightly as I could, knowing I was late for drinks. When I dashed into the drawing room the scene before me was eerily similar to the previous night, except there was no portrait of Alice above the hearth and, this time, my entrance drew stares from the assembled group. I was last to arrive, and everyone was already enjoying a pre-dinner drink. I took a moment to observe the reactions to my arrival. I noted that neither Rhian nor Dilys were present, which didn't surprise me.

Handing me a glass that promised the refreshment of a Bombay and tonic, Bud whispered, "You look great. You feeling okay?"

I nodded, took my drink, and sipped. *Tonic water and toothpaste do not mix well.*

Gwen approached me and complimented me on my outfit. I thought it a little odd that she would do so, but I reasoned that the seasonally appropriate red jacket that I'd teamed with my trusty black bouncy two-piece was a cheery addition to the sea of dark colors that everyone else seemed to be favoring. Gwen looked as though she was ready to accompany the male voice choir right there and then, as she was wearing a long black skirt and a white blouse.

Following her comments, I felt I had to indulge in small talk with the mousey little woman, so I began to wrack my brain for tidbits from our school days.

"Do you know what happened to the girl who sang the soprano solos the year you played the piano for the choir?" I asked. "I recall she had a beautiful voice, and I thought she might make something of it. Claire Williams, wasn't it?" I knew very well that was her name, but it helps if I sound vague about things sometimes.

Gwen beamed. "She was at the Welsh College of Music and Drama at the same time as me. She couldn't get into Cardiff Uni to study music, because she didn't get the grades she needed in her A levels. A shame I suppose. I think she's teaching somewhere now."

I was surprised. "Claire Williams was a very bright girl, and I know she was a good student. How did she manage that?"

Gwen looked as though she was trying to remember. "She ran out of her A levels with stomach cramps, so she only just passed them. She needed three A grades for uni—but they took her with three C grades at the college. I was glad, in a way, because we were great friends, so we got to be together for three more years after school."

"Sad for her that she missed her chance to study music, though," I replied. "I remember she had her heart set on a career in opera. Cardiff Uni had a great reputation for voice training in those days."

"I'm sure she was very happy being at college with me as a friend instead," replied Gwen a bit snippily.

I decided to not pursue what seemed to be a sensitive topic, and tried to think of another one. "Rhian mentioned that you used to visit Cambridge for music courses, or that you did at least once. Did you like the place?"

Gwen's sour countenance cleared. "Oh it's beautiful. I was only there once, for a summer school focusing on the music of Henry Purcell, at Queens' College. You were very lucky to live there for so long. You must have liked The Anchor Pub."

I sighed. "Yes, it was a nice pub." I'd spent many hours of my life there, not all of them happy.

"Did you prefer it to The Mill, and The Eagle?" she asked.

I nodded absently. I was grappling with ghosts from my past.

"I saw you there, you know," added Gwen quietly.

I snapped back to reality and forced a smile. "Really? Why didn't you say hello? It would have been nice to see you."

Gwen blushed. "You were sort of busy. You were having a bit of a row. On the street. You stormed off after shouting at a man."

I swallowed hard. "Really?" I tried to sound natural.

"You shouted after him, 'If I had a drink in my hand right now I'd throw it over you.' You were crying. I didn't think it was . . . appropriate to say anything to you. You walked right past me, but I didn't stop you. I don't think you saw me at all. But there, that's not so unusual. Most people don't." Her voice had trailed off, and I suspected self-pity was setting in.

I tried to sound like I meant it when I replied, "Oh, I'm sure it was something and nothing. It's a shame we missed having a drink together then, all those years ago—but, hey, we're doing it now, so cheers!" I chinked my glass against Gwen's, and we both smiled.

She took a sip of hers, and I took a great big gulp of mine.

I could hardly believe that Gwen Thomas had heard me utter the last words I ever spoke to Angus before he was dumped, unconscious, into my flat, a few nights later—the night he'd died. I found it very worrying. The word "coincidence" crawled around the back of my mind.

"You two reliving old memories of schooldays?" asked Bud cheerily as he joined us.

"Cambridge, actually," replied Gwen, suddenly bright again. "She didn't know it, but I did Cait a favor when I was visiting there. I owe her so much, you see, Bud. You're marrying a wonderful woman. She always encouraged me, when I was young, to follow my dreams. And I have."

"She's like that," said Bud, beaming at me. "She's still out there, guiding students on their future paths. And she does a great job of it."

I could feel myself blush. I'm not good at accepting compliments.

Gwen continued, "She told me I should never ever let anyone get in the way of me being able to do my best, and I took it to heart."

I held up my hand. "Oh come on now, you two, my head will be too big to get out through that door if you don't stop. Enough—okay? But thank you both. Though I'm not sure I'd have said you shouldn't let anyone get in your way, Gwen."

"It sounds exactly like something your teen self would have said,

Cait," remarked Bud. "Now, of course, I guess you know better. But, hey, we were all young once, right?"

I nodded. "Yes, the greatest folly of youth is possibly that we're only able to see black and white, right and wrong. It takes experience to discover that there are all types of grays in between, and that good and bad are not absolutes. We have to consider the consequences for others before we act, and not solely put self-interest first."

"Five minutes and it's on the table," called Dilys at the doorway.

I beamed. "Good—I'm starving. I've been imagining roast beef and Yorkshire pudding since Dilys mentioned it earlier. She's a good cook, isn't she, Gwen? Do you eat here often?"

"Not often," replied the woman. "They sometimes invite me to stay, so I like to come with a bag so I can—it's such a treat. But I'll leave when you do. I don't want to stay where I'm not wanted."

"I'm sure you're wanted," said Bud.

Gwen shook her head. "David's not here anymore, so there'll be no reason for me to visit again. I'll miss this place. It's magical. I feel special when I'm here. It's like a different world. I'll miss that lovely piano too. I know it very well. It's such a shame there's no one here who can play it as it deserves to be played. They don't like it, you know."

"What's that?" asked Bud politely as he took our empty glasses.

"Pianos. They don't like not being played. They aren't just pieces of furniture, they are instruments with their own voices. And every voice deserves to be heard." She smiled a strange little smile. "That's another thing you told me, Cait. That my voice had as much right to be heard as anyone else's—I just had to find a way that worked for me. And I've done that too."

"I'm glad for you, Gwen, truly I am," I said, as Bud took my arm.

"Time for dinner," he said as he pulled me toward the door.

I winked at Gwen. "Seems like this man wants me to accompany him, and he is a retired cop, so I suppose I'd better go quietly."

"Yes, you better had," she said.

Naw ar hugain

ONCE AGAIN I FOUND MYSELF in the round dining room at Castell Llwyd, but, unlike the previous night, Alice didn't insist that Bud and I sit beside her. This time it was Siân and Gwen who got the special treatment. I was slightly relieved, because I knew it would give me a chance to talk to Owain about what he believed to be the meaning of the riddle on the puzzle plate, and it would allow me to try to engage Mair a little about David.

Two things were immediately evident as we sat again at the table: no conversation about any of the recent occurrences was going to be tolerated by Alice, and it seemed that a roast didn't require a first course, so when Dilys and Rhian arrived, they were carrying trays bearing a glisteningly appetizing prime rib of beef and a triumphant Yorkshire pudding that, for all the world, looked like a priceless golden crown—it had risen to perfection.

"Almost as good as yours, Cait," whispered Bud as Dilys passed by.

His tone wasn't low enough for her to miss what he'd said, and she replied caustically, "My money's on mine being better."

Bud rolled his eyes as she passed. Laying her tray on a sideboard, she announced, "I'll carve now."

As she did, Rhian disappeared, then returned to the room carrying three tureens, which she placed on the table.

"Cauliflower, roasted potatoes, and peas," she explained.

Having taken a large spoonful of cauliflower, Bud leaned over and said, "What on earth have I just put on my plate? I thought Rhian said it was cauliflower. *This* isn't cauliflower."

I explained, "In Wales the cauliflower is sold with its large outer leaves fully intact. They aren't cut off, as in most other places. It's a shame. I love it this way, with the green and the white all mashed in together."

Bud nodded approval. "It's really good," he said. "We could do this back home with florets and kale, couldn't we?" he asked between mouthfuls, with enthusiasm.

I grimaced. "The day kale comes in through our front door, I'm leaving you, Bud Anderson. It's disgusting."

He grinned. "I'll get you to like it yet. Just give me a few years."

"You might die trying," I replied.

The cauliflower topic dealt with, I settled to my own, rather full, plate. Unfortunately the beef was ruined; I like mine to be pink, but this was just the way I'd grown up eating it—dark brown right through. That said, it tasted wonderful, and the gravy prevented it from being too dry. The vegetables were delicious too—glistening roast potatoes that were crisp on the outside, but light and fluffy inside their shell; perfect cauliflower that might well have been half butter; peas sweet and not overcooked at all; and gravy, running into the pits and hollows in the Yorkshire, that was absolutely divine.

"You said on your Ravelry page that you volunteer at the Perth Zoo, Siân," said Mair chattily, forcing me to concentrate on something other than my food. "Is it a good zoo? I mean are the animals well cared for?"

Siân nodded. "I believe so. They have some excellent breeding programs there. I don't think wild animals should be kept in captivity unless they are serving a real purpose—like helping to save their species. I volunteer so I can be sure they are doing things right. I don't like to see dead animals at all, and sometimes I can't help but think of meat that way."

Alice instructed Mair to serve her with wine, by way of sign language, as she said to Siân, "So are all our stuffed beasts giving you the creeps?"

I could tell she was making fun of Siân, but Siân didn't seem to mind. She smiled politely at Alice. "Not exactly, but I do think that taxidermists have one of the most dreadful jobs on earth."

I couldn't resist. "Hey, sis, don't knock the art of the animal stuffer. We only exist because of a taxidermist."

I knew my comment would draw some quizzical looks, and it did. Bud bit. "Do tell," he said, with a dose of mock enthusiasm.

"Well, it's quite simple, really," I said. "Our mum was a Blitz Baby—conceived during the Swansea Blitz of 1941, as were so many others in air-raid shelters during long nights with no entertainment. That conception was only able to happen because our grandfather hadn't gone off to fight in the war. He was a baker—a reserved occupation. And the only reason he was a baker was because his uncle—our great-grandfather's brother—had paid for his training with money he only had because he made a very good living as a taxidermist. He had a shop in an arcade up on Swansea High Street, and did a roaring trade between the wars. He even stuffed a mammoth that was on display at Swansea Museum for many years. He was a master taxidermist, and, if he hadn't done what he did, and if our grandparents hadn't done what they did during the blitz, then our mum wouldn't exist, and we wouldn't either. Ta da!"

Siân shook her head, smiling, as Bud gave me a little round of applause.

"So the next time I meet a taxidermist I should shake him by the hand and thank him and his ilk for allowing me to ever meet you?" said Bud.

"I'd check where his hand has been before you do," I quipped.

I felt I'd done my little bit to lighten the mood at the table. With wine, good food, and not bad company, the meal was over in what seemed like a very short time. It was as though we could all breathe again—as though we'd all agreed to lift the weight from our shoulders for just a short time.

As folks chattered, I did my best to try to find out how people had felt about David Davies—and I felt the mood was sufficiently brightened for me to be able to do it.

I gathered that Idris had liked him, though he felt he could have generally achieved more about the place, and more quickly and efficiently. Eirwen seemed to have had little time for the man, who she accused of "swinging the lead" at every possible opportunity. Gwen praised him as a hard worker, dedicated to his music and his choir, and a man with art and artistry in his soul. Mair's comment—that he was slow to fix things, but usually did a good job when he got around to it—seemed to match that of Idris. Owain claimed to hardly know the man, which I found difficult to believe. When I finally got the chance to ask Janet what she thought of David, I noted that the muscles along her jawline tightened as she told me that he'd always been very polite to her, but that she didn't see much of anyone except Alice, because of her duties.

It seemed that Alice had overheard Janet's comments, because she butted in with, "That was a good thing then. He wasn't a nice man. Danuta, the one before you, didn't like him. Never trust a man with feet that small, I've always said it."

"Mother, you might as well just say what you really mean, that no man on earth should ever be trusted under any circumstances— whatever his foot size, or choice of footwear, or socks, or *anything*. I have no idea why you're like this. Father was very good to you. He gave you, and us, a good life. Why do you hate men so much? What have they ever done to you?" asked Mair.

Looking at Alice, and knowing how beautiful she'd been when she was young, I suspected that she would have quite a lot she could tell us on that score. But she didn't, she just turned her cold, green stare toward her daughter and said, "You haven't lived, girl. You have no idea what they can do. I've saved you from goodness knows what, I have, and this is the thanks I get, is it? Shouting at your own mother in front of guests? Terrible. All I can say is that things will be a bit different around here now David Davies is gone. Good riddance to him, I say."

Rhian was standing right behind Alice when she spoke, still holding the plate she'd just removed from the table in front of the old woman. Alice must have known she'd be within earshot, and yet she'd still made her spiteful remarks—and everyone at the table knew it. It felt as though there was no air in the room any more. Even the fire seemed to lose its spirit.

Moving deliberately, Rhian carefully placed the used plate on the sideboard, then ran out of the dining room, almost colliding with her mother, who was entering.

Dilys called out after her daughter, "Rhian, Rhian! What's the matter with you? Where are you going? Come back here when I call you." Her angry voice echoed in the empty hall. We could hear Rhian's sobs fade into the distance.

"That was very, very cruel, Mother," said Mair, expressing what I think everyone felt.

Alice surveyed each face around the table, her eyes sparkling with hatred. "Stupid girl, marrying a man like that. She's got what she deserved, and so did he."

Gwen began to squirm uncomfortably in her seat, and Mair leapt up at exactly the same moment that Janet did.

"Mother—you're disgusting." Mair pushed her heavy chair away and stormed off toward the grand staircase, calling back, "I'm going to my rooms."

Janet said, "Come on now, Alice, I think it's time we got you up to bed, isn't it?"

Alice smiled with cruel satisfaction. "My work here is done," she said, "more than any of you will ever know."

She looked up at Janet and said, "Take me to my lift, and be quick about it. Then you can tell my daughter I want to talk to her in my apartment. Come on. You're so slow I could jump over your head."

"You'd have to get out of that chair first," said Janet, "and I know how long that takes you. Slower than the second coming, aren't you?" She dared a wink at the old woman.

Alice's mouth creased with a sly smile, "You know very well I can manage without you," she said. "And girls like you are two a penny, so be careful you don't go too far. You can be out in the morning and a new one in by lunchtime, remember."

"Well, maybe not quite that quickly, Alice," said Idris. "Your requirements are rather exacting, and the agency has warned me that our turnover is quite high." He looked panicked, and Eirwen clutched at his hand.

"See, even they think you should hang on to me," said Janet. "Besides, I know all your favorite treats now, don't I? And not everyone would be as understanding as I am, would they?"

Alice became less haughty and tried for winsome. "Oh come on, you know I'm joking, right? Time for some special milk and an early night with you reading to me, I think, Janet," she said. "I'll leave Mair to cool her heels, and talk to her in the morning."

As she raced across the dining room in her speedy chair, she raised a hand from her little steering column to wave to us all as though nothing had happened. She left an uneasiness in the room that we could all have done without.

As guests, I wasn't sure if we were supposed to leave the dining room, or if a dessert was due to be served—and if one were due, whether it would arrive, since Dilys had disappeared.

Eirwen stepped up and donned the mantle of hostess. "There isn't anything else, just the roast, so we could all move to the drawing room where Dilys will have set up coffee, if you'd like some."

Everyone began to move away from the table as I glanced at my watch. It wasn't even 6:00 PM. There was a very long evening ahead of us, and now the mood was as black as the night.

Deg ar hugain

"THIS ISN'T YOUR AVERAGE HEN party, is it, Cait?" said Eirwen sympathetically.

"We could have port, by way of a little celebration," suggested Idris. "We have a couple of bottles of very good port in the dining room. Mother used to drink it, but Janet has banned her from doing so. Just a moment—I'll get it sorted."

Idris moved with ease and was rapidly followed by his wife, who explained, "He doesn't know where anything is, I'll just give him a hand."

Owain, Gwen, Bud, Siân, and I sat in silence. I decided it was time for me to start poking about.

"So, Owain, any luck putting that plate back together?" I asked.

Owain squared his shoulders and replied defiantly, "Not yet. I was busy with other things this afternoon." Having seen his reaction to its being broken, I couldn't imagine what had been more important to Owain than working on his precious plate.

He continued, "I had Idris prying into all my stuff, at your behest, for a start." He sounded wounded. "There's nothing out of the ordinary in my library," he added, "nothing to find, nowhere for an interloper to secret themselves. It was a pointless and, of course, fruitless exercise." He dismissed me with a twitch of his beard.

I decided to press him. "But you told me you have some wonderful old passages and staircases hidden in the walls of that part of the building. Couldn't someone be lurking in there? I'd love to see them, Owain."

Owain's brow furrowed. "Well, you are *not* welcome to do so," he said abruptly. "I covered all the ground, and there hasn't been anyone in those passages who shouldn't have been."

"Who *should* have been in there, then?" I asked. "Or who might have been in there? Where do they lead to anyway?"

"This is unspeakable," said Owain. "All this, just because someone fell down the stairs? Preposterous. I'll tell you, just so you stop nagging at me. The doors in the bookshelves lead to little corridors, and they lead to narrow staircases. They go up and down, that's it. They are blocked at the bottom—where there's now soil and general detritus, and they are blocked where they abut the new wings. They were simply bricked across when they built onto the older building. They are without purpose—mere follies, nowadays."

"What was their purpose—when they were first built?" asked Bud. *Clever boy!*

"I couldn't say," replied Owain, too quickly. I wasn't going to ignore that.

"Do you mean you don't know, or that you choose to not tell us?" I asked pointedly.

Owain chewed his bottom lip, making his beard bob up and down. He looked as though he was eating a wriggling furry creature. *Very odd.*

"There's port, some sherry, the remainder of the wine from dinner, and I also found some whiskey, which we could add to the coffee," announced Idris as he and Eirwen rejoined us.

Their arrival created a rather jolly atmosphere. I poured some whiskey into my coffee, choosing to ignore Bud's barb about me becoming a wide-awake drunk, and also took a glass of port. We all settled down again in a much more cheery mood, and there were several toasts to Bud and myself, which was delightful.

Dilys Jones's appearance was greeted with inquiries about Rhian, who, we were assured, would be much better in the morning. Dilys cast a judgmental eye at the alcoholic beverages and left us to our own devices with what seemed to be a warning, rather than a promise. "I'll be back to do a final clear up at nine o'clock, then I'll be off to bed."

"Idris," I began, gaining the man's eager attention, "I wondered if you know whether the old Roman bridge was realigned when they laid the tarmacadam on it?"

"I know that," interrupted Owain before Idris had a chance to reply. "But why do you want to know?"

Idris looked embarrassed. "It doesn't matter why, Uncle," he said. "They were very careful to move the bridge and reconstruct it according to the original Roman design, but it needed to be widened, to allow for the proper installation of the newly invented process to lay the surface, and they took the opportunity to do some excavation work on the river. I believe they realigned the river somewhat, then built the new footings, then rebuilt and expanded the bridge." He looked pleased with himself. "I have all the papers and plans if you'd like to see them," he added with enthusiasm. "I've pulled them all out so they'll be ready when the engineers get here in the morning. They've been very good by the way—I managed to get hold of a chap on his mobile this afternoon, and he understands the problem we have, being stuck here with no one able to get in or out, and, you know, the body and so forth. I also mentioned your wedding."

"Thanks," I replied.

Owain was quiet for a moment, but couldn't resist the urge to speak. "I bet you don't know why they moved the bridge," he said.

I felt Bud sigh beside me, knowing what was about to happen. Siân tensed and took a glug from her coffee cup, as I replied, "I believe it was because it was in the wrong place for the major landscaping that was undertaken at the same time. The original Roman approach to the temple, and therefore the original road to the castle, would have been built in a straight line—as Roman roads were always built. Now you have a curved, sweeping roadway down to the driveway surrounding the temple. It sits well as a part of the early twentieth century landscaping, including the artfully positioned trees and the location of the stable block. But the new design necessitated the bridge being moved to a higher point on the hill. I suspect that the original location was closer to the sea. I further suspect that the river's original path brought it right into the temple, passing through where this very wing now stands, then out again, toward the sea, through where the Gothic-revival wing was built. Would that be correct, Owain?"

Although there wasn't very much of Owain's face to be seen, I could tell from his bald pate that he was flushed with anger. I heard Bud tut quietly next to me.

"Why do you say that?" blustered Owain. "Nothing can be proved. You're surmising. Wildly, if I might say so."

"That pendant you were wearing today was a clue," I replied. Owain absentmindedly clutched at his midriff. It was interesting to note how automatically he did it, and it suggested to me that he was wearing the medallion beneath his white shirt and sad old evening suit.

"It's a very ordinary pendant," he said defensively.

"No, it's not," I replied quietly. Everyone was alert, but puzzled. "It shows what I thought were the two faces of Janus, but each face had a river of water flowing from it. That's not 'ordinary,' is it, Owain?"

He shook his head like a small boy. "I found it when I was exploring with my brother, Teilo, when we were young. We each had one. I believe they were made especially for this temple—as offerings to Neptune."

"Like when they take collection at chapel?" asked Gwen.

"In a way," replied Owain.

"Gold doesn't change in water," I said. "It doesn't tarnish or diminish. So, while water is Neptune's element, as it is Llŷr's, the Welsh god of water, so gold is the way with which they can be honored. Where exactly did you find it, Owain? Did Teilo come across a way into the Roman temple when he went missing overnight, as a boy?"

The anticipation in the room crackled like the logs in the fireplace.

Owain looked at me with surprise. "You know about that?"

I nodded. "Mair mentioned it earlier today."

Owain seemed to sink into his seat. "It was a very long time ago. Such a long time. I was a very young boy, I remember. But when Teilo showed me the shiny thing he'd found, I knew I had to find more. And that's when it all started."

"The tunneling?" I said softly.

Owain nodded.

Idris and Eirwen were on the edge of their seats. "What tunneling?" said Idris.

"Your uncle's spent the last fifty years or so gradually working his way from the coal chute to the base of the Roman temple, haven't you, Owain?" The man nodded. "And yet you haven't found mounds of gold coins, or a hidden treasure anywhere, have you?" Owain shook his head sadly. "And when did David Davies find out about it all?"

I heard a sharp intake of breath from Siân and Gwen.

"More than six months ago." Owain was close to tears.

"And he forced you to let him join in with the hunt, and he began to make you uncomfortable about it, didn't he?"

Owain leapt out of his seat, his coffee spilling everywhere. "He was horrid to me. He said if I didn't let him in on my plan, he'd tell Mother. I knew she'd put a stop to it. But I'm so *close*. I must be. I've opened it all up—I have stood where the ancients stood, and have looked into the mouth of Neptune. But all I've ever found are the two coins that Teilo and I discovered half a century ago. There *must* be more. The plate said there'd be enough to save the Cadwalladers. I know we haven't any money any more, Idris, and I know that you and Eirwen worry about that. If only I can find the treasure I can save us."

Idris stood to comfort the distressed man. "Come on now, Uncle Owain, try not to get upset. I don't think any of us believe there's really a treasure. It's a lovely idea, but it can't be true. Please don't tell me you've been doing all this, all these years, just for us?"

Owain was very close to tears. I felt sorry for him. It's a terrible thing to see someone lose their belief in their dreams, especially when their dreams are the promise of stability and security for a whole family.

As Idris hugged his uncle, I said, "But you're wrong, Idris. There *is* a treasure. It's just that it's not what Owain thought it was, and it certainly isn't to be found where he's been looking."

Owain glared at me. "There you go again! You're quite something. Here two minutes and telling me about my own home, its history, and our birthright. You know nothing. You can't. So you can just shut up now, and let us be. I hope they fix the blessed bridge so you can get married and go away. We like being here, alone. We're all happy here. At least we were. We don't need you, and I certainly don't need your pity, your encouragement, or your stupid theories."

Owain stamped around a bit. Eirwen helped him with his spilled coffee, and he finally said, "I'm going to my library, and I'll thank you all to *not* join me."

As he slammed the door behind him, making Eirwen start, Gwen said, "Do you think Owain could have pushed David down the stairs because David was forcing himself into his little world?"

"It's definitely one theory," I replied.

"But you have others?" asked Siân with trepidation.

I nodded. "Yes, a few." *I don't think it was what anyone wanted to hear.*

Un ar ddeg ar hugain

IDRIS POKED AT THE LOGS in the fire, adding a couple of fresh ones while he was at it. Sparks flew, cresting, falling, and dying within seconds.

"That's all we are at the end, isn't it? Ashes."

We all turned to see Rhian standing at the door. Half-dazed, haggard, and utterly deflated, she walked unsteadily toward the fire.

"I'm cold," she said simply. Holding her hands toward the flames that had yet to take hold of the new logs, she finally crouched down, her pale cheeks reflecting the yellow and orange glow.

"Would you like a drink, Rhian?" Eirwen spoke quietly, and Rhian seemed to not hear her. Eirwen rose from her seat and moved to stand behind Rhian. She touched her hunched shoulder tenderly. "Come on, Rhian, don't stay there. It's not good for your skin."

Rhian uncurled herself and stood upright. "Alice said some very hurtful things at dinner," she said. "I know what she's like—I've lived here all my life so I should do by now—but today? That was bad. Why is she so horrible to me?"

Eirwen tried to comfort Rhian with a hug. "She's horrible to everyone, Rhian, not just you. Don't take it personally."

Rhian shook her head. "It's not right, Eirwen. We all let her get away with murder, just because she's old. And, yes, I know you all rely on her to let you keep living here, but she really shouldn't act like she does. It's inhuman. Treats us all worse than dogs, she does. I . . . I think I'm going to start looking for a job in event planning somewhere else, Idris. I know it's really only you and Eirwen it'll affect, and I'm sure you'll be able to find someone to replace me. If they don't live here, they might last quite a while. Of course, then you'd have to pay them a good deal more than you pay me—but I think it's time for me to make the break. Time to get away from this place. Get out into the real world."

Idris and Eirwen looked horrified. "It's not the best time to be making such a big decision," said Eirwen. "Let's get the funeral and so forth over with first? There'll be time enough for you to think about whether to stay or go after that."

I judged that Eirwen's concern was focused on Rhian, the widow, but I suspected that Idris's nervous twitch owed its appearance more to the idea of having to pay a living wage to her replacement. It hadn't occurred to me that wages for Rhian, David, and Dilys would likely be very small because they lived in, but it made sense.

I could also tell that Idris was impatient about the break in our previous conversation—not because he was interested in my theories about David's death, but because he wanted to know more about my thinking regarding the Cadwallader Cache. His entire body had become taut before Owain stormed out of the room, and I could tell he was eager to hear what I knew—or, at least, to hear what I thought I knew.

But we were all consumed with the sight before our eyes. A fellow human being was in deep distress, and we couldn't ignore the needs of a woman who'd lost her husband.

"I'll pour you a glass of port," said Idris, rising once again from his seat. "Or I could go and get some brandy, if you'd prefer?"

Rhian shook her head and allowed Eirwen to guide her to a seat close to the fireplace. "The logs will get going in a minute," said Eirwen gently, "and you can get cozy here. How about I go and make you some hot milk, and you can have a drop of whiskey in it? It's Alice's favorite, and it might help to warm you through."

"It's not really Alice's favorite," said Rhian gloomily. "Janet puts doping stuff in it. Alice just goes off to sleep in a fog, drugged up to the eyeballs. Janet's been doing it since she got here. She told me she does it to all her old biddies, so they don't fuss in the night and wake her up."

Idris shifted in his chair uncomfortably as Siân said, "That's a very bad idea. Believe me, when I worked on geriatric wards, before my specialist training, I'd have liked nothing better than to be able to give all my patients knock-out drops so I could have quieter shifts, but you just can't do things like that. Idris—where did you find Janet? Is she qualified?"

Idris and Eirwen exchanged a glance. Idris was the one who spoke. "We've used the same agency for years, but they . . . well, they sort of kicked us off their books when Danuta, Alice's last nurse, left here. They said that Alice was too demanding, and suggested we try an alternative company. Janet is the first girl we've had from them. She's not actually a nurse, but a health care assistant."

"She's *not* a nurse?" Siân sounded horrified. "But you refer to her as 'Nurse.' What is she exactly?"

Idris puffed out his cheeks and took a gulp of his port. "She's a member of the Royal College of Nursing—and she's studying for her National Vocational Qualifications in health and welfare. She'd been working at a care home not far from here for about eighteen months. The agency said she'd be a good fit—though, to be fair, they didn't seem to have a lot of people on their books who wanted to live in a private home, albeit a castle."

The logs in the fireplace shifted and finally began to burn.

Siân looked stern as she responded to Idris. "If she's got no qualifications, and she's not working under the supervision of a *real* registered nurse, then why is she allowed to administer any sort of medication? Unless it's something prescribed by your grandmother's doctor, for example, she shouldn't be doing it."

"I know," said Idris. "I didn't know she was. What Rhian just said is the first I've heard of it." He looked guilty as he turned to his wife. "Eirwen, what have we done? The agency fee was so low, I suppose

I should have known they might not have the best people. But Alice is so difficult to please, and she seems to like Janet a great deal. She's been a lot easier to live with since Janet arrived. Thinking about it now, Alice has mentioned how much better she's been sleeping recently. It didn't occur to me that Janet might be taking things into her own hands."

I looked at my sister, who was alert and engaged. For the first time since she'd arrived at Castell Llwyd, Siân's body language seemed to mark her out as a person, fully formed, with a purpose.

Even her tone of voice seemed different as she said, "Rhian, did Janet say what she was giving Alice?"

Rhian shook her head.

"I should check this," said Siân. "It's my responsibility as a nurse. And I think I should go now." Siân stood and stretched her arms above her head. "Oh dear, I'm still not right after that flight," she said, and I noticed her grimace as she arched herself, her hands in the small of her back. As she stretched, she said, "If Alice is on the same sort of powerful painkillers I've been prescribed for our common condition, there are a lot of sleep aids that would be contra-indicated, because of possible negative interactions between drugs. Alice's health could be in danger. It's best to check right now. Cait, will you come with me?"

"But Cait was just about to tell us . . ."

Eirwen kicked her husband as he spoke, then glared at him. "Idris," she snapped. "It's more important for Siân and Cait to find out if Alice is being dangerously drugged by an inadequately qualified caregiver, hired by us on the cheap, than for you to have the chance to talk to her about some mythical treasure. Go on, you two. I hope this is something and nothing, but you should find out. We'll wait here."

Deuddeg ar hugain

AS SIÂN AND I WERE just about to leave the drawing room, Bud called after us, "Cait, I'm sure Siân will be just fine dealing with medical matters on her own—and I think it would be a good idea if she was accompanied by a family member, don't you agree?"

Across an expanse of mismatched furnishings and oak flooring topped with aged, handmade rugs, and within a womb of wood panels, I saw my fiancé, my love, pleading with me. He hadn't said the words aloud, but I knew exactly what he meant.

"I agree," I said firmly. "Siân, you don't need me for this—medicine is your field, not mine. I won't be any help at all. But Bud's right, this is a family matter, and Idris is the one who retained 'Nurse' Janet, so I think you two should tackle these matters together. I'll stay here, and you can come back and tell us how you get on, okay?"

Siân's smile spoke volumes. I saw pride, gratitude, and sisterly love there, and it felt good. I usually like to be in charge, but I knew it was the right time to step aside for my sister.

"I'll walk up with you," said Rhian. "I'll get myself a cardigan. I can't seem to get warm."

"Let me go and get it for you," said Gwen, rushing to Rhian's side. "You stay here by the fire."

"Thanks," replied Rhian, "but I might just go back up and stay there in any case. I don't think I'm going to be very good company."

"I'll come with you—I'll settle you in and make sure you're comfy," insisted Gwen.

Rhian and Gwen joined Siân at the doorway. Eirwen pushed Idris out of his seat, and he trotted behind the women as they marched out of the room. I could hear the soles of Siân's shoes clatter across the tiled hall, then they became silent on the carpeted stairs. It set me thinking.

I asked, "Eirwen, what can you tell me about that lift that Alice uses? Was it installed recently?"

With only Eirwen, Bud, and myself remaining in the once-again-cozy drawing room, it seemed that Idris's wife was glad to have something to talk about.

She gushed a little as she answered, "No, it was put in about twenty years ago, I believe. Obviously, long before my time here. I think Alice's back started to get really bad when she was in her early seventies. She really just uses the chair because of the stairs, and this place is so big, of course. It makes life easier all round."

I was on full alert. "To be clear, are you saying that Alice is perfectly capable of walking about the place?"

I could tell that she was choosing her words carefully when she replied, "I wouldn't say she can get about easily. She has an old walking frame for getting around her apartment, but the stairs would just be too much for her. And, even in her motorized chair, she tires quickly." Eirwen paused and added, "Mind you, maybe that's not natural, if Janet's been slipping her sleeping tablets."

"So the little lift was put in to accommodate a non-motorized chair?" I asked.

Eirwen nodded.

I continued, "I noticed yesterday that the new chair doesn't fit into the little cab-thing very well, so I guessed that. But I also noticed that the lift is exceptionally quiet. That's unusual for something as old, and as basic, as that."

An emotional cloud passed across Eirwen's eyes. "David did that," she said. She looked up at me, and her eyes seemed suddenly tired—hooded. "When he and Rhian first married, and he moved in here, he seemed to be everywhere at once, doing so many jobs for everyone, and making us all feel . . ." she searched for the best word, "looked after." She nodded, pleased with her choice. "He wasn't a stupid man, and he knew how important it was to have Alice on his side, so he was especially careful to give priority to the jobs that directly affected her life. That lift was number one on his list of things to fix, and fix it he did. It used to make the most dreadful grinding noise as it went up and down. David fitted some rubber shoes—I think that's what he said, but I might be wrong. It was a very long time ago. It's been wonderfully quiet ever since." A wan smile curled her lips. "It was something that affected all our lives, because, in those days, Alice was up and down in it much more often that she is now, and it drove us all almost mad." A broader grin cracked her lips open. "Of course, the trouble with it now is that no one ever knows she's coming. So there's a definite downside to what David did." Eirwen paused, then added, as much to herself as to Bud and me, "But then, there always was."

She snapped back to reality and smiled brightly. *Too brightly.*

I decided to take my chance, with Idris out of the room, and be direct. "Eirwen, did anything *personal* ever happen between you and David Davies?"

"Don't be *twp*," snapped Eirwen, "I wouldn't."

"He wouldn't," added Gwen at the same moment. I didn't know how long she'd been hovering at the door, but she reappeared as she spoke. The two women gave each other a surprised look, and Gwen deferred to Eirwen who was, to all intents and purposes, her hostess.

Eirwen composed herself as she said, "David was . . . well, he was quite forward on occasions. But he was always quite the gent. Gallant. Helpful, you know? But not feely touchy with me, or anything like that. Though I will admit that those eyes of his could be very—well, I suppose that 'hypnotic' would be going too far, but they certainly pulled you in. Such long, dark lashes. The effect was extraordinary, if you know what I mean."

"Do *you* know what she means, Gwen?" I looked directly at my mousey ex-schoolmate who was settling herself near the fire, having returned from making sure that Rhian was comfortable.

Gwen blushed. She nodded, dropped her head, and looked at the three of us as though she were a sad puppy. "He always knew what to say to make me feel better. He always made me feel special, that I'd done a good job, you know? And his eyes? Smashing, they were. Deep blue, with flecks of gold. Everyone said they were amazing. But, like Eirwen said, he was always very proper with me, too. Rhian and I are good friends, you see. Lovely man. So talented. I'll miss him a lot."

I was beginning to get an inkling of exactly how much Gwen would miss David Davies, and it dawned on me that she was a woman who could quite easily find herself clinging to those who paid her any attention, however small. I wondered how the dashing David had coped with that attention. It sounded as though he was accustomed to using his appealing eyes and charming manner to ingratiate himself with women. He might have gone further.

With all the talk of eyes, I managed a quick glance into Bud's. They are pale blue, and whether kind or stern in the moment, they are always full of emotion. Best eyes in the world. Then I couldn't help but think of Angus. Angus with one green eye, and one almost blue. Angus with the mop of unruly hair that always made him look disheveled. Angus with the looks that were a cross between Tony Curtis and Robbie Williams. Angus with the wicked temper, and the rapier wit.

Bud must have noticed that I was deep in thought, because he stood and said, "Should I be doing something with the fire? Or could I maybe bring more logs into the room? We seem to be almost out of them. I guess I take this to carry them?"

"Thanks, Bud," replied Eirwen, as Bud picked up an old coal bucket. "The logs are kept in a dry lean-to outside the music room. If you wouldn't mind, that would be super. I'll come with you, show you where they are."

Bud and Eirwen left the room, so our entire group had dwindled to just Gwen and me. I forced myself to stop thinking about the man whose psyche had sought to destroy mine, then whose death had ruined my life even more completely, forcing me to run from Britain in an attempt to escape the tabloid press. I wanted to consider Gwen herself. I stared into the fire, always a comforting thing to do, though a log fire shifts and moves differently than a coal fire. The body of the fire glows differently, the sparks move more swiftly, the smell is so very different.

Once again the "coincidence" that Gwen had been in Cambridge when Angus and I had taken our last painful jabs at each other niggled at me.

"You're very quiet," noted Gwen rather sulkily. "That's not like you."

I wanted to say, "How would you know?" but decided against it. Gwen seemed to feel we had a stronger connection thirty years after I'd left school than I had even believed we had when I was there. *Odd.*

Before I had a chance to say anything at all, Bud came back into the drawing room from the music room. I'd expected him to be carrying a brass bucket full of logs, but he wasn't. Rather unexpectedly he was carrying a kitchen knife with its handle wrapped in an old rag. "Look what we found, stuck in amongst the wood in the log pile," he said. "I think this might be what someone used to slash Alice's portrait, otherwise why would it be there?"

"Good point," I replied. "Is there anything special about it?" I noted how carefully he was handling it.

"Other than that it was hidden, not much. But, having found it where I did, I'm going to get a paper bag from Eirwen and put it somewhere safe, so I can pass it to the authorities when I can. It might not tell us anything, but it could tell them a whole lot. So that brings us to the big question, Cait—have you managed to work out how David's death and the vandalism here are connected?"

I looked up at Bud and said, "Maybe."

Tri ar ddeg ar hugain

THE SCREAM WAS LOUD, AND it couldn't be ignored. Bud, Gwen, and I ran from the drawing room toward the staircase. It was clear that the noise was coming from Alice's apartment, so we all three ran up the stairs. I could see Eirwen trying to catch up with us.

When we arrived at the apartment, Bud didn't hesitate; he swung the door open to its fullest extent and I rushed past him. I hadn't known what to expect, but nothing could have prepared me for the scene that met my eyes.

Alice Cadwallader might have been ninety-two years old, but she had managed to attach herself to my sister's back, and was beating poor Siân about the head with her one free fist. Janet Roberts was lying at my sister's feet, her arms wrapped around Siân's knees, and was biting at her legs. Idris Cadwallader was lying on the floor next to a window, a gash on his head and a broken table lamp beside him.

Bud leapt into action. I joined him, and we attempted to pry Alice off my sister without hurting the old woman. Rhian rushed into the room and began to pull Janet away from Siân's legs, while Eirwen wailed over her seemingly unconscious husband.

Alice's grip on Siân's hair was tenacious, and I knew we were causing Siân more pain by trying to pull the woman off, but there seemed little else we could do. At one point, Alice smacked me in the face, and I knew a black eye would follow.

Rhian managed to get Janet away from Siân, but as soon as Janet was on her feet, she started lashing out at Rhian, who hit back with all the ferocity of a woman who was allowing her grief to flow out of her as anger. A full-fledged catfight ensued. Eventually, Janet hit the floor with a thud. At the same moment Alice lost her grip on Siân's hair, and Bud was able to split the two of them apart. He carried Alice to a daybed that sat beneath a window, and told her, in no uncertain terms, "Stay there, Alice—or I'll have to do something to make you do just that." Alice shrunk into a little ball and began to cry like a baby, wailing and sobbing.

I took one look at my sister and told her to sit in a chair, which I pulled toward her. She had scratches and cuts on her face, as well as bite marks on her legs. She was shaking with anger.

"What on earth happened?" I asked her as I tried to help with her tangled hair.

"Don't worry about me," she snapped. "I must check on Idris." She pushed me away and moved quickly toward the man who was still lying motionless on the floor.

Getting Eirwen and Gwen to let go of him was Siân's first job, then she rolled him over, checking his vital signs and the wound on the side of his head. Almost immediately, Idris opened his eyes, a shocked expression on his face.

"You're okay," said Siân soothingly. "You've had a nasty crack on your head, so we'll give you a moment or two to get your bearings. Then I'll do some tests to see if you've sustained a concussion. I need you to make all your movements slow and steady, so we don't jar your head or your neck. Understand?"

Idris nodded.

"No, don't nod your head, Idris, just speak. How do you feel? Can you see me properly?"

Idris croaked, "Yes, just fine." He put his hand to his head, pulled it away, and saw the blood.

Eirwen gasped, "Who did this to you, Idris? Tell me, who did this?"

"Alice," he whispered. "She hit me with a lamp. When Siân accused Nurse Janet of over-medicating Alice, both Alice and Janet went berserk. Have they calmed down now?"

Eirwen looked around and noticed Bud standing in the middle of Alice's sitting room. "They have, and Bud will make sure it stays that way."

"What in blue blazes is going on in here then?" Dilys appeared at the door to the apartment. "Oh my giddy aunt. What's happened?" She spotted Alice, who was rolled into a ball on the daybed, and made a beeline for her. "Alice? Alice, what's the matter, *cariad*?" She stroked the woman's hand, and Alice began to uncurl.

Looking up at Dilys, the old woman said sweetly, "Hullo, Dilys. When's dinner going to be? Will it be beef? I like beef. Let's have beef, whatever Idris says about the cost. I can have a little treat when I fancy it, can't I?"

Bud and I exchanged a glance, and I wondered how long Alice had been having violent episodes like the one that had just resulted in Idris being knocked out. I quickly reasoned, however, that, whatever mental challenges Alice might be facing, Janet had been the one wrapped around Siân's legs, biting at them. That was a greater cause for concern, so I allowed Dilys to handle Alice, while Siân and Eirwen continued to attend to Idris. I moved to the area of the room where Rhian was standing triumphantly above Janet, who was cowering on the floor with a welt across her face.

I reached out a hand toward the "nurse," who took it and pulled herself up. "Keep her away from me," she said, angrily eyeing up Rhian. "She'll take it all out on me, she will. It wasn't my fault. I didn't give him the come-on. He didn't need one. All over me, he was, two minutes after I got here. Gagging for it. Sorry, Rhian, love. It was all just a bit of fun really. I'm sure he still loved you. Said he loved me, but I didn't believe him for a minute. Knew his type only too well, but it's very boring here and, well, you know. It filled the time."

I wondered if Janet cared as little for David as she claimed.

Rhian sagged. "Don't say that, you horrible girl. Don't talk about my husband that way." She clenched her fist, and Bud was on guard in an instant.

"Come along now, ladies," he said. "Let's keep this calm. Janet, would you please come over here and sit in this chair, and Rhian you sit in that one." Once the two women were at opposite sides of the room, Bud stood between them, while they glared at each other.

By the time Owain stuck his head into the apartment, comparative peace had returned.

"I heard a kerfuffle," he said. "I thought I should come to see what was going on." He looked puzzled at seeing almost everyone in his mother's apartment. "Where's Mair? Missing all the fun, as usual?" he quipped.

I looked around. He was right, Mair wasn't there, and she was only one floor up from her mother's room, while Rhian had made it all the way down from the top floor of the wing.

"I'll go and check on her. Owain, show me the way, please." I knew that I was barking at the man as I grabbed him in the doorway. He dawdled along the landing as he followed me. "Owain, come on," I snapped. He seemed to slow down. I returned to stand in front of him. I looked up into his beetled brow and tiny eyes and said firmly, "Owain Cadwallader. There's been a near-riot going on in your mother's apartment, which I'm guessing you heard from your library." He nodded. "And you came to find out what it was all about, didn't you? Because you thought it was something serious, right?" Again, he nodded. "Then what do you think would stop your sister from coming down one flight of stairs from her rooms to find out why her mother was screaming her head off?"

"I don't know, I'm sure," he said haughtily.

"Nor do I," I snapped back. "But I think we should find out, don't you? It must be a very good reason, after all. So if you don't want to come with me, then don't, but at least tell me how I get into her apartment."

I could tell that Owain was pursing his lips into a boyish pout because of the way his beard moved.

"Up the stairs at the end, through that door," he said. "Hers is the first door you'll come to. She's at the sea-end of the wing, above us here." He waved an arm above his head.

I didn't bother to thank him, I just abandoned him and sped toward the door he'd indicated, the one Bud and I had used to get up to the top floor earlier in the day.

Two minutes later I was panting and knocking at Mair's door. "Mair? Can I come in, please?" No answer. I knocked louder and tried the handle, just as Bud joined me.

"Let me go in first, Cait," he said.

Bud pushed the door, and it creaked open. The room was in total darkness, the only light coming from the landing. Bud reached around and found a light switch. An overhead chandelier sprung to life and we saw a scene of total devastation. Broken mirrors, chairs turned over, books and knitting projects all over the place, balls of yarn tossed across the floor.

"Mair?" I called. "It's Bud and Cait, can we come in?"

Bud motioned for me to follow him. We picked our way across the room and into Mair's bedroom. Another light switch, another room in disarray, but no sign of Mair. I even checked inside her massive wardrobe and under her bed.

"Bathroom?" I asked. Bud nodded, and we made our way to the final room in Mair's suite. This time the room was empty but nothing had been disturbed.

I sighed. "I thought she might have done something to harm herself."

Bud nodded. "I know you did, and so did I. But looking around the place it's hard to know what's happened here."

"Someone might have been searching for something," I suggested, moving back through the bedroom to the sitting room. "But you know, I don't think that's what this is."

"I agree," said Bud, sounding grim. "This is anger, temper. Someone's crashed around the place not caring about the destruction."

"Maybe Mair did it herself," I said. "When she left us at the dinner table, she was a very angry, unhappy woman. I know the profile, Bud; she's a solitary person, she has no, or few, friends, and her anger had nowhere to go. This is her world, and she's just destroyed it. Of course I'm glad that she hasn't turned her anger on herself—but I think we should try to find her. I'm very concerned about what she might do. This is both a good and a bad sign. Her rage might have dissipated to the point where it's played out, on this occasion. Or this might be the first sign of her having decided that she no longer has any use for this part of her world—or any part."

"We should ask the family where she might go," said Bud. "Find out if she has any favorite places." He peered into the blackness beyond Mair's windows. "It's very dark out there. I know the rain's pretty much stopped, but the cloud cover is still thick enough to prevent the moonlight from coming through. If she's off on a ramble, she could lose her footing very easily—it's all so wet out there."

I looked at my watch. "It's gone eight o'clock, and she must have left us in the dining room at, what, about six?" Bud nodded.

I paused. "Why didn't we hear the noise of all this happening when we were in the drawing room? You'd have thought it would make a real racket. And even if we didn't hear it, what about her mother, who was directly below her?"

Bud shook his head. "I don't know why we didn't hear anything, Cait. Noises seem to move around this place in the most peculiar way. But our priority now should be to ask the people who know her about where she might have gone. Come on, let's leave this as it is, and go ask."

We re-entered Alice's sitting room as a pair.

By this time the room looked as though an informal soiree was taking place, with people sitting, and seemingly lounging, about the place. It was only the variety of injuries on display that gave away the fact that something very unusual had taken place.

I nudged Bud, indicating he should take the lead. He did. "We have checked through Mair's rooms, and she's nowhere to be found. I wonder if any of you might be able to suggest where she might have gone."

Good job, Bud—start softly.

Idris, who was by now upright, with a large pad of gauze taped to his head, said, "Where would she go at this time of night? None of us usually go out after dark. Why would we?"

Eirwen added, "That's quite right. I don't know of anyone who ever leaves the castle after dark. Unless they're driving into one of the villages, or into Swansea, you know."

Rhian sighed. "I quite often go out to the stables after dark. It's a good time to find some peace and quiet and get some work done at the office. I used to see Mair out and about sometimes."

Owain muttered, "Preposterous," then glanced at me, blushed, and shut up.

"Where would you see her?" I asked.

"Out somewhere smoking her face off, I dare say," sniped Alice. *She seems to be back to her old self.*

"I'd see her sitting against the stones in the stone circle," said Rhian, ignoring her employers. "She spotted me one night and asked me not to say anything. She didn't want anyone to know how much she loved the circle. She told me it made her feel calm—connected to the world, yet disconnected from it."

Owain harrumphed. I ignored him.

"Thanks," I said. "Anyone else got anywhere to suggest?" I thought I should check before I went tearing off.

"I think it most unlikely she's anywhere near the stone circle," said Owain sulkily. "She's been openly dismissive about it her whole life, so I cannot imagine it holds any significance for her."

As I motioned to Bud that we should leave, I said, "People and their habits change, grow, take a new course, and, sometimes, adopt new patterns, Owain. Maybe it's something you should consider for yourself."

I knew it was a mean-spirited thing to say when I wasn't giving the man a chance to respond, but I was utterly annoyed with Owain "my way or the high way" Cadwallader. As far as I was concerned, he could stew in his own particular brand of "preposterous" juice until Bud and I returned with Mair. *If we could find her.*

Pedwar ar ddeg ar hugain

FOR THE FIRST TIME SINCE we'd arrived in Britain, Bud and I didn't need our wet weather gear as we headed out of the castle. It was a cold night, and blustery, but it was no longer raining. Flashlights in hand, we trudged across the pea gravel driveway toward the stone circle. As we called out Mair's name, the wind carried our voices inland, away from the ancient monument. We knew we'd have to get close for our shouts to be heard by anyone near the jagged obelisks, which were still invisible to us in the blackness of the night, so we put our heads down and pushed against the force of the buffeting gusts.

The stones were black with rainwater, and the beams we played upon them dazzled us. But, although we completely circumnavigated the entire site, there was no sign of Mair. I recalled the cabinet full of old guns in the stable block, and my concern deepened. When I shared my worries with Bud, I noted that his mouth became a thin line and his chin thrust forward in his most determined manner.

We set off toward the stable block. It was dark and we couldn't be sure of our footing, so we stuck to the tarmac roadway, rather than cutting across the uneven grassy banks as we had done earlier in the day. It was a longer, more meandering climb, but we both agreed it was the safest option. As we made our way, we fell silent.

With no rain to blur our vision, we looked down upon Castell Llwyd. Light spilled from the windows of the drawing room, Alice's apartment, and the great hall. While walking up and around one particular bend I saw something that made me grab Bud's arm.

"Look, someone's in my room," I said. There was a light shining from the turret in which my bridal boudoir was situated, right above the dining room.

"Siân?" replied Bud.

I shrugged and pushed on.

We finally reached the stable block. There were no lights to be seen inside the building.

Bud cursed under his breath. "Idris locked it when we left. So either she couldn't have got in, and we've come on a fool's errand, or she had keys and might have locked us out."

Despite his words, Bud tried the handle of the stable door. He gave me a grin and the thumbs up when it turned, then we switched off our flashlights and pulled open the door as quietly as possible.

Our breathing was the loudest sound in the place. We both agreed, with a nod, that we were alone. Switching on our flashlights we swept the place for signs that Mair might at least have been there at some point since we'd left the place hours ago. Nothing seemed to have been moved. Bud tried the door to the gun cabinet. It was locked. He looked as relieved as I felt.

Not having found Mair, we were just about to leave when we both stopped in our tracks. A groaning, crunching sound was coming from behind the canvas-covered Aston Martin that Idris had told us was David's special project.

I grabbed Bud's sleeve and dragged him in the general direction, and we both turned off our lights once more. But it wasn't dark for long. Rounding the car we had no problem seeing, because light was flooding up out of a trapdoor that was being noisily pushed open. Let into the floor of the stable and covered with a flagstone, it would be almost invisible when it was closed. The light from the opening shone onto the back wall of the stable, and someone was coming up a ladder set into the abyss. A head appeared over the trapdoor. It was Mair.

Obviously startled to see us, she let out a little cry. She seemed to consider descending the ladder again, but, realizing there was little point, hauled herself out of the opening and brushed herself off as she came to stand beside us. Her hands, face, and clothing were all grubby, but with a whiter dust than I'd seen anywhere either inside or outside the castle.

She noticed me examining her clothing, looked down at herself, and said, "Limestone."

I nodded. "I'm sure the temple is quite a sight. Carved out of the limestone bedrock, I suppose?"

Mair nodded. Bud looked puzzled.

I said, "The dust on this canvas car cover has taken a very long time to accumulate. I thought of that when we saw it earlier on. David wasn't working on the car at all. He was working on the temple."

Bud nodded. "We already knew he was searching the temple. He'd found out about Owain's secret passage from the coal cellar."

"Owain's got a passage from the coal cellar to the temple?" Mair sounded stunned.

"You didn't know?" Bud looked skeptical.

Mair shook her head vigorously. "But that would be typical of Owain—I mean, why *wouldn't* you choose the most difficult thing to do and dig uphill, when there's a perfectly good channel running downhill?"

"The old river course?" I asked.

Mair nodded. "It used to run right through where they built this place. All David and I had to do was gain access to it, follow it along, clearing it out a little here and there, and then get into the temple itself. I wonder where Owain's passage enters it. I've never seen another entry point."

"I believe his passage comes up into the cistern," I said.

Mair nodded. "Oh, I see. I think."

Again, Bud looked puzzled, but instead of pressing me to explain, he said, "Mair, we've come to find you because we're very concerned for you. Are you alright?"

"Yes," said Mair, clearly implying there was no reason she shouldn't be. "Why do you ask?" A look of panic crossed her face. "What's happened? Has something else happened? Tell me—is Mother okay? Owain? What is it?"

I explained the situation that had arisen in Alice's apartment as best I could, and then told her about the damage in her own rooms. Her reaction suggested she hadn't caused the damage herself. I'd misjudged her, which is unusual for me.

Mair walked across to the workbench and grabbed a coat she'd pushed behind it. "I am done with all of this." She waved her arm in the air. "Mother clearly isn't well, you've told me that Idris has hired some unqualified girl to look after her to save a pound or two, Owain's been lying to me for years about the temple, and . . . and David is dead. I . . . I don't know what to do anymore. I can't actually *do* anything, you see. I wouldn't know how to earn a living away from this place. Well, let's be honest and just admit I wouldn't know how to *live* away from this place, let alone earn a living. It's as though I've spent my entire life in a prison. I am totally, and irredeemably, institutionalized. I wouldn't make it out there, not for five minutes. I get panic attacks in Swansea Market because there are too many people there, for goodness sake. What use am I to anyone, for anything?"

I spoke as reassuringly as I could. "Your mother needs people around her she knows and loves, whatever might be happening to her right now. Maybe it's as easy to tackle as getting her off a lot of medications she shouldn't be taking together, which I am sure my sister will address. Or maybe it's more difficult, like night terrors, or the beginning of dementia, or even Alzheimer's disease."

"Loves? You think my mother loves me?" Mair laughed in my face. "She's obviously not the only one who's nuts around here. You've heard how she talks to me. She hates me."

I knew there was little point following that particular line of discussion, especially while the three of us were standing in an unheated stone building in the middle of a winter's night.

Bud clearly agreed. He said, "Mair, we came out to look for you. Everyone back at the castle knows that, and I'm sure they'll be worried about you. Why don't we walk back down together and talk about this in the warmth?"

Pulling on her coat, Mair said, "Fine. There's nothing for me here anymore, anyway." *Odd.*

We pulled the outer door closed behind us and Bud locked it up. I said to Mair, "So you and David didn't find anything then?"

She smiled sadly. "Not a sausage. But it was so exciting to be looking. The most thrilling hours of my life were spent here, underground, when David and I were off on our secret hunts. It made me feel very special."

The walk back down to the castle wasn't as difficult as the walk up had been. I noticed that there was no longer a light on in my room, and that there was just a dim light in Alice's apartment. As we drew close to the white stumps of columns that had once surrounded the Roman temple to Neptune inside the bluestone circle, we had a good view of the castle. I could make out the movement of bodies inside the drawing room. There were only heavily decorated lace curtains at the windows, so it was easy to see movement, but not shape. I hoped that the room, and our welcome, would be warm, because I was beginning to worry that my fingers might never regain their circulation.

With steps to go before we entered the double doors of Castell Llwyd, the wind sent a bank of cloud scudding across the sky, and moonlight shone through the thin cloud remaining. The halo effect of the moon behind the cloud lifted my spirit.

"Look, Bud," I said. "There is, in fact, a silver lining." We both took just a moment to look up, holding hands in the suddenly brilliant moonlight.

"There always is, my darling Cait," he said, and he kissed me on the forehead. "And I bet you tomorrow will be a beautiful day," he added.

"We have to get through tonight first," I said, and with that, we walked into the great hall, to be greeted by Eirwen.

Mair explained that she was fine, that she'd simply gone for a walk. The women rapidly exchanged family news, with Eirwen reassuring Mair that her mother was fine. I was glad to hear that Idris was asleep. Siân had elected to stay in Alice's apartment to oversee Janet and the old woman, while Rhian and Dilys would both be staying in Dilys's apartment that night. Gwen would be able to get a good night's sleep in Rhian's bed, rather than on a couch. I didn't quite see why no one had seen fit to offer poor Gwen the guest room next to Siân's that wasn't in use, but that wasn't my call.

When Eirwen took her leave of us, I said to Mair, "Where will you sleep tonight? I can't imagine it'll be very easy for you in your rooms."

"It can't be that bad, surely?" said Mair blithely. Of course, she hadn't seen what we'd seen. I tried to explain.

She looked more concerned than she had been. "Well, of course I want to go and see what's been damaged and broken, but I'm not in any mood to do anything about it tonight. Maybe I'll sleep in the bed in the upstairs library," she said.

"There's a bed up there?" I asked.

Mair nodded. "Owain often sleeps there—he says he loves it. That it's the only truly quiet part of the castle. Of course, given that you've just told me that he's been scrabbling away underground for years, maybe he's never slept there at all. Maybe that's the knocking I've heard at night—the *bwca* noises. Just Owain, after all. Maybe he's been laboring all night, then napping in the library in the day—when we all thought he was working on his historical texts. I wouldn't put it past him, he's such an idiot. But, there, he's my brother."

"Given that he's clearly been keeping some rather big secrets all this time, can you be quite sure he wouldn't have been the one to damage your belongings?" I had to ask.

Mair looked amazed. "Owain? Never. Not a spiteful bone in his body."

I wanted to mention that he'd displayed exactly that trait toward me on a few occasions, but I bit my tongue—which was still a little sore where I'd bitten into it the night before.

Bud and I offered to help Mair sort through her room, but she declined, forcefully. So she went her way, and we went ours. Once again Bud and I stood outside the door to my room. It was gone ten-thirty, and I was dog tired.

"Not quite what I'd hoped for in terms of my last night ever as an unmarried woman," I said as Bud hugged me.

"Cait—none of this is what I'd hoped for, but we're still in the middle of it now. Tomorrow we *will* come out the other side. So tell me, how do you know so much about what's going on? And do you know the full story yet?"

"Bud, I understand that you want me to tell you everything, but we're both very, very tired, and, who knows, tomorrow might still be our wedding day. So let's just allow the Cadwalladers and all the other people who live here to sleep tonight, and we'll do the same thing. I cannot wait to get into my bed. I don't envisage any trips to the kitchen tonight, because I really believe there *is* such a thing as beauty sleep, and I haven't had any for days. I've got a sore tongue, I suspect I'll have the beginnings of a black eye by the morning, this cut on my arm is niggling at me, and my back might not be as bad as my sister's, but it's giving me gyp."

Bud grinned. "Are you aware that you and Siân sound as though you never left Wales now? Siân's Australian accent, and any hint of Canadian you might have picked up, have gone completely. It's quite amusing, though I'm having to listen even more carefully when you speak. It's a bit odd, but I think I like it."

I laid it on thick. "Well then, my lovely boy, you'd better get used to it, hadn't you, 'cos when I sees you in the morning, I'm going to come over to sit by wherever you are, and tell you all the secrets everyone here's been hiding. Tidy like."

"And with that, I'll say goodnight, Miss Cait Morgan. I love you lots."

"Goodnight, Mr. Bud Anderson. I love you more."

"Love you most," I heard as I shut my bedroom door, flicked on the light, and headed for the bathroom.

One up to Bud.

Pymtheg ar hugain

AS I SNUGGLED UNDER THE covers, my feet were so cold I could only warm them up by stealing warmth from my other body parts. I tucked each foot into the back of each knee, turn and turn-about, until I could feel some lessening of the chill. Of course, once I was lying down, my mind started to race, and I found I couldn't stop it.

Having had such a horrible experience with my normally useful wakeful dreaming technique in the bath, I decided I wouldn't try that again, but I knew that my brain wouldn't let me sleep until I'd given the mystery of David's death, and the acts of vandalism, a thorough thinking through. I toyed with the idea of getting up and making some lists. I like lists; I'm good with lists. But my room was too cold for that to be an appealing idea.

My body ached and wanted me to lie still. My head spun, running through all that had happened since we'd arrived at Castell Llwyd, trying to sort it all out. My head won. I pushed back the covers, put on the bedside lamp, scampered to the wardrobe, pulled it open, hauled out my carry-on, located a pad and three pens, shoved my bag back into the spot where I'd dumped it upon our arrival, and rushed back to my bed, which, I was pleased to discover, had held onto the warmth my body had created.

I pulled the covers about me, so as much of my body was covered as possible, and gave the matter some thought. Just the process of making a list is a wonderful thing for me. It forces me to organize my thoughts, even before I write them down. So I started with the matter of the treasure, because it was the easiest place for me to begin. For me, when it comes to lists, the output might not look like much, but it's the thinking that goes into them that counts.

Regarding the treasure, all I really needed to write down was GOLD, SALT, COAL, FACES, PORTRAITS, WATER, and MIRROR, and I was done.

Next I tackled the question of the vandalism. PORTRAIT, PLATE, RAVELRY, CHRISTMAS DECORATIONS, and MAIR were all I had there, plus the key words DAVID, INVISIBLE, ADVENTURE, and LOVE.

Finally there was David Davies's death. TIMING? UP OR DOWN STAIRS? IN OR OUT OF DOOR? LEGS? COAL DUST? CHANGING CLOTHES?

This last point needed a lot more thought. But almost an hour had passed, and my brain was truly tired, as well as my body. I turned off the bedside lamp and floated off on a sea of feather pillows and the sound of the wind beyond the windows of my very own turret. I didn't give a thought to the adventure that my sleep would be.

I am sitting in a boat that's being pushed along a meandering river, while all about me men are trying to make the river flow in a different direction, using their hands to try to shift soil and water. I laugh as I sail past, because I know they will never succeed. Arriving at a shore made of grains of pure gold that glitter beneath a sun that is etched with the two faces of Janus, I spring lightly onto the sand, only to feel it burn my feet. As if from nowhere a man bumps into me. He is in a full evening dress suit, and is dancing on his toes, like a ballerina. Although he has no face, I know he is David Davies. He whistles at me, and the sound is that of a full male voice choir. I follow him, because that's what his whistle is telling me to do, and I am crossing the bridge that is painted on a willow-pattern plate. I know I am in that landscape, on an actual plate. I am blue, and the water beneath the bridge is merely blue and white wavy lines. I am laughing that it has been such an easy task for me to cross the river. I shout that I don't need him to lead me at all, and that I can find my own way.

Gwen Thomas rears up from the water beneath the bridge. The bridge shakes and collapses into the water. I know I cannot swim, and yet I am swimming. Gwen is holding my hand, telling me that this is the biggest favor she could ever do for me. She is saving my life. I thank her as I step out of the river, where Bud greets me, though he looks just like Owain. He hands me a shovel and tells me to dig. He tells me, in Bud's voice from within Owain's beard, that if I dig he will marry me, but if I stop he will not. I dig and dig. I dig until my hands are rough and blistered, until my fingernails are ragged. The shovel is very short now, and I am bending as I dig and my back begins to ache, then I feel it begin to snap.

Siân is beside me, as is Janet Roberts. They force me into a wheelchair. I am screaming that I don't want to stop digging—that my whole future depends upon it, but they are wheeling me away from Owain/Bud, and from the hole I have dug. As they wheel me we go faster and faster. The landscape is a blur. I hear the air as it passes my ears, rushing like a mighty wind. Within the blur of the passing landscape I see scenes as if in a tableau. Janet is slamming the door of the little lift in the great hall against Alice's wheelchair, but the motion, and the contact between the two, is silent. Dilys Jones drops a plate upon which was balanced the magnificent stuffed head of a spectacled bear—as it crashes to the floor the bear's head comes to life, grows legs and runs away, a long baguette in its mouth. Bud is lying on the floor of Mair's room, bleeding from the head—the sight shocks me, and I try to scream, but when I try to turn to Siân and Janet, who I believe are pushing my wheelchair, there's no one there, and I make no sound.

Again I see David Davies in front of me, but now he is Angus. I will the wheelchair to run him over, and it does, but he pops up again behind me, laughing at my inability to kill him. I will the wheelchair to stop, but I only do so when I crash through a massive mirror that splinters and rains down upon my head. When I get out of the wheelchair the shards on the ground are not from a mirror, but from the puzzle plate. A man in a uniform I do not recognize helps me pick up the pieces. He is speaking to me in a language I do not know or understand. It's gibberish. As he is laughing at my lack of comprehension, he transforms into the Gryffudd Cadwallader of the portrait I have seen, but he is now a living person, sweating profusely under a suddenly present summer sun, and pointing to something in the clear blue sky that I cannot make out. It comes closer. I see it is a large seagull, about fifty feet across, and it is planning to eat me. I begin to run. I can hear the seagull screech at my back. I don't look around; I know that when people do that in movies they always trip and fall, and I mustn't do that, because I will break.

I see Bud in the distance. He is calling me toward a cave, where I know I will be safe. I run inside and find myself atop a never-ending flight of steps. I don't want to go down them. I turn to run back out again, but the wing of the seagull pushes me and I fall. Down and down I go, bouncing off steps, rolling and banging about, though nothing seems to hurt me. When I stop, I'm in the dining room of the castle, but I know I am not safe. The seagull is trying to follow me. The seagull has found me. It is smothering me. I beat at it. I feel its warmth, and, beyond that, the chill of the winter air.

I woke to find myself tangled in my bedding and in a lather of sweat. I got out of bed, cursing the chill of the room. I pulled open the curtains and shutters and there was the sea, glittering to the horizon where a beautiful sunrise was not quite complete. Sure enough, seagulls were playing on the breeze, calling to each other, and I knew that the storm had passed completely. It would, as Bud had promised, be a beautiful day.

My watch told me it was almost eight o'clock. I rushed through my morning bathroom routine and pulled on some stretchy corduroy slacks and a matching big, baggy sweater. I sat at the dressing table and examined the discoloration around my eye. It wasn't blackening yet, but it would be soon. I considered whether it was worth putting on any makeup. Maybe some concealer? I decided against it, because I knew I'd want to make a special effort for the wedding later on, if it took place at all. But I decided I'd get my wedding outfit out to let it get some air. I opened the wardrobe, grabbed the hanging garment bag that covered my lovely two-piece, and unzipped it.

Both the pants and the top had been cut to tatters. I couldn't believe it. It was ruined. I was so upset I didn't even cry. I threw the bag on the floor and tore out of my room, heading for the dining room.

Nature causing a flood that washed away a river bank and made a bridge collapse I could almost cope with. But this? This was deliberate. This was nasty. *And this will not go unpunished.*

Un ar bymtheg ar hugain

AS LUCK WOULD HAVE IT, everyone—including the dismissed, but unable to leave, "Nurse" Janet—was already in the dining room when I arrived. Dilys and Rhian were hovering and attending to the tea and coffee.

"Good morning, everyone," I said very loudly. All heads snapped up. Bud got up from his seat and made to move toward me, but I waved him off.

He was beaming as he said, "I have some news . . ."

"Good," I said, interrupting him. "So do I."

The light in Bud's expression disappeared, and I sighed. I mouthed "sorry" at him before I addressed everyone else. He could sense that something catastrophic was coming, and he left his toast to stand beside me.

I made sure I could see everybody as I announced, "Someone has been into my room and has hacked my wedding outfit to pieces."

I measured the responses, which ranged from gasps to almost no reaction at all.

"Don't you mean your wedding *dress*, Cait?" asked Siân, which I couldn't help but think wasn't an appropriate response.

"No," I snapped. "It was a two-piece. I didn't want a dress."

"Why ever not?" asked Siân.

I sighed. "For goodness sake, Siân, that's hardly the point! The point is it's ruined. And, FYI, I didn't want a dress because I stupidly traumatized myself by watching ten episodes of a ridiculous reality program about brides choosing wedding gowns. I swore then I'd never go to one of those bridal salons, so I got a two-piece at a department store."

"When did it happen?" asked Bud, his arm about my shoulders.

"I don't know. I didn't look at the outfit from the time I pulled the garment bag out of my suitcase until just now, so any time since we got here."

Bud was standing so close to me he was able to almost whisper, "Do you think it might have been when we were out looking for Mair last night?"

I knew he was referring to our having seen the light in my bedroom. "It might have been," I acknowledged. I squeezed Bud's arm and motioned that he should sit again. He did.

"Well, I'm very sorry to hear it," said Dilys as she made her way, with Rhian's help, toward the door to head to the kitchen.

"Hang on a minute, Dilys," I said. "You're not going anywhere."

The cook looked shocked, as did everyone else.

I tossed my head and said, "Today I am a bride, at least I am supposed to be. So I make no apologies for doing what I'm about to do. No, I'm not turning into some sort of 'Bridezilla,' so don't panic on that score, but I am going to, finally, take control, and sort out all this mayhem once and for all."

The only person in the room who wasn't puzzled was Bud. I looked at him and said, "You'll be up soon, officer." Bud nodded once. He knew what I meant, and I was also confident that he'd know exactly what to do when the time came.

"As for the rest of you? Alice, I'm going to make full use of a bride's prerogative and invite Dilys and Rhian to join us all at the table for a cup of tea, and even some breakfast, if they'd like. I wonder if I could have a cup of coffee, please. Bud, if you'd be so kind?"

Bud nodded and took action, rejoining me with a perfectly made cup of coffee.

I continued. "So, I hope you're all sitting comfortably, because I have a story in three parts to tell you. No, it's not going to be *Jackanory*—which is something Siân and I enjoyed when we were little. It begins a long time ago, and far away from here, but, I'm sorry to say, it does involve a death—your husband's death, Rhian—and a rash of wicked, destructive acts, all of which, surprisingly, sprang from a misguided type of love. So, ready or not, here I go.

"I will begin by acknowledging the one thing we all have in common. We are all trapped. Trapped here because of a collapsing bridge, yes, but we are all also individuals within our own, personal traps. I touched upon this when I was talking to Siân yesterday, but I now need to bring it to everyone's attention because it is at the root of all that has happened here this weekend."

The logs crackled in the grate. Most people continued eating toast or sipping tea.

"I'll begin with me," I said. "It's only fair, after all. More than a decade ago I met and fell for a dashing, handsome young man by the name of Angus, who I believed to be someone with whom I wanted to share my life and my home. He turned out to be a sociopath with a violent temper and an addiction to alcohol and pretty much anything else he could get his hands on. I'm not going to go into the various definitions of sociopath and psychopath, suffice to say he did some very bad things, and most of them were done because he wanted to have power over people. Mainly me. And I let him. I was trapped by my love for him, and my hope that he would change. I had made a prison for myself. I had constructed it out of self-delusion and an unreasonable amount of self-loathing. I couldn't see how to get out of it. Because I had built it."

I noticed that every woman in the room looked uncomfortable. *Good.*

"It wasn't until Angus threatened to turn his jealous rage toward a perfectly innocent acquaintance of ours—we didn't have any friends, you see—that I found the strength to throw him out. I'd told myself he was my problem, but once there was a chance that he would hurt others by his actions, I knew I had to act. I managed to make him leave my home, but he followed me for weeks. He'd show up everywhere I went. He'd stand outside my home at night. I was almost no better off. Then, one day, I confronted him in the street and we had what turned out to be our final row."

I turned my attention to Gwen. "I believe that's the fight you saw me and Angus having in Cambridge. I know that 'If I had a drink in my hand right now I'd throw it over you' were my last words to him."

Gwen nodded. "Yes, that's exactly what you said."

"Anyway, a few days later he was dead, and what followed was the worst time of my life. If I'd thought that living with Angus was bad, then having him found dead on the floor of my bathroom turned out to be an unimaginable nightmare. I am guessing you all know how that played out. I ended up having to leave the country to escape my new prison, the one the tabloids had built for me—the prison that exists when your face and your name are known and connected to a violent crime, even when you're later proved innocent. Then, in my new home of Canada, I eventually allowed someone into my life again. Bud. And now I have a chance to build a new life. No more prison for me. No more being trapped by my own choices or by the manipulation of others."

Alice wriggled in her wheelchair. "But what's all that got to do with us?"

The expressions around the table told me she was voicing a common query.

I cleared my throat. "I'm not the only one in this room who's trapped. You all have your own prisons, and you are all trying to make your escape. Siân? You live a rich and full life, with a loving husband and two wonderful, healthy children, and yet you are frustrated. Your life needs to be the way it is, you chose for it to be the way it is, and yet you couldn't see the joy in that."

Siân jumped to her own defense. "I can really, Cait, we talked about it. I was just having a bad time with my pain, and my painkillers,

236

that's all." I hoped the hurt I'd caused would heal quickly, when she saw more of my method.

I nodded. "Yes, I know, but it's an example I wanted to share." Siân looked deeply miffed.

"Bud," I said next. He looked alarmed. "When your wife, Jan, died, I think you realized the nature of the prison you'd built for yourself."

Bud swallowed nervously. I knew he would be up to my challenge, and that he'd follow my lead. Eventually, he nodded, resigning himself to taking part. "I lived in a cocoon of work. Total immersion. Of course, it comes with the job. It's essential. But when you have your life ripped apart like that, it changes the way you look at things. I'm sorry to say, Rhian, that's what you're going to be going through now. I packed in my job, and I've started to build a new life with Cait. We even have a new home to begin to make our own. It's hard—but I'm out of my old prison, and I won't be building another one any time soon."

"So, because David's dead, we should all run about giving up work and—what? Starve? Be homeless?" said Dilys. "Stupid thing to say," she spat at me.

"No," I replied, "I don't just mean work. Some people work their whole life and, while their job gets them down, it's their home life that's their real prison. Prisons are how we become 'institutionalized.' You said it yourself last night, Mair, and you were spot on. You, Owain, Dilys, and Rhian have never known a life lived anywhere but here. Castell Llwyd has become your literal, and figurative, prison."

"Don't try to dress it up with fancy words," snapped Dilys. "You're being nasty about my life. Belittling me, you are." She seemed to be the most uncomfortable person in the room. "Have me sit here at the big table, telling me I'm rubbish? There's nice for you."

"But you do things that allow you to have an escape, Dilys. Your cooking is excellent, I'm sure you're highly thought of by those you know in the local community, like your friend Audrey Williams, and your collection of cookbooks shows me you know of a world beyond these walls. Rhian, too. You use your connections with those around the world you do business with to allow you to see outside these walls. Mair, you have your online friends. Owain, you escape into history. Alice, I know you enjoy thinking about times gone by. Janet—well, you gave us a hint last night about how you've indulged while living here. Idris and Eirwen—you're rooted in the world outside because of, and for, your children. And of course there's Gwen who, although she doesn't live here, still will, like all of us, have her very own personal prison. What would you say that is, Gwen?"

Gwen shrugged and looked a little uncertain. "I don't know. I love my work, I enjoy being with talented, musical people. I don't have many close friends, but then that's not so unusual. I don't think I feel enclosed by anything, or anyone."

"What about those you admire, Gwen? Those people you put up on a pedestal, and won't ever let climb down?"

"I don't know what you mean," she whimpered.

"Gwen, since we ran into each other here you have acted as though you and I were great chums at school. We weren't. In fact, we didn't really know each other at all."

Gwen looked shocked. "You were a great influence on me, and it's clear you remembered me. When we met here you recalled me exactly."

I sighed. "I recall everything exactly, Gwen. I have a very strange and wonderful memory, which hangs onto stuff and never lets go. Whether I want it to or not. But I'll come back to that."

Gwen slumped in her chair and glowered at her coffee cup.

"Thanks for the analysis, Cait, but how does all this connect to David, and all the other stuff?" said Siân.

"Because David was trapped in a prison too," I said, "and he was trying to escape."

"I never meant to be a part of a prison for him," said Rhian plaintively. "He loved it here at first, but then he got restless. His rehearsals got longer, he had more meetings away from the castle, he spent more and more time working on his music projects and that flaming car out in the stables. Especially the last few months."

"He wasn't working on the car at all," I said. "He was working with Mair to try to find the treasure he believed was hidden in the Roman temple."

Rhian looked puzzled, and Owain exclaimed, "With Mair? He's been working with me, too. More or less blackmailed me into letting him come into my tunnel with me."

"Your what?" asked Alice. "Did you keep going with that stupid thing you began as a boy?"

"Okay, stop," I said. "I'm not going to sit here and listen to all this. I'm just going to cut to the chase, as they say. For years Owain's prison—which he began to build for himself as a boy—has forced him to believe that the puzzle plate told him that a treasure was hidden in the Roman temple. He never realized that the plate was a fake, a very clever fake—in that it was relatively modern—though it did, in fact, point to a treasure."

"Please explain that, Cait," said Idris with some urgency. "You said it last night. What do you mean?"

I said, "David was onto something. I found a book in a locked drawer in the stables that was about Bletchley Park, where they had teams of code crackers and creators during the Second World War. You told me, Alice, that some hush-hush stuff went on here during those years, and I know for a fact that the Welsh language was used during the war for secret communications. Code crackers would enjoy working with a wealthy man who could make a fake puzzle plate. They'd see it as a great joke. I believe that's what happened; your husband worked with the eggheads to create the plate. It had to be more modern than you thought, Owain, if only because the 'Cadwallader' form of your family name was used, rather than the original version of 'Cadwaladr,' which was in use during the period when the Swansea Pottery was working. You also mentioned, Alice,

239

significant renovations being undertaken before you moved back here permanently after the war, especially to the fireplaces. And then, of course, there were the portraits of you and your husband. Having seen both of them, and being able to imagine them in their original positions, they, and the puzzle plate, told me all I needed to know. Do you want me to go through the verse, Idris?"

"Yes, please, so long as you tell us all what it means," he replied eagerly.

"Right then, the first two lines—'Where the fire meets the earth, where the water meets the air / Where the face of beauty smiles, the treasures will be there'—frame the whole riddle and set us up for the rest. The next two lines are a couplet containing a specific clue—'Black gold in a seam, now popping with a spray / For every humble man, there is a time to pray.'"

"Exactly," interrupted Owain. "My tunnel from the coal cellar— 'black gold in a seam'—to the temple of Neptune, which is mentioned in the next two lines. See?"

"That's a part of your own, personal prison, Owain," I replied. "Coal in a coal cellar doesn't 'pop with a spray,' it only does that when it's burning. Those two lines are referring to *fireplaces*. And you kneel down when you pray like a humble man, so all you ever had to do was kneel down in front of the fireplaces, and that's where you'll find your treasure."

"Well I've done that hundreds of times, thousands, in fact," said Dilys, "and I haven't found any treasure."

"You don't have to 'find' it," I replied. "It's in plain sight. Every single fireplace in this entire castle is lined and faced with gold tiles. *Gold* tiles. They aren't just glass tiles backed with gold leaf. I believe you'll find they are actual gold, covered with a glass film. Someone will have to have enough guts to pry one off, but I bet you'll see I'm right if you do."

All heads turned to the fireplace in the room, and I could see eyes grow round. All except Owain, who said, "So, what does the next couplet mean?"

"Ah, yes," I replied, "let's consider that one. 'The breath of Llŷr and Neptune's tears—the same, there is no doubt / When they are gone, what gold is left, we cannot live without.' What could that mean? What can no one live without?"

"Water," said Owain. "The Roman temple has a cistern at its heart. The water came down the hill into the cistern through a gaping mouth of Neptune, was held in a cistern, and when the cistern was full, the water came out of the mouth of another face of Neptune and flowed into the sea."

"I agree that's how the temple worked," I said, "but the answer, in this case, isn't water, it's salt. And, of course, when sea water evaporates—when water meets the air—what you have left is salt."

"Preposterous," exclaimed Owain, gleeful that he had another chance to throw his favorite insult at me, no doubt.

I glared at him as I responded. "Alice's, or should I say *Alicia's*, mother was the granddaughter of a Bolivian salt miner and a Patagonian weaver of wool. You told me that, Owain, and the portrait of Alice certainly contained enough Bolivian creatures, and even a Bolivian landscape, to emphasize that part of her heritage. There's also a great big pile of salt on the table next to Gryffudd in his portrait, in which he's holding a map of South America. The map even has an X on it, for goodness sake! I believe that, somewhere in your library, you'll find papers that show that Alice has significant land rights to an area of the Salar de Uyuni area of Bolivia, the world's largest salt flats. They're shown in the background of her portrait."

"I own salt?" said Alice. "Why is that good thing? Isn't there enough salt in the world? Salt's cheap, isn't it?"

I nodded. "Yes, Alice, it is. But the impressive thing about the Bolivian salt flats is that they have been discovered to consist of a crust of salt that covers what is likely to be somewhere between fifty to seventy percent of the world's supply of lithium."

"They make batteries with lithium, don't they?" asked Idris.

I nodded. "Yes, they do. And the world has never been more in need of batteries—especially with the way things are moving toward the greater adoption of electric cars." I noticed that Idris sat more upright, a gleam in his eyes.

"Don't get too excited yet, Idris," I said. "The Bolivian government has made it quite clear that they will only allow nationals to exploit the lithium reserves. I'm sure that Owain's genealogical research will prove very useful when you're required to prove that there is a Bolivian bloodline, which might allow you to capitalize upon your land rights."

"Good work, Owain," said Alice with pride. "You've always been a clever boy."

Owain looked at his mother with great surprise, then returned his gaze to me, sullen again. "So what about the next two lines? What about them?"

"Ah yes. 'The worthy man sees treasure through the silver and through glass / The vain man only ever sees the beauty that will pass,' is something that I came to understand when I was talking to Siân last night. I was recalling an instance when I'd seen how blood had managed to get between the silvering on the back of a mirror and the glass to which it was adhered. Although the fireplace shown in the portrait of Alice seems to be a fantasy fireplace—I haven't seen one like it in the castle—I know that the dressing table shown is real. It's the one in my bridal boudoir. Did you move that dressing table out of your own bedroom, Alice?"

Alice Cadwallader shook her head. "Not exactly. The dressing table didn't move, my bedroom did. The room you are in used to be my bedroom. The dressing table was far too big and heavy to be moved. The bed, too. They just stayed where they were. And that fireplace in the painting? The artists made it up. Said it was something he'd once seen, and it would make a nice background."

"The bed is massive," said Eirwen, "so I can see why you'd leave that where it was. It suits the room. But why would a dressing table be that hard to move?"

"I believe you'll find that the mirror is entirely backed with gold," I replied, "behind the silvering, between the mirror and the wood backing. Did you have any other mirrors in your room, at that time, Alice?"

The old woman nodded. "Gryffudd used to say I was a woman who was unable to pass a mirror without looking into it, so he made sure I had a lot of them." She thought for a moment. "The old boy was making fun of me, wasn't he?" She chuckled. "Well, maybe, I'll have the last laugh after all."

"Where are all the mirrors now, Alice?" asked Eirwen, now as eager as her husband.

"Here and there," replied Alice. "Don't go making a load of bad luck for yourselves. I'll point them out so you don't have to break every single one in the house. It could mean there's a lot of gold here."

I nodded. "So the rest of the verse might be right. 'Cadwalladers will never leave the castle of the gray / As long as ancients rest in peace and old walls not give way / By the rushing of my lifeblood, I swear this on my grave / The wise man will discover them, and my kin be ever saved.' By the way, Owain," I added, "I believe the reference to walls not giving way is a nod to the fact that the river was diverted, and presumably walled to allow it to do so, by your father's father, thus preventing it from running straight through this very room."

Owain slurped his tea very noisily. I could tell he wasn't going to admit defeat until he was surrounded by gold tiles and plaques.

"So did David work that all out then?" asked Rhian in disbelief.

"No," I said, "he didn't. Though he did work out that the plate was much more modern than Owain believed, and I think it likely that he was on the right track about the mirrors. I noted as I looked around the castle, and particularly in the music room, that anything that was metal, and everything that was gold-colored, was scratched and marked.

I know that everything here has age, but I don't mean in that way. I found a collection of items in David's desk in the stables that are used to test for gold. Magnets don't adhere to gold, so metal can be checked that way. But, otherwise, if you rub a stone against an object you want to test, then apply certain liquids to that scraping, you can find out if it's gold. Being in everyone's rooms to 'fix their radiators' would have allowed David to test everyone's mirrors, metal radiators, and even furnishings. Of course, it allowed him to partake of other activities as well." I glanced toward Janet, who blushed. "If David was, as you told me yourself, Rhian, one for the ladies, and I understand there's been a fairly good supply of young ones coming and going as Alice's nurses, then he'd have probably been in many parts of castle, at many times of day and night. Lots of chances for snooping."

"But I still don't understand why he got pushed down the stairs, or who did it," cried Rhian with frustration.

I said, "Rhian, there's no easy way to say this. I'm pretty sure that your mother had her suspicions about David's less-than-husbandly activities, and I think even you had more than a clue, too. I knew that he and Janet were involved because she had the faintest trace of his aftershave about her uniform—which is why being close to her yesterday gave me a bit of a sore throat." I responded to the puzzled expressions around the table by saying, "But that's a long story involving childhood tonsillitis. And I picked up a note he'd written to her on what I discovered to be a pad of paper he used for ordering items he needed for his 'handiwork.' That said, there's one person here who cannot have been in any doubt about David's penchant for Janet, and the other nurses, and that's Alice. Right?"

"He was a very unpleasant, and frequently unfaithful, husband, Rhian," said Alice sharply. "I saw what he did to those poor girls. They were disposable to him. He broke their hearts. You said I could probably tell a tale or two about men, Cait, and you'd be right. I was a very attractive girl, and I don't deny that I made a very good marriage, at a young age, to a man much older than myself, with whom I had little in common. I will also not insult you all by denying that my husband and I had relationships outside our marriage. But it was David who really turned me against all men. Showed me how nasty they all are when it comes down to it. When the nurses came to me, desperate to leave, I told them to say it was my fault that they were resigning, so that no blame would attach to them. Then I'd see him do the same thing to the next one. This one? Janet? She wasn't here a week before he started on her."

I added, "He liked to work on women who thought themselves less than perfect, invisible in many ways. Women who hadn't had much attention paid to them, am I right?"

Alice's lips wrinkled into a sneer. "Easier for him to control them that way. And I put up with it. Until he started on Mair. I'd heard it all before, and when I heard him try it on with her, well, that was it. You know, don't you?" she said, directly to me.

I nodded.

"Very well then, no point denying it." She sounded resigned.

"What do you mean, Mother?" asked Mair. "David never made any moves on me." She sounded almost disappointed. "We were friends. We had adventures."

Alice shook her head sadly as she looked at her daughter. "There's no point denying it, Mair. I heard him. You know very well the way sound travels around this place. It's all those passages in the old walls. I was having a nap. Janet had given me some of that lovely milk I like so much. It was yesterday afternoon. Oh no, it can't have been yesterday—it must have been the day before. Or before that? Anyway, I was lying there, just dozing, when I heard him tell you that you had to slow down, that you wanted it too much, and that he'd have to start to ration you. You were very upset, Mair, don't deny it. I heard you crying, and I've heard a lot of them like that. Of course I was shocked—especially when he said you wanted 'too much.' But then I'm your mother, I think of you as a child still. But I knew I had to act. I got into my chair right away, took my walking stick so I could close the door of my little lift, and got myself down to the top of the stairs to the kitchen. But he wasn't there. So I went to the other door under the main stairs, and tried that side. I found him. And I told him in no uncertain terms that he was to leave you alone. He laughed. *At me!* And I pushed my little controller to go forward to be able to smack him one with my stick, because he deserved it, but my foot pedals must have hit him and pushed his legs from under him, because the next thing I knew he was bouncing down the stairs on his chin."

Silence.

Alice looked more deflated than usual. "I didn't mean to hurt him more than a slap. But I had to save you, my dear child. You mean the world to me, you and your brother, and I didn't want you to have your heart broken. Because that's what he would have done." Alice's voice was more tender than I'd heard it, and Mair was beginning to cry.

"Mother, he wasn't my *lover*. Nor would he have ever suggested that. We were arguing about my cigarettes. He used to buy them for me, and bring them to me, here. Yes, we've been having a bit of an adventure grubbing around in the temple, but even I knew he was a bad lot, and I wouldn't have done that to you in any case, Rhian. You have to believe me—there was nothing between us."

"I believe you," said Rhian quietly.

"Cigarettes?" said Alice in disbelief.

"Yes, Mother, cigarettes. David was the one who brought them to me. You know very well I hardly ever leave this place. How did you think I got them?"

After a moment Alice said to me, "How did you know it was me?"

I said, "There was a transfer of paint from the interior of the door of your little chair lift to your foot pedals, and then onto the front of David's jeans. The line where your pedals hit him left a mark. By the way, Dilys, did you change David's trousers after he was dead? Just to make sure he looked neat and tidy when he left here?"

Dilys nodded. "I wanted him to look respectable," she said. "Nothing wrong with that, is there?"

"But you couldn't change his sweater because his body had already become rigid?" I pressed.

Dilys nodded.

"But what about the hand prints on his back?" asked Bud. *A good question.*

"Janet? Maybe you'd like to explain that," I said.

All eyes turned to look at the young woman, who was anything but bright and bouncy.

She flushed. "I didn't have a date with David that day, because he had a meeting with you, Bud. So I really did go for a nap. But something woke me. I didn't know what it was at the time, but this place is weird—banging and knocking and voices from nowhere. With what you've just said, Alice, it might have been you going back into your room, I don't know. Anyway, I decided to go down to see if I could find him after all, and there he was, at the bottom of the steps, dead. I didn't know I'd left handprints. I rolled him over a bit, just to see if he really was dead, so maybe that's what happened."

"Probably transfer of coal dust from his jeans to his back," Bud said. "About that coal dust," he added. "Why did he have so much on his clothes? Didn't you and he have coveralls, Owain?"

Owain blanched. "A bit of fisticuffs earlier on, I'm afraid," he said. "We'd been in the cellar just after lunch, and he told me I wasn't working hard enough to break through the cistern walls. I was still in my coverall, and he'd taken his off."

"And how did you know it was David and Owain down there, Cait?" continued Bud.

I allowed myself to smile. "The boots in the cellar. I eventually realized that the sizes on the boots were British sizes, not Canadian ones, and I didn't even know if they were men's or women's sizes. I take a size 4½ in the UK, but a 6½ or a 7 in Canada. It was quite possible that the British size 7, so a Canadian women's size 9 or 9½, could belong to a man—especially one with small feet. Although I noted the selection of shoes that David had in his room, I didn't look at the size he wore, which was a serious omission on my part. But I'd seen for myself that he had small feet, and that fact had also been commented upon by others. Also, there isn't a woman here with feet that large. So David, plus someone with size 11, or Canadian size 12 or 13, feet. Idris's feet are too small, but Owain's are large."

Everyone was silent for few moments, then Alice Cadwallader asked quietly, "What will happen to me? I didn't mean him to die, Rhian. It really was an accident. I—I was very upset when I found out he was dead. I'd never have done that to you. Nor him, of course. You do know that, don't you?"

Rhian nodded.

Gradually, Bud became the center of attention. He looked uncomfortable. "Please don't expect me to have an answer about anything that relates to British police procedure. I don't know what might happen."

"Will they arrest me for murdering him?" asked Alice. She sounded like a small, scared child.

Bud looked worried. "Alice, I just don't know. Of course I, we, are duty-bound to tell them the truth, when they get here. We can't change what happened, but how it's handled by the authorities from this point on remains to be seen. All I can do, all we can do, is present them with the facts."

"Rhian—you won't let them do anything to her, will you?" said Dilys. "The missus is ninety-two. It would kill her."

Rhian sighed. "I'm not sure it's got anything to do with me, Mam. It'll be up to the police when they get here." The young widow turned to her aged employer and said, "Oh, Alice. If only you hadn't decided to do something so spiteful—even if you were doing it for what you thought was a good reason . . ."

Silence.

Dau ar bymtheg ar hugain

EVENTUALLY MAIR BLURTED OUT, "WELL, Cait. You've told us that our family is wealthy, and that Mother is a killer. But none of that explains all the other things that have been going on here, does it? What about all those terrible, malicious things? You said everything came out of love, Cait." She looked at her mother. "I can see that Mother might have loved me enough that she wanted to save me from a man she thought was going to break my heart. But the rest?"

I nodded. The only way I could press on was to try to compartmentalize things. Two puzzles explained, one more to go. I plunged in. "You admired, and maybe even loved David, didn't you, Gwen?" I said.

Gwen tensed.

"It's alright," I continued, "you don't have to answer that, I know you did. David gave you the attention you craved—and you let him use you too. I don't mean like he used Alice's nurses, but he used you to carry a heavy load for him with the choir, used you to run about and fetch and carry for him, I heard. But you put up with it all, because you got to be in the limelight with him. And, when he died, you immediately suspected that someone here had something to do with it. Slashing the painting, breaking the plate and the Christmas decorations? At first I thought they'd all been done to throw people off the trail to the treasure, but your only plan was to destroy things beloved by certain people—Alice, Owain, Idris and Eirwen, and, last night, Mair, when you wrecked her apartment, all to avenge David."

"But what about Mair's Ravelry account being hacked weeks ago?" asked Siân.

"Shall I tell her, or will you?" I said to Mair.

Mair shook her head, so I spoke. "Mair wasn't hacked. She wrote a lot of nasty messages in a fit of temper, directed toward herself. Last night, when we saw her rooms, Bud, we both thought she might have done something to harm herself, that the mess up there was a symptom of self-loathing. It wasn't, it was Gwen's work, but I believe that the online incident was Mair's. An attempted escape, if you will, but one she regretted. After posting angry messages, she covered her shame by saying she'd been hacked. That's right, isn't it, Mair?"

Mair nodded.

"So there weren't two different modus operandi in play," said Bud.

"No," I replied, "just one. And I believe that Gwen has acted this way for many years. I suspect you managed to make your 'good friend' at school so sick that she didn't do well enough in her exams to get into university, so she had to go to college with you, Gwen. I dare say that if someone took a good look at your life, they'd find other, similar examples of your spite, vindictiveness, and ruthless pursuit of your own ends and desired outcomes."

"*You* told me to do it," snapped Gwen. "You told me I shouldn't let anyone, or anything, get in my way. And I haven't." She looked around the room at the assembled group. "You were all horrible to David, and you all deserved what you got," she spat. "Not you, of course, Rhian. I really like you. You're my friend. I did what I did for you, as much as for David." Rhian looked shocked.

I said, "And what about *me*, Gwen? What did I do to deserve you sneaking into my room and ruining the clothes I was to wear for my marriage ceremony?"

Gwen looked at me with the coldest stare I'd ever seen. "I told you yesterday that I'd done you a big favor, and you never even said thank you. You should have said thank you, that's what."

I took a deep breath. "You mean you did me the favor of not talking to me in the street in Cambridge one day when you were visiting, because I was upset after an argument with my ex-boyfriend? Well, thank you very much for giving me my space, Gwen." I could hear my voice get angrier with each word.

"No, that's not it," replied Gwen dismissively. "That day I heard you say you wanted to chuck a drink at that bloke you were arguing with, I followed him to a pub and I threw a pint of beer all over him for you. So there. See? I did you a big favor, and you never said thank you."

Automatically I grabbed for Bud's hand. He immediately knew there was something very wrong. I felt my entire body begin to shake. And it wasn't only Bud who could tell that something was awry. Siân began to rise from her seat.

"What's up with you now?" said Gwen harshly.

"What's up with me?" I managed. "I'm going to say this, then I'm going to leave, because, otherwise, I won't be responsible for my actions. Gwen Thomas, you think that all you did was throw a drink at a man that day. Let me tell you now that, no, there are no coincidences, there are only choices, and actions, and consequences. What you did that day changed the course of at least two people's lives. The beer that you threw led directly to Angus getting involved in a bar brawl, which resulted in him sustaining a ruptured spleen. That's what killed him, and it was why he ended up dead on my bathroom floor a few days later. And I ended up being arrested for murder, hounded by the press, being in a position where all the research I'd done would go up in smoke unless I left the country and started again in a place where people wouldn't point and stare, referring to me as 'the criminologist who was arrested for murder.' Your action, like that of Alice, was born of spite—or born of love and admiration in your mind—and had terrible consequences."

"I meant it to be a kind thing," said Gwen.

"I do understand that throwing a drink at someone might seem like a small thing, Gwen, but do you now see how the consequences of that choice you made, and that action you took, led to the death of a human being, and the absolute upheaval of my life?"

Gwen nodded. Her chin puckered. The faces around the table displayed a range of emotions, from horrified to sympathetic. I thought I'd reached my limit, but Gwen's next words pushed me right over the edge.

"If I hadn't done it, and you hadn't gone to Canada, you'd never have met Bud, and you wouldn't be marrying him today," she said slyly. She even added a sweet smile. "You told us all about your great-great-whatever spending the money he made by being a taxidermist to get your grandfather trained up as a baker, and that's why your mother, then you were born. See? Everything's connected. Really, you've got me to thank for you and Bud being a couple."

I literally heard the blood rushing in my ears, and I worked hard to slow my pounding heart. Eventually I was able to speak. As I did I could hear my voice quiver. "I see," I replied, seething.

"It wasn't my fault that he died," said Gwen. "I did it so you'd have your revenge on him, and it's all worked out for the best." She sounded almost proud.

"I could have thrown a drink over him myself," I said. "But I chose not to do it. Actions have consequences. When I told you about our family history I told you about people making decisions—decisions to work hard at their lives, their careers, to invest in the next generation, to apply themselves. It wasn't all just a series of connected coincidences that allowed me and my sister to exist, but a series of decisions, actions, and consequences. And if you want to invoke the idea of 'but good came from the spiteful thing I did' then you also have to consider what I'm about to say now. Before I made the final move to the University of Vancouver, I went to visit the place, and they offered me a trial run. I took it. It was a chance for me to get the feel of Canada, the university, the people and the systems I'd be working with. I rented a small apartment for six months, and left a lot of my belongings in storage with an old friend in Cardiff. Once I'd decided that I would make my new life in Canada, I asked my parents if they'd take some of the things they'd been keeping in their attic for me since my schooldays to that same friend, so that I could ship everything to my new home from one location. Oddly enough, Gwen, the Llwyn-y-Bryn School magazines they were transporting for me probably had photographs of you in them, because I know there were some of our House Choir."

Bud squeezed my hand. He knew what was coming.

I pushed myself to finish. It was important to me to do so. "So, on a sunny Sunday afternoon, Mum and Dad loaded up their car and set out for Cardiff, happy to be a small part of helping their daughter to start over, after a very tough year. Because you threw that beer over Angus, Gwen, my parents died in a fiery car crash, on the A48 between Swansea and Cardiff. Your actions led to Siân and me losing our mother and father. Your choice. Your action. The consequences."

I stood and walked to the doorway. "I hope you all prosecute this woman, who has caused physical damage to your property, to the fullest extent of the law, because there's nothing I can do about the fact that she once hurled a drink over a man in a pub. All I can do now is work out how to live my life from here on."

I looked down at Gwen, then at Bud, and tried to soften my voice as I said to him, "Bud, this is not how I wanted our wedding day to begin. I'm so sorry." My voice broke. "Now I know what they mean when they say a person can be so sharp they might cut themselves. I didn't know what Gwen had done in Cambridge. I saw her as a woman with a borderline personality, whose warped sense of love, loyalty, and retribution had led her to carry out the wanton acts of destruction we have seen here. I never imagined I'd meet the person who began the fight in which Angus sustained his fatal injury, let alone know her—slightly. I need some time to process this, Bud. It's big."

I looked across the table at my sister. "I know how you felt when you saw David's corpse, and it brought back all the emotional turmoil you thought you'd managed to deal with. Like you, I'll get through this—and I won't have to deal with jetlag and strong painkillers at the same time." I forced a smile, as did Siân, through her tears.

"So sorry for you, sis," she half whispered. "I know you'll be fine. You've always bounced back."

"But never from so far as this," I replied, my tears turning to sobs. I turned and ran up the stairs, crying.

Bud came after me, calling, "You're not dealing with this alone, Cait, wait for me."

I stopped and said the hardest thing I'd ever had to say, "I need to do this alone, Bud. I have to allow this to come to an end, for me, without you being a part of it. Let me do that? Then we can start on a new path, together. I know you understand, because it's what you needed to do after Jan died."

"You're right," he said simply.

Dim

WHEN BUD KNOCKED ON MY door half an hour later, I knew
I still had a long way to go before I could even begin to cope with
what had happened, what I'd discovered. But all my psychological
training allowed me to know it was a journey, and that it wouldn't
go quickly, but it would go less well if I tried to rush it. It would be a
voyage through grief, and that takes time.

Bud sounded excited as he knocked. I pulled open the creaking
door. Bud was smiling. "Do you care what you're wearing when we
get married?" he asked, gazing into my eyes.

At least he hadn't been stupid enough to ask me how I was feeling.

I managed a smile. "Not at all. It's completely immaterial to me.
All I need to marry you is you, Bud Anderson. Though I know we
must have registrars and witnesses as well. But that's it. Oh, I suppose
we'll need our rings—and Siân, of course."

"Good," replied Bud, "because I need you to dress for the weather,
and come with me. I have a plan, and it involves a bit of climbing."

"Climbing?" I knew I sounded horrified.

"Yes—but just down a set of steps, and a bit of a pathway, not up a
cliff, or anything like that." He grinned. "Do you think you can cope?"

I nodded.

Ten minutes later, I was dressed for a walk on a sunny winter's
day, and Siân, Bud and I, Idris and Eirwen, and Mair and Owain were
picking our way, carefully, down the path toward the beach below
Castell Llwyd. It took a while, and as we went, Bud explained that
the bridge was still unusable, but it would be repaired sufficiently by
the end of the day for us to be able to drive over it in the morning.
Apparently, with the discovery of huge panels of gold behind various

mirrors, as I had predicted, money was now no object, and Idris had hired a mass of people to make sure it happened.

Knowing we'd be able to.leave the next day gave me a sense of relief, but Bud still wouldn't tell me why we were making our way down to the beach. Eventually, we all stood on the golden sand, the sea rippling at the low tide mark, the sun pale and round in the duck-egg blue of the clear sky. Our footprints grew into large, dry-looking patches as we moved around. Bud held my hand.

"Don't go too far," Bud warned. "Idris—are we okay here?"

Idris nodded, then he and his wife, as well as his uncle and aunt, pulled some oars from a pod attached to the cliffside. They shoved them into the sand so that they met in a makeshift pointed arch.

I was even more puzzled when two men, who seemed to be out for a walk along the sweeping sands, began to approach us. The younger of the two was carrying a large backpack.

"Are you Bud Anderson?" said the short, round, gray-haired man in a Barbour jacket as he greeted Bud.

"I certainly am," replied Bud. "You must be Mr. Williams, the superintendent registrar."

My tummy flipped.

The man nodded. "And this is Mr. Hobbs, who will assist us today." He turned toward me. "Are you Miss Morgan?" I nodded. "Good," he continued. "We're the most nimble people in the Swansea Register Office, so we were picked to clamber down the path to Three Cliffs Bay, and then walk all the way here." He winked.

"Thank you, Mr. Williams, Mr. Hobbs. Bud—you're brilliant!" Then I panicked. "But the license is only valid at Castell Llwyd, isn't it? Do we have to climb all the way back up again? You poor things have already walked so far."

Idris smiled and said, "The Cadwallader Estate owns one hundred yards of this beach, and, as such, it is a part of Castell Llwyd. We never enforce it, of course, but this is the bit we own—right here."

He grinned. "So it's just the same as being inside the castle. Except for the wind, and the spray off the sand. And this," he gestured to the oars, "is a structure, for now. Will this meet your requirements, Mr. Williams?"

The registrar looked dubious. "Our rules do not allow marriages to take place in anything but a permanent structure, and certainly not in the middle of a beach. As you can imagine, we'd have people getting married all over the place, willy nilly, if we allowed that sort of thing." His stern expression softened as he looked at me, bundled up against the elements, with a bruised face and eyes still red and swollen from crying. He also glanced up at the climb he'd have to make to the castle. Eventually he said, "Under these very unusual circumstances, it will be acceptable."

I was hugely relieved.

The paperwork, which had been in the backpack, was quickly sorted out by Mr. Hobbs, then Mr. Williams took the lead.

Ten minutes later, Caitlin Morgan and Börje Ulf Dyggve Anderson were married.

"A new year begins tomorrow, wife," said Bud immediately after our embrace, and a lovely kiss, "and we face the unknown future together."

"And here's to no more corpses!" said Siân as she pulled me aside and dropped two tiny stones she'd picked up from the beach into my palm. "If you stick these where the two stones are missing on the picture frame I brought for you from Perth, it should say FAMILY again."

I could feel tears pricking my eyes.

"I have a little something for my bride too," said Bud, suddenly beside me.

"I thought we said no presents for each other," I gasped.

Bud smiled. "We did—but this is a gift for both of us, not just you."

He handed me a thick, glossy brochure with a picture of a sleek ocean liner on its front.

"A cruise?" I was astonished.

Bud nodded. "Hawaii. It'll be our honeymoon."

I stupidly blurted out, "But I can't swim! I've never been on a ship. What if it sinks? And, anyway, you have to get all dressed up for dinner, and I haven't got anything suitable."

Bud and Siân laughed. Eventually I joined in.

Siân said, "You'll have a smashing time, Cait. Todd and I have cruised, and it's right up your street. Food everywhere, all the time. So many bars you won't know which way to turn. The Hawaiian Islands are lovely. You'll be safe on a cruise ship, Cait. Lovely. And you'll be with your husband, of course."

"You'll be with yours soon," I said, seeing her misting over.

Siân nodded. "Yes, not too long now. But I'm not leaving the Gower, or Swansea, until we've had a chocolate sundae together at Joe's Ice Cream Parlor in the Mumbles—after we've had sausage, chips, and gravy at Dick Barton's Chip Shop, of course. Tomorrow? All three of us. Agreed?"

"Agreed," I said. "Does that sound alright to you, husband?"

"Whatever you say, wife," replied Bud.

Pronouncing Welsh names and words

First of all, don't worry about it! You're the one reading this book and, unless you choose to read it aloud, no one will know or care if you mangle the pronunciation of anything. Just enjoy the story and let the words that look unfamiliar find their own shape in your head. But, if you enjoy learning as you read, here are a few general, and specific, hints and tips about Welsh pronunciation.

Welsh is a living language, but it's also a very ancient one, so it's not unusual to hear Welsh speakers using borrowed English words when they speak Welsh. I was queuing (standing in line!) in the Marks and Spencer store in Carmarthen, South Wales, recently, and the lady in front of me was returning some items. The entire process was conducted in Welsh, with the odd interpolation of English words and phrases like "credit card" and "PIN number." This is quite normal. Indeed, in many parts of South Wales, especially in and around Swansea and the Swansea Valley areas, a specific "dialect" is heard, which has been labeled "Wenglish." As you'd expect it's a mix of Welsh and English, but no one can agree if it's a dialect of Welsh, or English, so it's really a hybrid. It's what I grew up speaking, though, of course, I didn't know that at the time.

It was quite normal for me, or anyone else in my family, to say things like, "Don't be twp now, 'ew. Silly mochen, she is. Don't take no notice of 'er. Come over and sit by here, and we'll have a nice cup of tea and a cwtch, is it. Tidy like." Yes, I know it makes little sense, but to those who grew up in South Wales, especially in Swansea in the 1960s as I did, it's perfectly normal. It means: "Don't be so stupid. She's a silly pig (horrible person). Ignore her. Sit next to me and we'll share some tea and a cuddle. It'll be fine."

As television, with its Standard English and American accents, proliferated, so many of my generation began to "speak properly." However, as with most aspects of one's childhood, the language I used to speak is bubbling just under the surface.

I grew up in an English- (or Wenglish-) speaking family, but studied Welsh at school until I was sixteen. Although I have forgotten most of my Welsh vocabulary, the accent, and often the syntax, remain with me. What also remains is my ability to read the Welsh language aloud, using the correct pronunciation of the twenty-nine letters and diphthongs in the Welsh alphabet. I rather take it for granted that when anyone sees a Welsh name or word on the page they know what it sounds like, even if they don't know what it means—which is really not true. With that in mind, here we go!

Below is a list of the Welsh words from *The Corpse with the Sapphire Eyes*, along with their phonetic pronunciation (the italics show what to emphasize).

Main characters:

Siân: Shan "Si" is pronounced like "sh" as in "shape"; this word is pronounced with a long "a" as in "arm," as signified by the mark above the letter "â". (English: Jane.)

Cadwallader: Kad-*wol*-u-dur "C" is always pronounced hard, as in "can," and the rest of the word is this way because it's an Anglicized name.

Mair: *My*-r It sounds like the word "my," followed by "rrrrr," so it doesn't rhyme with the word "hair," even though it looks similar. (English: Mary.)

Owain: *Owe*-eye-n "Ai" is pronounced like the word "eye." (English: Owen.)

Idris: *Id*-riss "I" here as in the word "in." (Welsh name, so no English version, though it is also a Muslim name.)

Eirwen: *Eye*-rr-when "Ei" is also pronounced like "eye." (Welsh name, no English version.)

Dilys: *Dill*-iss In this case the "y" is pronounced like an "i" as in "in." (Welsh name, no English version.)

Rhian: *Rh-ee*-ann "Rh" is a specifically Welsh sound, and is one of the diphthongs referred to as a "letter" in the Welsh alphabet. You need to try to pronounce the "h" almost before the "r" if you're to make it sound correct! The "r" is so soft it almost disappears. Rhian originated as a short version of the name, Rhiannon, but it now stands alone as a name in its own right.

Names of other characters mentioned, but not appearing in person:

Gryffudd: *Gri*-ffith "Y" can be pronounced like "u" in "under," or like "i" as in "win." In this case it's like "win." "Ff" is pronounced like "ff" in "fluff"; "dd" is pronounced like "th" in "the."

Ieuan: *Y-eye*-an "I" is a "y" as in "yellow"; "eu" is like "eye." (English: Ian.)

Hywel: *How*-el It sounds just like "vowel" but with an "H." (English: Howell.)

Eleri: El-*airy* Here the "eri" is pronounced like the word "airy." (Welsh name, no English version.)

Elena: *Ell*-en-a Due to where the emphasis is put in Welsh, this is Ell-e-na, not El-ai-na. (English: Eleanor.)

Teilo: *Tie*-low (Welsh saint's name, so no English version.)

Some other Welsh words found in the book:

Castell Llwyd: *Kas*-tel L-*oi-d* "Ll" is a tough sound for most non-Welsh, or Arabic, speakers to make. It's the sort of noise Donald Duck might make. You shove your tongue behind your top teeth, smile, and try to make a hard "chchch" sound in your cheeks. Yes, odd. Most non-Welsh pronounce "ll" as "l," and we put up with that! "Wy" sounds a bit like "Oi!"

Swansea: *Swan*-zee The Welsh name for Swansea is Abertawe, which means "the mouth of the River Tawe," so Swansea is an anglicized word. But so many people mispronounce it that I thought it should get a mention. The second "s" isn't soft like the first one, it's hard, like a "z" sound.

Bwca: Boo-ca "Bw" sounds like "boo" as in jumping out and frightening someone, as opposed to "book," and "ca" has a short "a," like "ha" in "hat," not like the word "car."

Mabinogion: Mab-in-*og*-yon Compiled from texts found in two late-medieval manuscripts (the Red Book of Hergest and the White Book of Rhydderch), this collection was compiled, edited, and translated by antiquarians William Pughe and Lady Charlotte Guest in the early nineteenth century. Although overlaid, some would say, with nineteenth-century intellectual input, the original texts, from the eleventh to fourteenth centuries, clearly captured much of the mythological lore that had been handed down through the spoken word for many centuries. If you have the time, and are interested in medieval mythologies, the Mabinogion will not disappoint.

Teisen lap: Tea-shun lap This is a traditional moist cake, with fruit, and it's cooked on a low heat on a plate. Yes, really!

Llŷr: Ll-*ee*-r Once again here's the challenging "ll" sound, this time followed by a long "ee" for the pronunciation of the "y."

Chapters and numbers:

I thought it would be fun to "translate" the chapter numbers. Here are some pronunciation points, which you can apply as the numbers increase.

Un: Een This sounds like "seen" without the "s."

Dau: Die This sounds like the word "die" as in the opposite of live.

Tri: Tree Just like the trees that grow.

Pedwar: Ped-waar In this case "war" is not pronounced like the English word for a series of battles, but like "far" with a "w."

Pump: Pimp Just as in "pimple."

Chwech: **Ch-*wé*-ch** "Ch" is another challenging sound. Make a noise at the back of your throat as though you're trying to make spit, or clear something that's stuck there—that's about it! Here the "we" is pronounced like the "e" in "café."

Saith: **S-*eye*-th** Again, "ai" is as in "eye."

Wyth: *Oi*-th

Naw: N*ow*

Deg: *Dé*-g This is the same "é" as in café.

Ar: **Are** Say it like a pirate would!

Ddeg: Thég

Pymtheg: *Pim*-thég

Bymtheg: *Bim*-thég

Deunaw: **Die-now** Not a threat, but the word for eighteen.

Ugain: *Ee*-g-en Here the "u" is pronounced as a long "e," as in "each," the "g" is hard, as in "get," and the "ain" is pronounced "en" as in "when."

Hugain: *H-ee*-gen As above, with an "h."

Acknowledgments

WITHOUT THE SUPPORT OF MY ever-patient husband, my mum, and my sister—who give me rapid, and sometimes challenging, feedback—I would probably never finish any book I begin to write. My dogs are my faithful writing companions, understanding every word I share with them, but never judging. Thank you to them all.

Special thanks go to Liz Jarvis, Superintendent Registrar for the City and County of Swansea. Despite her warning words, I have taken complete liberty and hope that the extenuating circumstances that prevail in this book do not encourage anyone to think they can get away with what Bud and Cait did!

I didn't migrate to Canada until I was forty years of age. That means I am not "of Welsh heritage," but am, in fact, Welsh. It is impossible for me to thank everyone who, over the decades, has helped me understand what that means, if, indeed, I do. Of course I must thank my mum and my sister, again, but I must also mention my late father. He would drive us all around the Gower Peninsula in our little Ford Anglia from my earliest days. I spent a happy childhood playing on the beaches, clambering among ruined castles, picking wild flowers (sorry!), and ambling across endless sand dunes. Visiting relatives near Slade Cross was always special, and camping trips, spring days plopping about in rock pools, or just singing "Ten Green Bottles" for the umpteenth time as we weaved between tall hedges, avoiding oncoming cars by a hair's breadth, are all ingrained in my soul. I love Wales; it never leaves me. As I know I have written before—always Welsh, always becoming Canadian.

Finally, I don't know how you found, or found out about, this book, but I very much hope you enjoy/enjoyed it. The team at